CHINA

CHINA

Shaheen Asbagh

authorHOUSE®

AuthorHouse™
1663 Liberty Drive
Bloomington, IN 47403
www.authorhouse.com
Phone: 1 (800) 839-8640

Published by AuthorHouse 10/05/2015

ISBN: 978-1-5049-5416-7 (sc)
ISBN: 978-1-5049-5417-4 (e)

Print information available on the last page.

CONTENTS

THE 7TH HISTORY

1

The command of nature, at 3:30 p.m., like other efforts of nature, is repeating itself in a cold and dreadful beat as during every year throughout the past millions and two times that as in every six months. Turtles can not fly, run, and even climb, and yet find it, alas, natural to be imprisoned in a shell as hard as a rock and somewhat heavy a burden that has come to mean protection and, however, not a burden. Yet around 3:30 they bury themselves in any concept of the woods that would keep them cool and comfortable and wait for the night to rush to the not-so-far shores of the ocean-they mean business. It is then time to lay their eggs that are due to bring birth. The cycle originates in the woods; the tropical zones and their surroundings where they play and can feel the desire for life and fun. What man describes as magic, a miracle that perfects life, the essence of nature, and what us beings associate it with-Mother Nature!

The ritual is undeniably familiar and for its commonality it is believed to be the root of tradition which only comes from turtles; these creatures do not think yet they strive and that's, however, the framework of a mere sign of population second to humans, at a land so antique and an historic age that rules the rainforest, the shores, the mountains, and even the cities. The people know it as well as the often fertile turtles which never hold a center to control their acts. They always hold an individualistic form of identity although it varies for millions of them as patterns of birth among a retarded species. What else could be said about the creatures? Except, for the freedom to reproduce and sacrifice half or even more of their upbringing at 3:30 pm at the shores there is a silence ruling the beach sand and therefore the dusk is to come boisterously, and the cooler breeze will entice the hardbacks the same way as the intelligent residents except those who convene one or two wishes hoping the sea would lay a reality upon the land through its ebbs and flows. Because, at 3:30 a life is being decided upon as in many a turtle who are just getting ready to live or die through the tidal stampede of the crabs or bigger fish! The life flourishes through its quadrupeds and seemingly they live; live life as they were endowed with it. Reproduction entitles them to a legacy and a power over the other species. The birds would be accounted for the same, but here, this island only knows the tranquil, pausing, and speculative beings that solely live to eat, hide, and reproduce when it's time. They are jovially waiting for 3:30 and etc. to pass as farther on shore the old man's 3:30 doctor's appointment is due anytime. Sitting rigidly cross-legged covering his thinning scalp with a skullcap and a peacoat he scrutinized the color photographs of a magazine of an unknown genre-he was preparing to make a legitimate and prudent statement to the physician. He knows only the ritual of greeting a literate man with earnest vibes and a sound consciousness for most of them know what they are talking about. *It took you ten years to become a doctor?*

"I have known you for how long now?. . . . . it is probably decades, many more years than the fingers on my hands. It has been since the birth of your son that we happen to meet during your annual checkup, then his graduation. . . . or even I still remember his ear infection and his polio, or that time, a little later, when I diagnosed your hemorrhoid, but I have to admit, for you as for all of my patients, I kept one thing secret and that is to sustain mind over muscle,. . . eh! To put it mildly I always try to keep your morale in top shape and I believe that is what keeps a man physically fit. For that, I insist that I am different from any other doctor, at least beyond a few hundred mile radius from this place, like those turtles-that everybody knows-who will hatch their eggs one of these days in the hope that their offsprings will live to see the days when their birth givers have seen. . . . . anyway. . . . well I've been smelling them just as I have every year and any year that we have had our visits (meetings!), and I won't ask you how life is treating you because my humble instincts tell me you have been having painful lapses of nausea and a metabolical crisis perhaps new to you such as lack of appetite that I hope somehow you have overcome and you are here in a good and sound mood and stature! I don't mean to give you a headache today but like one of those days that I am sure you have had many of during the seventy-nine years of tenacity and good deed that have kept you a friend of medical science and most important the sea time does no more allow me to keep anything from you. . . . ."

He was watchful, only about four or so miles from the shore; he sat motionless, his face toward the window which was exposing the fog and hidden trees behind the mist on the glass. The doctor's office was particularly of interest to him because he could hear his correspondence being read to him-the letters from his son and relatives, bills, tax reports, and any other habituary that was fancied by the formal side of an illiterate man like him yet having raised a few children with immense intelligence and education. Two of them exactly, he had raised two sons of which both had studied law. . . . The doctor usually read his communication to him and if the office was crowded he would wait for a few hours as he always brought a meal wrapped in a paper bag to his canonical appointments.

"Sir, you know I don't have time for this. . . . say what you want to say and get it over with. .. sir you always surpass my patience and for that I honestly hold no grudge against you but what's most important is that I have another letter from the prison and that is why I had to come in so soon because Victoria is away visiting her family and there is no one to help me out!!"

Doctor took the sealed envelope from him and set it on his desk in front of him without moving his eyes away from the old man's and sighed.

"You want to listen to me or hear your letter!?. . . . The choice is yours because I would've called you anyway!"

He rested his hand on the fat envelope and waited for an answer but he knew the old man had something else in mind. It probably had something to do with his older son's previous letter, but he left it to be indicated by the old man perhaps a bit later as he was still waiting. The old man's older son had been in prison for almost ten years on a twenty-five year sentence charged with treason, embezzlement, espionage, and whatever else they could pin on him. He raised his finger and with the other hand pointed to the doctor, "first things first. . . ."

"Do you have pain?" Doctor leaned back and rested on the leather chair crossing his hands on his chest and yet remaining inquisitive. He waited for old man's pride to subside and give up, "mostly after dark!"

"Any other feelings that I should know about like lack of appetite or wanting to throw up or anything at all. . . . . ?

"What's with you today doctor!? If it is new medicine .. . . let me have it now! As about the letter. . . ."

Doctor interrupted with an apparent sign of wariness.

"Will you relax, or maybe not, I will read it to you later!"

There is a knock on the door and the doctor allows the entrance of his secretary as she brings in a weighty file and a pitcher of water and a couple of glasses and sets them on the doctor's desk, apologizes, and calmly leaves the room.

"This is your file,. . . a report of your health for the past forty years or so, and I think I've done my share. . . now you need to see a specialist!!"

"I feel fine,. . . . I will live!!"

"Less than a year based on my findings. . . . !"

"Why do I need a specialist then!?"

"Just to be sure!"

"You know. . . before my son was put in prison and her mother dies I promised my family that we would again live in heaven and would be rewarded a medal for our respect for others and the good deeds we all, as a family, have committed to help others. . . .I know you still remember my wife, and I know her heart attack was a bad omen for all of us and that's why. .doctor. . .I have never given up on you. I don't think I need a specialist! Your word is enough for me. . . .I believe you but I have business to take care of like every day of my life. . . . . I don't know how long they're going to keep my son behind bars, and my other one I have yet not heard anything from. It's been five years since he gave up on all of us and left!! Doctor they are both educated and I am now to believe that it's my fault to provide them the education,. . . . .perhaps God (*Which God?*), my God, and your God. . . . will help me overcome the pain and leave this world with a peaceful spirit."

"Now that I have told you would you like me to read it to you?"

Doctor waited for an answer as he eyes the letter curiously. They sat, although not comfortably, in silence. It is this moment that forces the patient and the doctor to get closer. The old man did not seem hopeless yet held a grim and likely concerned impression. He seemed too wary and waiting for the doctor to say more but he does not. He had said his last word awaiting his patient patiently. Finally the old man swallowed and calmly waved at the envelope! The doctor picked it up, carefully tore it open and undid the trifold page. He waited staring at the old man. His humble posture, honest face, a figure unforgivable by any man and yet innocent as a member of this earth he kept the doctor waiting and the latter wondered if such assistance was in place for the devastated senior.

"Listen! On my watch next year you'll be hidden under a pile of dirt deep in the silence of the worms. . . !! What's this urge to follow up with him? He won't be out any soon. . . you should think about yourself and do the things you always wanted to do and never got around it. . . Please listen! If there was anything that could be done they would've done so. . . He knows why he is in a cell!! You should worry about yourself! There is not much time left. . ."

"I have an inheritance their mother wanted them to have. . . the house should be his! Everything in it bears a memory. . . It is their heritage that I am worried about! It has to be maintained and all those years we worked hard to raise them. . . after their mother's death I meant to keep a share of everything for them and now I am certain that everything belongs to my children. They never bothered me. I love them! They are good children. . . ."

The caretaker wondered eyeing his office with a desperate look on his face. He was looking for the right words for the umpteenth time just like the rest of a day; he consults his patients-each and every one of them. They see in him a member of their own family, certainly someone more than a mere physician, but this moment weighed heavily on his burden, only to be left alone to spell the final days of the father of a national hero! He proceeded:

Shaheen Asbagh

To my dear righteous head of the family:

My father:

Days go by, nights shelter the divine and the cellmates the same as dawn is always the judge of who will die and who will stay yet by noon everyday the contest is over and jailbirds have to eat their meal in the solitaire of their souls behind walls and barbed wire. It's been only a few days since they pulled out a number of the younger cellmates and shaved every strand of their hair except the eyebrows and took them all to the warden's quarters. God forbid what he wanted them for, because this prison is remote and far away from everything much less a place where guards could find relief and company. My contacts even mentioned passing those cellmates to herd owners for business in return for their conditional release! Father I hope you have laid this letter in safe hands as I keep in mind always your lack of ability to go through my writings although I'm sure and confident in your wisdom and noble virtues. To the reader of this letter I present my due regards and hope that this outline will remain a secret between three of us under any circumstance. The pillars of the legislation and executory powers have begun to suffer as decay and dishonesty have begun to corrupt all positions ascending to the highest echelon. My contacts have already predicted me to remain here for life as some of those members of the government are blaming the intellectuals for the growth of a deep resentment among the activists. I have tried to keep this within these bars but I have to admit that things look different from here and the word is that soon they will begin to scrutinize and inspect every active cadre and institution even the prisons for evidence of participation. They will be looking for individuals with the slightest contribution to this wave of awareness and those who pass on useful information among the common citizens. My dearest father as you know I'm in here for a twenty-five year sentence that of course no one would ever find out about its baseless and futile roots. I have to inform you that I might be kept here longer like many others. They have already begun to classify us as my cellmate is also an attorney who passed on to me these incredible news. I intend to maintain a strong heart and mind over everything that is and will happen and not to worry I will make sure that you will be protected and kept away from the ongoings, but I have to confess that there is a new color covering everything like a new air or tone like the promise of the future. I find it hard to believe and I am sure there is a price to pay, but believe it or not it seems like a familiar beginning, one that has only been seen by the people of this nation in books and distant tales. Justice has always been my directive, my service to my clients was what got me in here and I am sure the new face of the same justice will break the chains that have tied me down sooner or later. And add if I may, it is important that my correspondence and the future ones reach you through different hands, because they no more follow the code and I promise you it will even get worse that I might not be able to write to you at all. So, among us we came up with a team, contacts among the guards and those close to the end of their sentences, to create a channel or I call it a "paper tunnel" to reach our families as things might become worse. Correspondence will become vital and to whomever reading this letter I cordially make a request to continue reading him my father's correspondence from me and to keep them strictly secret without bias because I personally predict that they will soon concern everyone. My dear father I just tattooed my skin with the date of my imprisonment and my sentenced day of freedom, and the symbol of justice of our nation. In coming weeks I will tattoo the other side, right, of my back with the dates and titles of my diplomas and my legal certification so if I die I would feel suited to demonstrate who I am in the flesh. We, here, have a lot of time but cannot *write on the walls or otherwise end up in the cooler in solitaire so skin is the way to go! For me, now is a utopia, an egotistic path, and between the prisoners and the men in arms there is an enigmatic race of ideas and comradeship, but I need your help to survive and prevail. In here I feel it every single day that what my family has done for me is perhaps more nutritious than any act of nature or manhood of man. Why it is all here and not out there I still cannot determine but the pressure and stress mean differently than where there is still a morsel of freedom left among men. And that for every drop of sweat there is a reward to look forward to. We are at best a year away from the plan but do not question my secrecy father because the chance for victory depends on you and your generation. . . . .I suggest you stay put. Do not sign anything or give in, and most important of all forget about me until my letters reach you and make sure you bring it to whoever is reading it now. That will be less complicated! I have a feeling you are in good hands and I hope I am too. With that at last I leave you with your peace and wish you the best of health at the comfort of your soul.*

Cyrus

Doctor drops the letter on his desk and thoughtfully looks at the old man then he pushes the button on the intercom. While his secretary was listening from behind the door resting her head on it she was duly prepared for this interruption and ran back to her desk and answered doctor's page. She got a fresh trace of lipstick and fixed her hair and entered the room.

The old man needed a ride and the doctor asked his secretary to hitch him one, either a taxi or health services. She walked him out and made a couple of calls. The transportation would be waiting in fifteen minutes and she would charge the expenses on the old man's bill later. When he finally left, the woman walked into doctor's room and awaited further duty for which the physician had none and offered her to go home as soon as she desired. She closed the door behind her and waited in the reception area and eventually occupied her seat and still waiting until the doctor stepped out putting on his coat and holding on to his attache. He said goodbye and left. She picked up the phone and dialed a number.

"The old man was here!. . . . . Yes, he had received a letter from him!!. . . I heard it all and yes they are up to something. . . .ok!. . . In the usual place. . . . . don't worry I know the code!"

She hangs up the phone and heads for the door.

"Where are you going!? My place is by the shore sir. . . . !!!"

The driver steps on the pedal and strives through the streets and avenues of the central zone of the island. It was late in the afternoon and the drive took only about twenty or so minutes as he finally stopped in front of a newly projected building and honked three equally consecutive times. Two men came by and unloaded the old man and took him into that building, and through the elevator to the third floor; it was a four story building facing north. The taxi left but there was a passenger car which was parked cross the street from that building's entrance which had arrived right after the taxi. They waited in the car while scrutinizing the building with a pair of binoculars.

The secretary arrived shortly after the taxi had left and stepped into the building taking the elevator to the third floor. She knocked. A man opened the door and waited!

"Perhaps some turtle eggs for dinner."

"It is that time of the year." The man replied and stepped aside.

She entered and asked.

"Is he in the room?"

"He is! What did you hear? Go on!!" Another man in a suit sitting across the room inquired.

The secretary went on describing the contents of the letter she heard being read in the doctor's office, and explained every detail about what went on at her office as the man listened without a move. There was a telephone next to him, more like it was placed on that table for quick use unlike how they are placed at the corner of a room in the house. He listened; he did not ask any more questions and when the secretary finished he pointed at the door. She left quickly and did not say a word.

The two men in the car waited; it was getting dark and the cool breeze of the sea had already begun to poison the mind as the people began to get out and the street was suddenly amassed with a fresh crowd a bit different from the daytime pedestrians who were usually busy gong and coming, to and from work. The two men were careful maintaining a distance from that apartment and took notice of the traffic on the street. The driver drove around the block and parked further from the apartment building, and the passenger stepped out and walked to the entrance. He carefully memorized the four names on the ring plate and walked away as specifically not toward the car, and then waited at the corner of the next block. The driver, again, drove on around the block and after circling once he picked up his passenger and parked a little further away although maintaining a good view of the building. Now they knew that the secretary worked for them but they were not sure about the doctor; also, they knew that one of the four names on that ring plate would belong to the man they were looking for. As they were looking for contacts the passenger made a call on his mobile and awaited response and then read a code into the receiver and glanced at the driver warily. There was a voice after only ten seconds. So the passenger dictated the address of the apartment as well as the four names he had memorized off its ring plate and ended the call.

The dusk was beginning to entice the city with its presence and the lights now became clear and familiarly luminescent to sink the passers' statutes in shades of color; some laughed and others talked, the two men sat in the car without attracting attention during the early hours of the night. It was past eight when a man opened the entrance and stepped out of the apartment walking away from where they were parked. The driver glanced at the passenger and he steps out of the car as he threw his cellular on the seat and keeping his distance followed that man. The subject continued to walk and maintained his pace and the passenger kept his distance from afar. This continued for about ten minutes without the man stopping or producing a suspicious sign. The passenger looked at his watch and decided to return to the car. He is almost there when he realized that the car was gone. He went to the shop across from the apartment and asked to use the telephone. The shop was crowded with night goers buying liquor and some bought soft drinks, cigarettes, nuts, as it might come to be useful since the area did not hold a single bar and there was not a restaurant within a five mile radius of that area. People walked; it was the season, humid, cool, romantic, without a trace of rain or any tropical phenomena. Sea held her peace and so did the residents of the city. They worshipped the nights and this peace of mind was the only thing that kept them dancing, teasing, joking, and specially talking about it all. Men mimicked the hard shells, the women made signs and the street had turned into a flirting ground. The driver answered hurriedly. He informed the passenger man that they relocated the old man and he had to follow them and advised him that he should keep an eye on the apartment until the end of the night. He explained that his cellular had not rung yet and he would try to come back and pick him up and that the passenger man must call him in an hour and continue calling every hour or so as they tried to cover to gain control over this operation. The passenger bought some cigarettes and a bottle of coconut water. He did not smoke and was not even thirsty but pretended to be looking at the passing crowd and making signs and comments at the women while almost one hour passed-very quickly! He would hold the cigarettes without puffing at them and the water still sealed. This time he went to the shop and got some change. There was a pay phone across the street on the same side as the apartment about a quarter of a mile away. He carefully stepped in the booth and looked around while the lights of the apartment building were mostly on. The driver answered quickly and explained that they had tried to distract them by sending a man out so he had called another car to come and pick him up and it would be there shortly.

Passenger found out two days later that the apartments were forfeitures of the ministry of information and indeed deeded to a high ranking employee with no alleged connections to the old man. The two scrutinizers reasoned that since the government was under an international watchdog the torture chambers, prisons, interrogation rooms, and all other locations of hostile exchanges by the authorities would be monitored and inspected, and more, revealed towards the bad and rutting reputation of the government. The old man would not be released even after a week had passed. And the opposition decides to wait and tolerate. . . .

2

What he wanted is far away and completely absent in warden's agenda, but he has wanted it for the past twenty-three years and would probably persist for the next twenty-seven if he lives. He has not lost any hair yet, his weight brush him far short of a normal man. Everywhere he carries the mop in and out of the prayer room after spreading the scent of prison ammonia consumed in prayer water aroma and inmate sweat. There is a shortage of refined water and clean towels so they have to save what there is to wash the sheets and apparel. He also helps in loading them into those huge boiling tanks and then takes them out to dry. In that, he does get some help but it's mostly done by him for the past decade or so. He sits quietly in the prayer room without knowing a word of prayer, or perhaps anything from the book and he just sits there and stares with his muddy glowing eyes waiting for someone to call his name, and that ends his prayer; he knows how to say amen loudly and pretend cautiously, earnestly ashamed. He is senseless about apprehension and does not react anymore to news from outside, and has no visitors; but on the inside everyone recognizes what he stands for, the warden's closest confident if he could produce what he means to say verbally. The prison outfit gets deeper wrinkles on his frame every year and now probably a size or two bigger than what it was when they were assigned to him and even the new one that he seldom wears is too big now. Cyrus brought him a couple of books and magazines, and they are still sitting there at his spot in the prayer room while Cyrus squints at them not believing he is not even interested in the outside anymore. He wasn't even married yet when they took him in for treason. Cyrus couldn't figure what is left of him would work out for the remainder of his life or not, alas he worries if the guy would survive his sentence. Day in, day out, and same thing from the dawn of a guarded day to the noon, and they always surround him around lunch and hope for his usual appetite eating his leftover be it a lesson what prison could do to a man. Cyrus felt lonely and abandoned when he spent time in the prayer room hoping there would be solace; he even greets him everyday, just like a stranger, merely to attract his attention or what is left of him. Cyrus thinks of him as a maniac; to him, he is a scarecrow, a part of the plan-what the cruel warden wants from them all. He wants them to die on their own and never get back out there!

The penitentiary is becoming a black and white end game while the shape of this apocalypse has become so deceiving that Cyrus sees himself now washing clothes and performing speechless prayers with no words to utter and losing his stature and not wanting to ever get out. . . .He often spends his time in the prayer room without a sound and would read law and history; he prays as well except that he is not a man of God although the inmates all think otherwise only because he spends most of his time there, and his dad is not a man of piety much less holding on to religion as a hope for salvation.

They have begun to meet there since he took the habit of taking books to the prayer room as most of them by now know about his case and some respect him deeply. That's just because they see him read and talk like teachers and pauses when he discusses wisely all based on an attitude unfamiliar to most of them as some hate him for that as well and when comes time for prayer those wait for him to leave and then talk about him among a few of them who see nothing in it!! Or at least a way to escape, while there are changes made in the order of that prison. The cellmates are divided like in a game of spades; the others discuss politics making sure everyone hears as in a bid. They are closely attended and some one watching him very closely as the rumors flowing over the surface so reveal. It is, by now, obvious that the warden wants him to stay away from speaking to everyone or perhaps he's been ordered to keep a close eye on him. The sharpshooter up there in the watchbox always keeps his pointed his direction as if he's been paid for his head. Nobody talks in there; the plan is to get out clean and nice without any further hassle from the warden and get on back to the normal trail of life like family, a job, and a reputation or what is left of it. It is only fair to say that not all of them would make it, and surely not all of them are allowed to make it because the warden has his own hired hands among the guards and a lot of contacts in the government as he used to be the secretary of information for almost a decade and not more. So he knows some thing or two about the nuts and bolts of the system as so does Cyrus whose reason for incarceration is promised to be kept secret if he followed the given guidelines passed on to him after the court where they freed Omar, his partner at law. Omar loved his wife and had a deep affection for his partner and the clients when a friend in a successful attempt on his spouse persuades her into addiction and an unlawful relationship. Meanwhile keeping Omar as a business contact he plans for a proposal; so he brings it up during a secret visit to Omar's house. Later, then the woman asks him to get out not to be living together anymore. Omar can't find a reputable place to live in and his notorious contact and client invites him to live in his remote villa! "Think of it as yours. . . .!!" He is desperate and agrees to stay there for a week or so until the mud settles thinking he could probably ask for help from Cyrus. While he stays there his business contact raises the dosage on Omar's wife until she is unable to tell right from wrong. Now, then, she is ready to marry him and the business contact begins to kill time and procrastinate. He starts to share some unrelated issues with Omar who would not step out of the villa and is spending his time incommunicado. Meanwhile, the business contact keeps a tight control over both the man and his wife looking for a way to take advantage of Omar since his influence is well over the usual bracket and his powerful friends could help him help the government whose survival and victory would serve the purpose for the business contact who thinking of a plan, he considers defaming Omar, or penetrating into his business, by way of deceit or else indeed something of a life and death nature!

The business contact reaches to his friends in the government and even to some he secretly brings up Omar's name; they meet on occasions clandestinely and a couple of them once join at the villa and speak to Omar while pretending that they are only interested in creating opportunities to improve Omar's business, or perhaps promote him to a higher position by enhancing his professional reputation-both him and Cyrus! The intentions of these people are hidden and far from being revealed to Omar as he is still looking for a way to reach peaceful ends with his wife who is deeply hooked and far desperate in seeking more drugs and still keeping her addiction a secret. She has no respect for Omar or his partner anymore. Cyrus stays away from both of them, by now he senses something wrong as he hears hardly anything from Omar, the man he has worked with for so many years since his school days.

The island keep its limited usual climate as the midday heat of the sun brings the wild closer to the shore as well as the human inhabitants. Omar would occupy the backyard of that villa for hours in contemplation; he badly wants a way to come to terms with his wife not being aware of her abysmal diabolic involvement. She is deceived and stepped on; by now, physically involved with Omar's shroud business contact. The man and woman apart but in trouble, Omar sinks in thought and depression about his marriage that is in pieces; his woman has sold herself for a dose of enigma like a medicine that has kept mankind in the dark side for centuries and her dosage being increased day by day. However, Omar is living in a desperate hideaway and is gradually overcome by a ubiquitous helplessness that can only be improved through assistance from his nemesis, none other than his business contact whose watchful eyes bring him to the point of settling ties with Omar's wife as though she is a piece of elastic around his fingers, but he not only loves the woman yet he hates her more than anything. He is close to Omar now and keeps him at a distance by inviting Omar to stay longer and, yet, begins to reveal some secrets about the vicious present government and its immense corruption.

The tropical summers killed some and let reproduce some insects and beasts indigenous to the island. The heat broke hearts and cooked the minds of the inhabitants. Lovers and haters too, to the point where some only drank to get rid of the sticky hot, and deeply touching sweat that shaped the form of those beings in the island's small world; they drank water, wine, whisky, and again whisky, wine, and water, water, water, and again. Omar, too, was drinking perhaps only whisky and he had the best being given and served overt bottles of it which he drank only with water-a lot of it! Sweats of different kinds covered his desperate stature; wet shirts, pants soaked in between his legs, and he wore slippers and spent his time around the pool dipping his toes occasionally without meaning to swim in the water. He was afraid; worried that there might be some trap, perhaps the pool being poisoned or electrified. He also tests every bottle of whisky making sure the seal is authentic and now there he would eye the water carefully and every single meal he had to tolerate. His business contact spends an afternoon with him apparently meaning to talk to him; and by now, Omar has a good picture of the end. He has to wok for the government, and yes, it's all about recruitments, 'Join the army and become a do gooder!' But he feels the depth of the mission along with his experience in law and how he always pictures himself a liberalized man and separate from the system. All he wanted was his family back together like the old days. He was ready to forgive and forget everything that had happened. He wanted her back but couldn't tell his business contact about his wife; not a bit of it would go through his head and not only that but it would destroy the rapport, it would be mal-reputation. No sense in resisting even though he knew that they had high expectations, and perhaps, there was some money involved, but he didn't need it. He was careful and he heard Cyrus, like always, pointing out the possibilities, "There might be something worthwhile for us to dig into,. . . keep your head up!!" He thought about calling him but perhaps later since it would interrupt the ongoings and create doubts about his status. He had pretended enough and now was time to tell or listen. Omar wanted to listen! It was better to follow them and maybe it was not bad news after all, perhaps the business contact could help him, even bring back his family. But he began condescending Omar and inquired into his present condition. He also informed him that the government was paying for everything without expecting anything in return except one small detail.

They both drank whisky and constantly wiped the sweat off their faces with already soaked handkerchiefs. He inquired about Omar's affairs and told him that he would help him with anything he needs as Omar denied acting confidently and assured him that everything was fine. The business contact finally opened up and explained that his people, ministry of information, were after a group of individuals who had been involved in a crucial incident associated with the ministry. Among them, he explained, were a few persons remained under investigation through his office. They happened to be Omar's clients! He walked off the poolside and headed for bathroom to do his business as he had al day, every couple of hours. The liquid life and those blazing hours added up to his solitary presence and its frightening tension. The whisky had already gotten to him although he knew what it was all about. The return from the bathroom was accompanied with a fresh refill of the highballs, whisky and water on the rocks! He sat down and looked the other way without even reacting to the business contact. Omar whispered to him that it was out of the question and that client files were confidential and that was law. The law that everyone had to abide by; the law of the land that was enforced by its government especially the ministry of information. Omar also informed him that it would be impossible to access those files or leak any information about his clients. The business contact bursted into laughter and looked his direction, and assured Omar that no one would know; he persisted that it was in the interest of the country and the ministry. He told Omar that the persons he had indicated were already accounted for as criminals accused of treason and many other crimes without mentioning their names. Omar, still looking away, closed his eyes slowly and uttered, "You heard me. . . !"

The contact left his seat and refreshing his glass returned to the wide backyard and took a few steps around the pool while sun had stepped into her equatorial descent. The leaves seemed darker and the water in the pool was turning into a deeper blue like a mass of turquoise. He wanted to explain but his attempt died short of its final syllables. Omar, then, changed his impression as if ignoring everything he had heard so far and started talking about the comfort of the contact's villa. The two men were as savvy as two backgammon players feeling they had barricaded all the pieces yet knowing the dice would explode at any moment, and alas, there would be a turnaround. The two dodged around the palms which by then flowed into momentary trembles showing the strength of the evening breezes that could cool each man's torso provoking them to hold their glasses high and talk louder. The business contact, now almost yelling, still worked hard to persuade Omar into cooperation with his plan to reveal the identity and the record files of the aforementioned individuals. He finally turned to him, directly looking into his eyes, and asked the business contact about the pay while he had denied having mentioned any money and claimed it to be a service to the country. Omar wanted money, a big sum. He wanted it to be immediately delivered along with the deed to that villa and an automobile. He was quiet for a few minutes while the business contact refilled his glass and came back after making a phone call.

"Do you share everything with your wife?"

"Obviously! What kind of question is that?"

". . . . Just asking, don't mind me!!"

The telephone rang and he picked it up.

"Yes,. . .aha. . . .OK! Really? Well. . . Thank you!" He hung up and faced Omar calmly with a grin on his blushing face.

"It's done. . . !!"

———————————

The men, all at high ranks of the government, inquired about by the business contact brought a case against Omar and Cyrus accusing them for breaching the confidentiality code and could care less about what the court would uncover. They wanted blood and they got it! Once Cyrus blew the whistle on the business contact and the ministry the judge let Omar go for cooperation and would sentence Cyrus to prison. But things got severely tight because Omar's wife came to surface with a plea to addiction and the business contact was publicly identified. Omar committed suicide in his prized car. They said it was an accident off a cliff but had no proof of foul play. The body was medicated which was kept secret although Cyrus knew. He plead for appeal, but the judge's hackers had him hypnotized. He found Cyrus guilty as charged. The head of the ministry resigned once it was privately discovered that the villa and the car were originally yet indirectly properties of the ministry. They were deeded to an administrator in charge of public relations (business contact). That minister was reassigned as the warden of the prison once the judge found everyone innocent except Cyrus who was now left more than a few years of his heinous term. Omar's wife was relieved to a rehab and it took her years to figure out what had happened yet she persisted to see the business contact during her visiting hours until she finally sobered up.

After Omar's death his wife, Salome, gradually felt the extent of this puppet show. One day, she went to visit Cyrus in the penitentiary and told him what she knew. Salome even volunteered to stand court, she wanted them dead and done with. Cyrus, of course, having known better told her to stay away from the public (their public), and away from the associates of her late husband as well as visiting him as little as possible until he could put the pieces together. He tried to tell Salome that this whole thing was bigger than what they thought!

The warden kept a watchful eye over Cyrus's daily agenda. He often met him around the yard or, on occasions, in his cell or his office to make sure he was completely controlled while his cellmate reported Cyrus's private moments to the warden each passing week. The sun was brushing the skin wet with dampness as each islander awaited the dark side of the day to rid of the heat being it summer, or else as they all were one season which was a heaven for outsiders and a hell for the aborigines. A decade, what Cyrus owed to himself, and it was him that that knew he was innocent but through the first half of his sentence grief disappeared and compassion led on when others around that prison began to tell him about the outside during the prayers. He told them about his confidence in God's miracles and faith that should lead him the right way any moment. He believed he was lost in a time travel to finally find his path and become strong enough to help others.

Cyrus thought of a prison ritual, performed it every week in the prayer room, by burning all the newspapers they could find around the yard. He began to hate the press and persisted that others should do too while he delivered sermons of a new nature-all in the silence and peace of the prayer room-as he watched the guards being astonished and trying to control themselves. Surely, they reported everything to the warden who would puff his hand-rolled cigar and exclaim that everything was going as he had planned. Cyrus did not fight for his life as the prison walls were his sacred shield and the mates and guards his witnesses. It was every week that he burned the newspapers and performed a sermon aloud for all present to hear; he meant to provoke and stimulate the atmosphere as to escape insecurity and the sheer power of what he sensed to be a conspiracy. He had talked to the warden on occasions but could not trust him likewise when mutually the two men saluted as warden assured him that the walls of his cell were deaf to him and could not hear anything! He wanted to find out what Cyrus knew by letting him go about his way. For more than eight years or so, the man believed he was paving the way for a sure trap. He even had hired some boys on the outside who assured him nothing was going on although everyone knew it was otherwise. . . . *Leaving this man in peace would bring others like closer. The enemy will believe that we are in rebellion. . . .*

In the meantime, not only the prisoners but most of the island's established organizations including the government were beginning a fresh campaign to save the day as the towns and smaller communities became aware of the leader's status, and to some way, got to know about a scar on the face of this system that kept turning deeper and deeper. Cyrus was pushing hard to provoke the inmates who came forward and blessed them with rules of teamwork asking each of them to save any paper or burnable garbage in order to perform the familiar rite of praise and burn whatever they could find, and by that fire they sat and worshipped for their unity. This sensation prepared them for a future foreseen by him that would keep the prison authorities on their toes and warned the outsiders that something was wrong until the press or at least the newspaper decides to promote the story of Cyrus's trial allegedly linked to a source connected with the court. Warden's agents doing their best to avoid any outside contact began to secretly keep an eye on his family and friends whom by now outnumbered them. His name was all over the community and even mentioned on the television while leaving a good memory of what had happened in that court years ago. The newspaper held no importance anymore notwithstanding those news; they all wanted to participate and bring the papers to the prayer room and some even picked out the books written by designated writers deemed to be corrupting the mind, tow-timing, and plain out lied to bend the mates' beliefs and direct them towards a different direction in order to uphold the government and its members; they brought them all to Cyrus to have them burned and calmly talked about what went on. They began to divide and argue but Cyrus was keen. He was capable of building a strong theory to convince and make them believers of his ideology and it went so far that the cellmates bound for transfer carried his ideas with them wherever they went. He invited the boys to consider, think, and hold their opinion and be free to talk about it as freedom would someday have them surrender to its police power! Indeed, in every moment that passed, Cyrus warned them of this police power and told his protocols to beware of the long-time luring police power of this apocalyptic freedom. Cyrus believed in explicit alertness of the mind and ideas one learned during his life being it during prison days, at school, or among his family. He assured everyone that people liked the warden were capitalizing on them to be government agents once they got out and so it was best that they were on guard and prepared to protect themselves with stronger than the envisioned public. The cellmates, not only history but they began to burn political texts, social sciences and anything related to the educated mind including religion. Cyrus called it the purification of a fellow man and persisted in unity and teamwork to make the terms seem shorter along with his patriotism-that of an old tradition.

The bars no more hurt their feelings because they knew that they were able to watch over themselves. They knew that their families were safe because somebody was serving a sentence to pay the blood money which the regime expected, but it was the bars that had killed the rage among the criminals as well as inmates like Cyrus who were taken in for defying the government, and whose number now was on the rise. Cyrus could not hide his happiness and performed the rituals with more confidence in the comrades who surrounded him during the prayer room hours. Two, four, eight, or even up to sixteen, reason was clear as the multiples of two gathered to formulate into the frontiers with gaps! And those gaps filled the clear-conscience and the innocent never to be upheld as a lawman or else, or otherwise the faith would rule the prison of which Cyrus never wanted to understand even a sheer simple proverb or book, and whom cellmates took for a hoodlum that washed them off with peace and verses of, say, blank moments of meditation as though a multiple would be almost short of loading the proxy. A gun that went hand to hand until it was stolen and brought back to the hoodlum, Cyrus, who knew the words to its poetry! Still, the stink of burned palm tree skin, newspaper, and pages of multiples of books on general literacy flowed with sea water odor as the rain, to its reasonable portions, was stepped on by bare soles, boots, incognito tennis shoes, and brought into the lost complex. They would run after anyone willing to pay an ear. Two on two would later make four, sixteen, and thirty-two and the remaining each faced another cellmate to convince and share the honest ideas of the hoodlum orator. Cyrus had known and knew now! "Pure pattern of human tragedy should fall about each and every one of you who've been warm with fire and cleansed with meditation and adorned with elementary rituals of humanitarian nature for humans to remember during moments of solitary revolution when one needs to move for the sake of his solitude and take a step toward the utopia of growth and security. . . ", Cyrus said as he promised that they were awaiting every one of them to avenge and the vigilante would overcome. Yet without a conventional logic it was not possible for them to prove champions and the police power of the newfound freedom would fail and fall to its needs, and then, image and not flesh winning over the values that convinced-for every bite of bread-to put silence to more arms and would permit the cycle of ocean breeze to brush the island independent of insidious elements. *Enough with this sin, because I breathe the sea now with every cell alive, you breathe it too. . . let not freedom destroy the heat of this chained perdition; this proxy to our future should live, live long, yet lost in the lives of future sons and daughters while they are called to retrospect and generational prudence. . . they will know, eat, and think with us all as one.*

The cells almost empty now, let this spirit take over and syndicate every element of communication! They wanted him to pursue his better judgement and create the final form of his urges. He smelled the sea and used familiar methods of tradition on this small piece of land showing them how easy life was and could be if only they stopped learning and persisted on inventing a self that prudently and nobly dramatized their present status in the compound and continued the same on the outside so the police power of freedom disappeared! Thus, never again would they want to know who would be liable to impose a constitution. . . . "We don't want to know, we cannot, we are stupid but we care to protect the human race with peace and inner strength of the mind to prolong the life for others like us. . . . men, women, and children!" Cyrus taught not hate but he exclaimed that within man there was a treasure that allowed him to survive his own kind and loved them. He could use his hands to build and that was why science remains from within and against these small members of the enemy man needed not kill or die but to overcome through basic means of knowledge what one shared with the one next to him.

The sea had been calm. The correctional facility was the target of the waves set on a short cliff by that edge of the island nation less visited yet a short distance from the capital, and making a perfect square on the map with two other villages less populated and equal distance from the capital and the compound. A daily number of merchants continuously travelled between the three communities and that high spot of the island, the prison, at the peak of the cliff allowed the inmates to see them and their cars and trucks move around loads of domestic goods that fed the lives of the inhabitants. "What may this seascape have to ultimately offer does not quite meet the balance, fate, and faith! That human essence which insofar remains absent from the pages of the new history and the poor geography of shelter and industry never ends here. . . . among us there are the resilient who persevere at peace and comfort for the youth. The day that comes soon will show the clean hands of the people raised against this regime and it is about time to move now. . . ." Cyrus, relentless and out of breath, daily, through what short time left of his term could only persist in drawing colorful lines of speculation and dreaming with the last paces of his beating heart to keep that faith among his elite audience who called him "Preacher" and respected him to be one innocent rebel who merely wanted them to resist injustice and the miserable cycle that had the island nation to its knees.

The movement was growing. It had begun to provoke the youth and educated towards the promised paradise, that of a more obligated aphorism. The nation became more gullible as days passed; she was as innocent as an infant who sought only attention and food. Cyrus knew not any better but to keep his peaceful ground away from insults and savage strikes of the warden and his men similar to the other fronts that were shaping in different institutions. So he had heard and invited the cellmates, who were about to be released, to contact the active intellectual elements and share their ideas with them as he specifically advised them to avoid the books or any literature having been circulated by the enemy. That enemy was presumed to be prepared and ready to open its wings and play police. Those men knew now and, better yet, they would be wary without any irony to be inserted, as agents of a mortal front, into a pure form only so humane to seal the shadow of liberty and revival.

The year had now been targeting Cyrus. He knew!! Another pardon coming up soon, it might have included Cyrus as he was a possible candidate to be granted it and the taste of freedom again. He knew!! He was not anxious yet a bit weary and, more than anything else, unsure that he might sink into his own cage-one that he had built as he grew older in that prison. His responsibility had exhausted him now that he was looking up to others and he did not know where he belonged. What would he do out there?

Perhaps, someone could shoulder the burden he had meant to solemnly iterate and inform those close to the man to wake up, and to think, and to pursue immortal causes that would thus flourish in the eyes of history. He had started dealing with his own prudent cause; the one we call retirement from the fight, but could he do that or should it all subside? He was surrounded by so many that the guards were starting to stay away from his daily deeds letting him do what he wanted. In the yard, the muscle klan kept him protected and the guards had stopped listening to the warden's instructions looking away from him. He even received books, more books, food, and was met his other needs although did not smoke or hardly drink. He had long given those away. Cyrus was almost living outside the parameters by then. He knew!! His pardon was near and everyone was certain that they would let him go. He had less than two years or so left and he was strongly endorsed through the present media by those citizens which were ready and able to fight when, one day, he was informed of his father's abduction. . . . .

3

Among the sufferers, she was tall and grey yet she survived. The door to the garden was ajar but not welcoming and, although not far away, Eden stood between them as they were suffering benign illusions and a tender amnesia that touched not only self but its ego so drastically save for those who were among those survivors; alive and courteous, they were conscious of sin solely with regard to infants, the name of a child that at least could pick up 'yes' and 'no', and say 'potty'. Yet unlike rats and turtles, they pleased the outer paternal instincts that were accounted for while the ego flew the distance and conquered the kins and blood drew a picture of humanity-that kinship which man once burdened and promised for the better, the philosophy of the struggle of soul. She never carried a child for Omar. She behaved and no one stood between them as a socially high-rank family, well off, and prominently active in their community. Her status, if important and worthy of mention as she was humble and felt deeply trivial, was bound by a bipolar deficiency that occurred, say, after her extensive drug use in the hands of the man who pretended to be a friend and happened to be a prodigy in psychedelics and charm in possession of anything that could anyone from her center or his! This business contact persisted and Salome did not resist as she regretted yet hardly understood why everything happened as they did although it was too late as Omar took his life. . . .

She worked to forget the past along with a never felt hardship she would never recognize the cause for and a bam-bam, dirt-raising, smoke-filled, somber pink yard, and with its neighborhood remaining quietly in astonishment. Salome was under care of a therapist that knew everything; a benevolent partnership for all of one's private dreams and for the secrets to be let loose as Salome had minimal instincts for some days and things, but not for others while she maintained herself, spontaneously, to avoid Omar. Amen!

That she left the deck immaculate and left the table between games while still wanting to deal another hand showed the pure elements of her beauty aside from the prodigal soul that always was possessed within this woman. Or if she had or had not sinned, it was regretfully omitted from the proxy of the court yet she still enjoyed the testimony of the man of the hour as with an askance. The television was showing 'the preacher'. He was, again, denying the system while intertwined in repetitious exclamations of fear and denial, and that fraudulent cabinet that by then upset lives and the communion of the society by not allowing even a moment of peace among its people! Cyrus was to be taken back to prison while deliberating his inquiry outright on the media, the channel only accessible to the prosper. He solely repeated his predicaments as it only took him two or less months of freedom to be encaged behind the bars again. Salome only saw a familiar figure while rushing to the bistro as starvation had gotten the best of her. The poor psychotic heroine who still remained on the list to be called by 'the preacher' to the stand; alas, he was presently unable and indeed for a long time after. It was part of the outline that the island nation routinely implemented over its infidel elements and those who made unnecessary noise and raised a handful of dust! They better had burned! Heating the blood in the veins of this nation's masses would certainly be a lesson for others that might have learned sooner than later to forget about bullying the government.

Anyhow, everything counted; the elements, the members of the cabinet, the corruption that ruled the island nation, and those hatching turtles that only released and died in vain like million others, and those secretly terminated by death squads that by then were so common as a majority instrument of its rulers. Salome, at her usual seat, floating in tranquility eyed Cyrus on the television without surprise or yet a sense of doubt as he orated ragingly his father's abduction and house arrest under the orders of the ministry of foreign affairs and then the commentary that followed cynically produced by the national press. The community television, assigned and supported by the few who pulled most of the strings those days, smoking island's hand-rolled cigars and consuming heavy intakes of rum and rye. Thus, progress was an illusion, and people were a mass of slaves as Cyrus begged for help and was pushed away from the camera. Later they forced him to the motorcade destined for prison. Her lunch was always ready; and once ordered, it was prepared for her with the best attention of Mamma who did fried bananas, slices of meat, and a loaded rice that was her specialty-a token of Mamma's affection prepared best for whoever she cared to entice with such heritage. The rice was the oldest recipe that smelled of gravy and spices, spices that were prepared by Mamma herself. She dressed in her duty uniform and an apron that adorned her presence as *the* chef. Salome, too, was in a red uniform with a papillon and a beret that had a white cloth flower in the front and a name tag on her chest. The bananas were perfect as always but Salome was consumed in desperation and fear over Cyrus's capture. . . She was mumbling as she forked through them. The rat-infested bistro was quiet with a sporadic number of tables occupied by gamblers and onlookers alike. She strived and hid from her disability; one of obscenity and evil that those only half-absent from the reality of life could have shared with her their humble sentiments. Salome tasted the food without emotions although savory; it went down without a flavor to be felt and, too, being absent from the reality of this cycle she was not able to thank the creator properly or else that was a daily routine? Salome mumbled, murmured, and quietly laid a claim of revenge by just being an employee of the only casino at the island nation. She had been identified, recognized as an evidence of a heinous act-betrayal of dignity and the human bondage. The woman knew everyone well so much so that she was like a member of the family for Mamma, Baba the casino manager, Dama the co-worker that shared her poker table, and on she went by helping the others as they did on to her. Yet the moment of chaw was her moment, grub, a plate of it. She was left alone to rest in retrospect feeling an immense respect for individuality she upheld so deeply among the oppressed.

Floating and loose, at another phase of catastrophe, no one would admit but her who could care less having seen the worst of it; Salome had begun to gossip and exchange dreams and doubts with her shadow. A deep rhapsody that entails the status quo-one of desperation and sodden truth that would not stand. . . . "May I know what you are all about looking like you are all that. . . . !?"

"I can tell! Don't think I can't. . . . I can tell you what is going on, and no one else would know, and one more thing. . . . it's not finished yet! It'll happen soon. . . . that shining armor will finally overcome, we'll know it before you would!! Them thieves would have lost, they'll go to hell in the kingdom, and us, what am I talking about!!? Us poor beings will be saved and would be fed well and even better we'll be with our family. . . . Omar be seein' me and put his soft hands around me and . . . . don't look at me like that. . . like you. . . .. !"

She picked a morsel of fried banana with her fork and looked around and swallowed quietly saving the meat for last.

"Mamma knows, yes she does know what I like! We are bloods and there is no stopping that, she knows my favorites and I love her. . . . don't never bother the girl! Let her what she does, cookin' me some' different everyday. . . what you want. . . !?"

Salome dropped some food on the floor accidentally and pulled it under the table with her toes. She became quiet and continued eating. Suddenly a small rat appeared under the table which Salome could not leave unnoticed. She stared at it with curiosity although not very uncommon in that antiquated and ruinously old casino. She went on bickering at it without attracting attention. The rat ate the particles of what she had dropped quickly with hands and efforts of its sharp teeth persuading her still to show a bit of kindness and generosity. Salome obeyed her heart and deliberately dropped a bite of her meat over the same spot persuading the rat to stay and eat it. The pest, although rare, was not seemingly afraid of its vicinity; the noise would not scare it and it carried on by occupying that space under the table going back and forth while munching on what was left of all that Salome had dropped on the floor.

"Is that all you. . . . dirty and feeding on leftovers,. . . . you are a nasty little beast!!"

"Why did I feed you after all? You make me sick to my stomach. . . ."

"I have enough on my damn plate and now you. . . ."

Salome began to ignore the rat, now a bit enticed and awaiting another morsel of food which the woman would not drop. The animal made a sound as if to pass on a message to delirious Salome who was still talking by herself.

In a sudden change of noise the room became quiet when Salome felt she was starting to undergo another bipolar spasm due to acute brain attack as she heard that rat:

I am the princess of darkness as you are the princess of change, I am a fugitive although not quite safe of tragedy and you are a small kin of a big revolution; one who, as I know, exhausted the merciless claws of a psychedelic and has escaped death. . . I betrayed my family to be here and so did you, and at last I too am a creature of God left in his hands for bad and good. Listen to me because I admit that now I am a fugitive without a place, without a choice to do what I want while I am sheltered by you, a desperate and abused being. I repeat! I know what happened to you. . . don't worry because it is all for the good. You are part of the history as I hope that it will be the same with likes of me since the sentence I was honored is still death and I can not go back and am in your hands! I beg you to understand with care and regards and bestow upon likes of you to be watchful while scrutinizing what goes around you because now it is important, and then, it will be a major incident of solidarity and, later, suppression albeit with more than a few lives in line. . . . A sea of blood, as a lesson to God. . . what they have said, what all of them believe in. . . .God forbidden, pain-thirsty, bull-minded, and power-hungry. . . . they want to dictate the fate of the turtles in capital letters, an act of dominance, with intentions of sheer superiority and determining the lives of millions, those indigenous figures of peace on this island. . . . they'll be, someday soon, nothing but empty, dry shells laying around the sandy beaches as a souvenir of demons that would rule an archipelago of skeletons forever through the ruthless pages of its history! I have seen it with my own eyes, the rat poison, that medicine of man for such humble a creature! It's all there, every bit of it saved for those innocent turtles and more, and I had to get away from the God-ridden, equivocal, low-lives that can not look eye to eye at their newborns but to prepare them to learn to kill when time comes!! I am therefore in your hands among these last crumbs of food to perform my natural act exhausted with terror, partitioned among the nations, as an element, one of bilateralism, beware of the balance indeed because nature has always burdened man with her good and the bad times, alas, I hope I will not be a reason for further separation and betrayal of sexes among humans forsaken and underscored by that same signs of nature that are informative and alarming. . .. because letting me be, a fugitive, can only be the work of one God, the one and only creator, this entire presence, the last resort to save the signs of life and common cause, and instead wholly lure the weary tribes of turtle and rat to co-exist, but save for that wishful dream. Man is to be saved from the bloody horizon that would fall like a crimson curtain and smell of animal rot. . . .the sea will be contaminated with odor and filth, the shores horridly stripped of their refreshment and pleasantry. . . . The tribe has saved the poison and is ready to raid the turtle nests and fill them with it, they have saved the dead rats and are ready to feed them to the hardbacks! It is a conspiracy, I tell you, my guardian! And do not be surprised because you will someday be important as I know you as a fugitive from death, and be strong as I, too, mean to be, humble and proud of what I struggle to do which at this time can not be done, one against an empire, a poisonous one, with a plan for dominance and totalitarianism. . . Beware and do not forget for I might hold an important message for you as outsiders are fearful of such belligerence as a sign of radicalism and immoral behavior that has become common among the rats! They have enough poison now to victimize half of all the turtles and would feed the rest with morsels of poisoned ones. My hopes are for you to understand and share my deepest sympathies for nature is related by all of its elements. . . I don't have anything against the turtles as I have begun to participate in this game of conspiracy since I felt the dimensions of the plot and would regret every part of it later and now that it has brought me here hungry and exhausted, unafraid of human traps to pass on what I know to you. I feel free!! Let not leave anything untold as I am here by the works of God, and I know them, all of them, as they have intentions, indeed, deep-rooted, devil-polished, most undesired intentions that make an innocent soul want to give up life and join the dead than follow them. . . And how are they going to respond to their offsprings? There is no telling how many of them are actually believing in what they live for but the strings are pulled by a few and, perhaps due to a selfish hostility or an unwelcome encounter between a rat and a turtle as the former lives in dirt and the latter spends much of his life in the water making it more gullible than a rat, maybe. Every hatch hole will be installed with packs of poison and more of that would be contaminating every stream and grove while it is the last attempt to terminate the flow of natural balance on this land. The archipelago will be covered with filth, and although I do respect my generation, garbage which has fed us since inception. The fighting will start and go on for eternity to see and judge. To humans they want to show muscles but holes, sewer, attics, and tunnels do not seem to be enough because ambition is chewing their pride and provoking them to join the evil while I have to deny peace and uphold freedom the only way I know and that is fighting. That fundamental pattern of seeking and desire, that which breathes through the veins of life, any life that substantiates the existence of a society and that social club belongs to those rats that are following the scapegoats of a liberal nation like they fought rats of a different color or a different faith, or idealism. Indeed, my nation senses alarm but more, they sense a hazard, a useless hazard that has ruled the ideology of co-existence since the beginning of time. . . . our queen or king wants revenge because it believes in supremacy and can not see another species subsist and deny it its right to totalitarianism because the nature and what you humans call prosperity are limited and depend on time and season therefore the rats want a larger portion and, in fact, they want all. My kind, a male and a female, can produce a hundred offsprings in a year and wait till you see we are everywhere, every hole, home, or hospice. It will be a sanctuary of dictators what this requiem will result in. So help me God and Man as good as any, and what other powers there may be to stop this act! You, as much as anyone else, are responsible now that you know. . . . Our island without the presence of those peaceful and free-living turtles, the asset to which we dedicate pride and tradition, a statement made by the cycles of a natural habitat and an attraction unique in itself, and a sign of the purity of the wild and the sea. . . .

Salome played around over her plate forking the last pieces
of fried bananas and what was left of the meat on it. Then,
she began to repeat after the rat. . . . 'hmmm. . . the wild and
the sea. . . . !?' and looked around which was quiet now but
she playfully put the fork down and approached her plate
with her nose sniffing the food like the rat would do and
bust into laughter; loud but uncalled for she knew that in
order to understand that poor pest-that last virtuoso of its
kingdom-she had to find out what brought it to her when
she suddenly freaked out in her more familiar identity. . .
Calm and now in a serious tone she asks:

"Is that you darling?"

"I wasn't expecting you. . . and by the way you are early
because I get off at seven and now it's too early to go home,
or did you, darling miss me. . . ? I too got a few reasons to
miss you but it has to wait. . ."

Salome kept on babbling while Mamma started to notice
how she was brought back as she approached her table
and calmly set the desert next to the plate Salome had left
unfinished. Both, quiet and in a moment of deep inquisitive
surprise, looked at one another with awe struggling to hold
an impression or, yet, break the ice after Salome came
together but not losing her femininely familiar tone, that
which was hers before her husband's death. She asked:

"Is that for me? You're so sweet Mamma but I've had
enough. . . perhaps I should go back to the table. . . .!!"

Mamma smiled earnestly. A noble woman whose stature
was more a legend than a weighty cook. She was felt as
years had brought her up to be kind and be a source of

warmth and friendship like a logo, a silhouette that said,'We are the blood', and the blood ran in the veins of island nation so painfully now as she exclaimed, "Oh, I understand madame. . . I understand. . . .maybe a little later Mrs. Salome!!" Mamma stood on as Salome stared at her and she smiled like a servant would do and then stepped away obediently.

The serving area was quiet as the patrons headed for the tables to try their chances at the evening glory of the island while they still had a few hours till midnight when most of the tables were closed especially roulette and perhaps craps but poker and slots would do all night as usual. Salome rested at her seat while waiting to deal the second round of cards in a game of five card poker as one man looked at his tokens and eyed the caller contemplating an ante. Suddenly there was a couple of gunshots; it interrupted the lurking silence of the casino. . . . "Long live our island!!!" A fellow shouted without looking around. Then he walked toward the center core of the casino where the roulette table was located and fired another air shot. . . . "A new day in our history has started and we are not too far away from. . . ." The armed man continues to speak through his throat's deepest vocal cords, thick, fluent, confident, and hopeful as Salome had already hidden under the table like others when a tap on the back shook her up. She turned around swiftly but without any noise when a young man behind her whispered, "You are coming with me. . . !"

———————————

Feather blown, double image, and painful labyrinth of a cycle of messages each exceptional in tone and rhythm, those that make humans, beasts, and ghosts shiver the same or to believe that upon the ire of the men of Queen, or the gravedigger who owed it all to the Shah, the role of a venal undertaker to dethrone as many sinful members of the secret committee or the Round Table of the knights became having to repent and face the dilemma and relive the somber and pallid portrait of a hard-earned goal that beheld those solid facts of depression and repression, and again, a whole mass of social and whimsical elements that would loiter as long as time allowed to help scribe the pages of social and political eras in history. A man standing in front of the facade at Monte Mar, a filly at Westminster viewing the written words in the sky over the clouds about daydreaming that shaped the wind, the solar, and the lunar oath which endeared the nature's way. Sinking in the depths of such a cold case with regards for the bad and the good yet reached the depths of hell and, then and thus, they were able to find heaven while sending the heart of our virtue in paraphernalia and trash upon inhalations! Then, they eventually march with loads of explosives over dead carcasses thereafter planting trees, again step into war with more explosives and pistols, thereon, produce children brought up for another war. The human seeds of the soul solely bear with them the innocence of the society than accommodating them and that meant the demon and the ugly were were weary of redoing the roots and inflict blood in the upbringing of the blossoms changing the taste of the fruits of belligerence as though the Reich was reborn, and the Holocaust, again, culminated seeping the odor of savagery over the earth and spelled the human faith to be a battle between Man and the Books! But gold has the power over love. The endangered people rose and fell where treaties came short by a wedge in a deep quarrel while neither party was sober enough to decide on the fate of the argument.

Communication breakdown brought everyone together, and in pursuit of peace, they starved and gave blood and nursed the injured. All views of an exhausted nation that, for years, went through an epic too dire for its citizens to put up with. Aside from mimicking the center and, as well, for years to follow the colors of a different flag, they showed gratefulness and blessed the comrades without a lower or upper hand deeply contaminated by psychedelics and excess of useless freedom which I leave to your judgement because, after all, everyone was free to choose, to bear arms, and to speak his heart. Yet there remained a few choices in the island, perhaps they had a record in solely mimicking freedom; one that tasted more like being entangled in pain and corruption since the primes of liberty at the capitol, all the taverns, and the casino.

The cubist affairs of the artificial generations of propaganda tore down the doors and entered island nation with an urge to build networks and mass produce, more propaganda, and free sex for all like the fathers of socialism and the voice of those who long believed in freedom of their opinion. It spoiled the island and rutted its common roots and the music had never been played again in anticipation of the paradise lost and its musketeers-the clowns of the renaissance fair! The mimics faded and budded into shapes that were familiar now that people knew about who and whom to send their toasts to. The corrosion of the culture was evading the minds in a psychopathic process as the rhythm slowed and it became priceless yet these worthless anthems brought with them a tumultuous image of war or perhaps peace which, albeit, did not change the tone; it is all good over the flawless surface of sand. So quiet and soft that a man could find its most indelible instincts and was not able to speculate simply dying in vain. Indeed, the diagonal, straight, all of those calculated forms and formulas proceeded to be accounted for by a few while flesh undertook the task of deception toward nationalism in the island. *God bless the nation!*

Salome surrendered with ease and a melancholy typical of her mood of confidence in another without her bipolar symptoms only to l;eave her cage; the long-driven sanctuary was assigned to her by the conspirators of Omar and others. She let her hand loose without resistance to his words or the young man's warm and damp hand. He pointed his piece to the entrance signaling her to move on after him. Once they started for the door and coming to view he began to shoot a couple of rounds to stabilize the scene and rid of the moving patrons who started lying down on the floor. The half-prepared and intoxicated casino security too were scared. He was yelling "Freedom! Freedom for all! Once and for all!"

What could a man do, as a man did with an urge to profit from the end result where virtue dictated the atrocities and the human essence as capricious as the birds in the sky. Running through the obstacles without noise, so peacefully without a final result was only a deception of that human nature. Even years of work would not end its call to demise and commit finalization. The fire burns; it is an element but to the eye when peace was at stake it might be said differently in terms of an ultimate weapon, a thing that should have been retained, that which might have turned everything into ashes, and finally that which would destroy pleas of repent and mercy for the justice that would not have outlived its law. The men and women, children, brothers and sisters alike all breathed down this path; they remained hand in hand to embrace a prayer, a terminal cure to warn the black nature and the grey clouds and all that existed apart from them merely with a message that said man was free without any conditions. And how pain printed upon their footsteps the words of that ultimate messenger along with the entire wealth of their household and their capacity to hold trust in those last days of a confident nation. Although, island nation showed other scenes, more of a morbid nature, detesting the history and surrounding this sole issue, that was filth, or rage, and the latter was a betrayal of their immense senses, those of all the nation that was brought about through the four corners of the globe, and raised with sand, sea, and sun.

The nation, in itself, was a government of royalties, a segment of something much more complicated; the details of which were a manufacture of a Queen and thus the city, thereafter the principles of civic elements that had bent the generations into a shape more favorable to a colony and not a colony of beasts but one more attractive to the taste buds of the dukes, the lords, and the core of feudalism. Then, they tended the disputes and the city formed into circles of class and class action. *The result of that: Their city, their people, and their money!!* While the city grew into a main street, a boulevard, a tavern, and a crowded park the executive force dealt with groups. The tipping point became so attractive that life was only given for sufficient bribery and the innocent hid away to be overlooked their rights and keep the noise down before the dusks when the palms began to shiver through the sea breeze like a hungry soul seeking a morsel of bread in a chaos. The tropical blend drove one crazy as the sunset became more and more charming and was attested by the chosen few-those families that clandestinely ruled the city. In the streets, tavern, and even the butcher shops the virtue spelled in a whisper not so familiar anymore hat the mind of innocent was ticking until the last hours of the night to seek solace. The merciless waves of the ocean lethally punished the shores as the days dawned.

That morning the reincarceration of Cyrus hit some parts of the island that looked up to him; not many, not a mass, yet the few who knew him held a familiar pattern of importance among the inhabitants and often provoked them with every change in a day's life.

The man knows! They waited for a moment and then talked and told others; therefore decided what to be done like every other nation! The island had been devastated and that was why she, on a motorcycle ride was headed for a sanctuary unique in its form and cause, but not unfamiliar in human history. The tosses and turns finally led her to a dark corner of the docks. She was guessing the destination was the old fisherman's tents area unused for quite a time but the young man told her not. He dodged the minimal traffic and started back from the other end of the docks towards a popular warehouse having made sure nobody followed them when suddenly Salome began to vomit into the passing air and started a shiver.

"Have you been on a bike before!?"

"Don'y start that with me. . . . I have. . !"

"Sit tight we're almost there. . ."

"I am pregnant!!!"

4

"You owe me a couple and some change. . . better drink it soon before it gets cold! I'll be in PR. . . I need to talk to the new assistant, she seems to have some difficulty processing our releases!"

He leaves the paper cup on his desk and while the three of them are on the phone the heat inside the has become exhausting around half past eleven; a time when the ministry is usually at rest, and again they rest after lunch unless there is something of an urgent nature or like an audit or inspection of some kind like today. The doors of the ministry are closed to the public lately and, besides, normally they do not accept walk-ins but the mayor and some friends of the minister are always welcome, because the guards are told so. They have been busy keeping the entrance which is unusually crowded with groups of a new opposition who call themselves 'new awareness'. The ministry is quiet and not much is going on around the country while the officers have been on the phones to collect proxies for the upcoming elections and the affairs of the equivocal, flat-voice, and flamboyant new minister of information. The cheap and worthless, however global, exports of the island do not quite pay for the demand that its economy generates due to the inhabitants and the ministry's constant crackdowns on freedom fighters-nothing new! "The boys raising dust. . ." is what the mayor has to say about the latest ongoings. The nation yet survives on poverty; that beast of burden praised by mankind only to avoid a desperate death or the tragedy of an epidemics that might wipe men and women off the face of the island. Only then they will live with this course of survival-a poverty! Ministry, aware and in control, lives on the legacy of its officers; the men who bargain even death. It is this office that could trigger anything. A death trap, arrest, espionage are among many others the present and actual functions of this office. A full participant would be the minister who is now even more powerful than the prime minister yet clandestine. The employees of this organization buy blood by bribing, feeding, and letting go of the dough holders; they survive by taking away whoever is on their way. The afternoons are spent under the ceiling fan and action usually commences around the dark. The fan spins melancholily and, overcome by the heat and the indigenous humidity, it reminds one of the bilateral operations of this ministry, to the left and to the right like a machine gun on an endless round. . . .

That fan symbolically blows through his damply sweating inseams while he is jotting something off that PC-the central source and the only computer in that office. Flags cover every desk and he is trembling to the low and slim beat of the current in the room. He still recalls the day when the general, his father, has his last word with him, "You want reputation, career, this is it! My last word. . . otherwise you'd be in the papers. . . . . THE SON GOES OFF LIMITS, AN ALLEGED PROSTITUTION! COULD COST GENERAL THE OFFICE!!!"

He is brought in along with the paparazzi and the photos while he is still trying to get a grip of himself believing that he has been set up! The woman has been tipped and the whole brothel crowded with agents awaits him to take the bait. It's been four years now and his father still serves as the commander of the army having started after his induction to the ministry of information. He is worried about the future. How and why would he resolve his differences with his father who is now about seventy yet strong and steel-minded as ever, the most decorated officer in the history of the nation and the most eligible candidate soon to be prime minister. He is flattered by the respect he gets often than not granted because of his old man having an eye on him with big plans for his son. Things that are easy for the general and become easier as he practices power and authority like mad through every step of his tenure. The man is becoming a symbol of tyranny for the island nation. He finally gets up and walks to the other desk around the corner just opposite the wall size flag and leaves a handful of change for the coffee and nears the window to take a look at the street. That quiet street hardly has any traffic except for the service cars that usually leave after ten o'clock and begin returning to the ministry in the afternoon and until late hours; those are the ones that others cannot recognize but he knows most of the ministry echelon. The hours are quiet, the activities not so typical of that office but the ministry has a hand over everything these days. It seems that special attention is given to his team; three or four officers in addition to him that are younger and very loyal. They are the best trained among the staff and would probably last through a long career in the system. He knows everything now, everything there is about this ministry and even the cruelest ongoings-their functions and functionaries. He feels devoted to his service. They have said that they want him there. They even have proposed a raise and a promotion, but the last word comes from the top, the general! Some say he wants more for his son, yet the mighty general is puzzled by him wondering about all these years his resilient and hate-stricken forty year old son has served in discreet devotion and good standing. They are both together in command and stature but doubtful about the other according to the ones who know them closely. The relation although ends here, it has puzzling roots of indignation and is a path to absolute power over the nation, be it the father or the son!! In the spring during his fifth year of service with the ministry his father would be seventy-one and running for the highest office while promising every sod his seal of prosperity and freedom, due acts of an affair soon to be the skeleton of his diabolic campaign.

The harbor log-ins and log-outs during the hours of the sea as the steamships, boats, barges, and commercials in small numbers crowd it not so grandly but simply in a way underscoring that harbor's capacity while the signal horn and the lighthouse symbolize a minimal flow traffic, and at night through the darkest hours the sailors blow the horn to salute and step through hours of midnight intoxicated and out of control. Most cargos are delivered in the day; they are usually nothing but spare ammo for the small army and other constitutional pro bono forces. At dark, they are drunkards waiting for procurement and heading off the shore in noise and rum.

The captain is in his cabin eyeing a feminine product of the island and the skipper is at the foghorn playing a song to keep the sailors singing to sea. They get plenty of the best rum; one that does wet their lips in style and provokes the nerves far stronger than rye, one that the island is well known for-the magic! Hours and rum bottles add up as the ship is surrounded with half-burned cigarettes which they throw every direction. Those boys from the ministry don't mind them a bit. After all, the moment is seized by the best of what happens around the harbor. The boys know it and, not only, they are following orders. The few women on the ship gradually take the night away some at large and others are agents of the government; they are to keep the sailors rested and safe. That foghorn goes off a couple of more times and so does, in response, the ammo ship's whistle. This is an after-hour activity that the locals know about very well by now. The ministry keeps a low profile, no high-rank officers, and minimum transportation; everything is arranged through groups of desperate civilians who either have relatives in the prison or owe money to the ministry for unpaid taxes and other duties. That's how the nights are relieving the dark burden over his neighborhood while the horn sound has kept him up sharing his pain with that bottle of rum. The moments that become the final scene and a forlorn silence of the soul to draw the lines, and rum will help sustain the strength that carries him on. He thinks of his discreet journey through the short history that keeps him a part of it all. As his father stands as a legacy to the power that might someday possess him as well just like the man himself. He, his father, now the uncontested head of the nation in full control to seize the system believes in kinship; his persistence for him to remain with the ministry and constant participation in the old man's political affairs has taught him all he needs to know to replace him. Indeed, his private companion, rum, distilled through struggles and painful rites of the island that separates the poor from the rich, has momentarily cleared all the wounds inflicted upon him and the higher class-those who know that they know everything and not those who don't know that they don't know what is to be known! The hidden eyes of the rum still bears witness to the tumultuous streams of the process while the ships around the harbor subside to fill the ghettos with armed men only to anticipate what the militia call the future. They don't know what is out there yet, but indeed the silence is a different one, merely like one felt elsewhere in the memory of those who live on. Plenty of rum fills their minds with hot blood and flowing veins provoking arrogance and a strange thirst for more once an islander knows it is his turn to put in his two cents and be a part of the nation. The nation whose roots are transformed and heavenly unified by the eternal red dust that poisons boys and takes away the chastity of the la femmes and together they lay the stones for the next generation, as gullible and innocent as those shielded creatures of the sea. That harbor could see better days and a future which could change in solace and peace would dawn!

But among men of peace, this sacred breed not often found on the streets of the island is said to be in crisis. No more! A boy would dread to pick a stone and throw it at the other and as long as such serenades survive the streets and alleys peace would find its moral ground on this island. There will be more ships to come and unload the sinister cargos pid for by gold and salted with rum. The innocence seems to have lost its seat among them and the devil gradually consumes the patriot's desire for reincarnation. For such removal, the removal of the sin and, perhaps, the death of a Mr. Fizzle who went to church, fed the pigeons, and brought bread for the poor all in one form of peace and harmony they would say he is a colonist, a man of ambivalent ideology who solely appeals to kings and other persona of that nature like him who spends time drinking rum and speculates what his father laid down as the future of this island. The son even peaks through the writings of Brother X for advice and reads his attested logic that may one day help in mending this overdue system. He seeks equality and searches for truth; one that would sit him fairly in his rank and indeed would escape the old man's horrifying plans. Although such equality has long been forgotten according to the books. A tsunami flees the shores in a silence, one of a secret masked invader, unlike the past. His nights consumed in meditation and anticipation uselessly leaving him fear-stricken and at large-the desperate kin of number one. Then, one dark night, around eleven while he floats and sweats through the pariah of delusion sustaining his uncalled wisdom with no options to choose from, the phone rings. . .

Jay-jo jangle, hay-ho hankle and doodle-dom. . . . the morning starts with a breeze when he sticks his head out to feel it and he looses his nose, his sense of smell deceives him with an artificial yet superficial scent of the living sea and wet bricks so grimly green and damp that only a usual life's day could explain except that it was the new minister of information who decides to buy everyone coffee knowing that he would be driven to work in a four-door stretched town car to see the present one on duty in order to exchange plans and orders. That is who called him; he was invited to lunch yet it is to stay a secret until later. He throws a bundle in front of a coworker, "Go buy all the coffee and cigars you can buy,. . . .hurry!" He looks at him with a questionable face and follows the request quickly while the first hour is the best hour of the day for that purpose. *Something must be going on!* The general impression turns into a solid somber mood once they guess it was all about promotion and whispers reveal his ride in a chauffeur driven carpool. It is the building guard that passes on those facts before he has a chance to tell. Everyone with the right hand over left chest as a sign of higher up, government order, superiors, or an official call waited for him to explain. The appointment has been endorsed by the top. It needed to be executed as he knew other; after all he has only served the ministry for a few years. He doodles, loiters, and chats in interrupted segments without getting anywhere just to pass the morning hours once he steps out of the ex-minister's office. The cubicles are filled with talking heads but it seems to be speculation and should not be anything of importance, just another day. However, he remains standing and eyeing the office as one last scrutiny. He would eventually tell his friends; only that he doesn't think it is right save for the sake of friendship because it could be too early or not duly prestigious. The coffee is brought in. He is paid the change and he begins to hand out the cigars. . . .The future is smiling yet it might be luring him toward an end. He doesn't know but soon would find out. Who would be better than his father to tell him what the hell is going on? But he has been apart from his father and a bit of separation has kept the two away and forlornly in bad term with each other. He now has to find a way to break the ice; he knows he can and he goes to his cubicle as he requests a line to the general's office.

"Now we got to find you a woman!" The general coughs without a greeting and goes on to fill the receiver with his dominant tone.

"You know better that a minister has to have a family of his own. . . . first thing that came to my mind when I heard the news, well you've been doing some excellent work. . . !"

Shaheen Asbagh

"What is this all about father?! What do you want? Couldn't you let me be. . . ?"

"Listen, I don't know what you're talking about. . . beside this is no time for this kind of nonsense!! Go buy you a new suit. . . it's on me! Take your friends to dinner, be happy, you hear me!?"

"What I want to know is what you are up to, father?"

"Son. . . there are two different kinds of men out there. . . the brave and then there are the cowards!! I let you take a pick. . . You know, when they told me I said to myself: Now I have a son, a man,. . . a man I could depend on!! Don't disappoint me son!! Go on! This is time to celebrate. . . ."

A metamorphosis bleeds through the veins and whitewashes the guilty skin of the elite but people are felt to have the right to know as Island Herald writes:

"LIKE FATHER, LIKE SON. . . !!"

Two days later the vice minister of information is assassinated at the Gentlemen's Private Spots Club in the capital and doubts are raised about the appointment of the new minister while a conspiracy has been committed and the hostilities are refreshed but the members of the government, per say, the rich and poor could not idolize anybody anymore. Even the traditional arbitration of the aged is not possible because of the immensity, alas, so sudden and apocalyptic to say the least. They would say,

"For the better and for all!" and that's the last they would say about anything while the press merely dramatizes pulling forward single-issue publicities as if they are dealing with and taking responsibility for the scoop. No one issues any statements and dubiously the source is in oblivion not to be known or uttered because of all the strange segments of an artificial terrorism that never has stopped for quite a while now. There are, of course, and according to myth, two sides to the ongoings but a smog is covering the incidents so swiftly that the island citizens could only point out the right hand over the left chest (Government!)! The religious processions through the alleyways and the stucco covered tropical villas continue to be distracted while the crowds noticeably scrutinize the writings on the eggshell white paint: Liberation, Liberation! Knowing is guilt. . .

The elements of a crime always dazzle the rich which do not care and worry the poor because they put the wealth at the strong hands of the former. In this case, it could be completely a symbolic version as forlorn as a tax evasion while the gossip brings to surface the relation between the ex-minister and the vice minister. However, the first is successfully delivered to the legislation for a seat in the house and that's that!! What could have happened in that ministry during the last few months, years, or perhaps weeks and even days could probably solve this crime. As palm trees now have yellowed in the sun and quickly drying. . . Liberation. . . . through an alley where they cannot relive the tenure but could and have shown the rebellion of a new force. That people stare at those words and then at each other is a promise of a contraband justice while the news channel through the boiling communities of the capital. The market, and the barrios, in the fields of illiteracy, is where people talk, communicate, and now even understand.

Liberation, Liberation,. . . . knowing is guilt. . . . !!

"THE CURRENT HISTORY STILL IN DISGUISE HAS TO DETERMINE THE PLACEMENT OF THE NEW MINISTER! THE SON OF THE MOST POWERFUL MAN OF THE ISLAND!" Island Herald,

He and island are close now; closer than ever where the old man could only seek power and mercy in a merciless dust of terror. He begins an operation to secure the island from outside help and proceeds to use his son's help in espionage and a few border issues against his lack of desire for cooperation, but the general has the son's lacks all in heart. The crisis between the two begins to root famously among the power sharers of the nation. Hopes are raised that it is all over once the island is back on her feet again and the country would be out of the hands of the few returning to its common and innocent people soon. Under the watchful eyes of his son the general takes over the police, customs, and other forces of security beginning to control the affairs in order to place everything in the hands of his privately hired klan. He pledges to bring the island back to success yet for that his terror is limitless, and his mind diabolically blasphemous and belligerent.

The hand-over-chest messengers increase into a large number of the people and they are everywhere even around the offices and the ministries as the gesture is found to be a ceremonious and professional act that is inserting a few drops of responsibility against terror. It is around the office that general's son holds his cigar and begins to use his charm righteously in the way of the prodigal fate that now vehemently throws him to the lions in one direction or the other nonetheless unable to surpass his inherited resiliency.

His cigars come from the desk of the minister where he leaves them for him as a token of respect for the newcomer. They are the best and rolled by the genuine hands of skilled rollers who are indigenous of island nation well known to the visitors and the locals the same if they could afford them. He feels he has tolerated enough and now decides to win over the ministries affairs as the least he could do. His plan is to trigger the human factory that deems absolutely effective in comforting his doubts about the future. The factory that would produce homo sapiens that would have his ears, his vision, and the rest of him that wants to free himself from fear and conspiracy, to live through this moral high ground he is granted through and away from this dictatorship. *But why?* His human factory will only last because the time is on his side as not only his father but others now keep a watchful eye on him. General's controlling manner is a lesson to the son, and the old man's bitter legacy sinks deep in his heart but still he knows that there is a way to protect himself and help the island nation survive. His unbeknownst thirst for solidarity provokes him to take action constantly and, too, he is desperately and absently informing his minuscule proteges, his contacts, early on begin to feel his pain which is caused by the general's actions and they realize that the wind could devastate the sun blazed palms only one way. His human factory, in simple terms, soon takes on numbers and the homo-sapienism becomes his secret hobby in a way to inform whom his innocence he knows of. . . .He produces human morale and tells them about conspiracy in order to help separate peace and prosperity and to choose one over the other because the sea does not allow them both on this island. As the night fog spreads around the alleyways and hides faces by coloring the night in mysterious and secretive shades, the natives do not recognize each other in the familiar dusk anymore. It feels like an after hour freedom from identity where they could go any direction and eventually he chooses that after hour for his plan; he seizes to spend too many hours at the ministry uselessly smoking cigars and obeying his father's referenda until no one knows what he really wants. He seeks sympathy to, somehow, rest his mind and go his own way and that's why now too often he cites ideas or dreams to his inferiors or friends that have known him for many years since the beginning of his service to the ministry. The small crowd that makes up his acquaintance begin to understand his pains and his venue in regards to the general. He is tenaciously occupied and the belief that someday he will make a difference constantly persuades him to deliver the principles of making a promised land to others, those homo-sapiens of the human factory that are perhaps-one could say-illiterate but willing to accept the terms of compromise and cynical suffrage just like the path to human evolution that started with the origins of its living amoebas.

Deity, are you a woman? You shall not, but be it that you appear as son, the son of separation and determination, the kinship of old kingdom and not the colony of homo-sapiens, the general has been stabbed at least about ten or eleven times! His butler admits that everything that day was so usual as he asks for his usual pint of beer, imported as island nation does not produce ale at all, and as usual defies and bad-tongues the domestic rum as gutter filth and spends the evening at his desk in the bedroom and goes to sleep early as has been permitted so by the general himself. He even gives him a hand-rolled while he is served dinner and he tells the butler he wouldn't need him for the rest of the night. . . . . Calling him on the special line can cost him an alert for the ministry but it also gains him prestige like his late father has promised him. They finally decide to call him on that line officiating his position although a year later the district attorney and the other pieces on the board see the son as a puppet and a decoy in his father's legacy. *He kills him who believes in humanity!* The next on the list is the confidante ex-minister of the information, now the voice of the senate and the cadre that has power over the powers of the nation, per say, in officiality and solely when the general would be absent and this way more than many the leader becomes entangled in the woven web of red tape. A division between the general, the strongest man on the island, and the senate led by the ex-minister who initially has set up this politick to be able to transfer the power allegedly into the hands of the military and the coupe runner-ups. "We have to move quickly. . . the island is in critical shape! I suggest a meeting to visualize what may happen, but more important we have to replace him!!" The district attorney who leads the executive power in the island promises to broadcast a press conference to inform the people that everything is in control and the nation will be under discreet control of the forces regardless of any unspecified circumstances, and that the elements of this heinous act shall be duly and soon punished by the solemn hand of the justice led by his office.

The shakeup puts the government in limbo and the intimacy between the power holders and the general has turned into doubtful and backstabbing speculations about who would take his place. The government communication, although poor and useless, is now limited to private lines and paid for by the private owners of those facilities-the senate, judiciary, and the higher echelon of the army who are looking like heroes to some and descendants of evil to the likes of the human factory, homo-sapiens. Now is the time that those who pull the strings be forced to distinguish and tell 'homo-sapiens' from the samaritans if necessary and put in place the floating humanity to bring the divided classes a sense of skepticism for the better. It is the son's homo-sapienism of the third degree that divides the wit and the virtue, peace and prosperity, and finally fanaticism and atrocity, to calm the turbulent waves in search of another paradox-a quiet sunset. As men or women, homo-sapiens, pro or con, free or detained, senior or junior, and at last good or bad, they all are waiting as the press conference goes on the air. The D.A. announces the death of the general without citing the nature of the incident, because it might trigger turmoil or fear that the regime is threatened by outsiders. Although some of the natives speak English, the announcement is not aired worldwide and it is rendered in local tongue yet it seeps through the international networks placing a different perspective in the eyes of the globe. The sailors around the port all remaining in the ships soon begin to feel the insecurity penetrating through the harbor. The late general has been recognized as the protector of the ammo cargos and most other importing carriers. The crews of the anchored ships soon appeal to armament and some of them even hide their flags while maintaining transmission by curfew. The office of the minister of information is to be in control of the ongoings regarding the spirit and morale that at this time has overtaken the nation as the burial and mourning for the death of his father (general) echoes across the island nation as many foreign dignitaries also participate in this uncalled for tragedy.

"Oh Lord, oh the holy, there is need for those blessings. . . .those that bring together and those that make us feel the greatest being of all, for his good deeds! We need thy blessings to stay humans and homo-sapiens, and do-gooders, and to tell the good from the evil in this chaos, and thereafter. . . ." The conclusion of the son's broadcast eulogy grasps the island with his sad tone that was as honest and solemn as the breakout taking over the nation. He points his hand as a sign to end the broadcast and while the daily program resumes with messages of hope and revival, he is awaited outside the broadcast cabin by four officers. One which is the righthand commander of his deceased father. He knows him well as he, not long ago, had placed his national medal of honor on his chest as there are at least more than a dozen pinned to his uniform on his chest. The other three are also in official gear as he is wearing a white linen suit entirely wrinkled as it has been exposed to the year round humid climate which is typically the cause of perspiration and tears bringing the procession of the general's funeral to a peak; hot air, tears, and the blazing faces of the islanders have crowded the capital's main street and it would take all day. The high-ranked confidante of the dead general has an envelope for his son which he opens just as he was handed it. It is written to him in person as the officer explains that he has been personally ordered by his late father to deliver it to him at the time of his death or disappearance or any critical circumstance that would necessitate help beyond his capacity. Thus, this is now the moment; he is informed that the code to general's safe is in the hands of the three persons cited in the letter as he reads those names without uttering them. The officers are dismissed. He looks for a phone as the heat and humidity pose a lack of breathing room in the small radio station. The crowds outside still mourn while the coffin is transported to the private site of burial of general's choosing escorted by a motorcade of

SUVs and a couple of official government carpools that are filled with army and police officers to protect and escort the undertaker from the surge of people pushing and shoving to touch the vehicle.

Following the content, in the order written, he calls the ex-minister of information and blatantly requests immediate contact on a secure line as he introduces himself to his secretary. The ex-minister admits that he has been anticipating this call and momentarily returns to the phone after securing the line by request from his secretary and says,"24 left. . . three times!!" and suddenly sinks into silence and after less than thirty seconds or so apologizes, "How did he know!?" The son stipulates before any answer is given and responds with a sigh. . . . "There is more for me here as, hereby, I appoint you as the new warden of the national penitentiary!!" The son suddenly holds his breath and finally is able to respond,

"Why?"

"Because I will get my job back! That's what your father wanted. . . we should have had a meeting . . . . don't you think so? It would been appropriate!?"

"Minister congratulation! I hereby transfer all of my duties to you entirely! I should say. . . a formal meeting would not be in accordance with my father's wishes and the secret nature of his correspondence! All the best!"

Next, he calls the chief of police and requests that general's note be revealed and the chief agrees. He says that he has been expecting the call. . . . "He has written 35 right, one time, and there is also a note in addition to the combination that I have kept near to me. It is to remain a secret; however, you will probably find out later! It concerns the police force. . . !! You have my word that you will be under strict police protection sir!! All the best!" He hangs up the phone and writes the combination on a notepad while he requests a secure line to his office and as he is connected he asks his secretary o connect him to the office of the assistant minister. He answers promptly as expected.

"Hello sir! I know why you are calling and I am sorry I have not mentioned anything about the general's letter! I was discreetly asked to remain silent!! I am relieved now!

Don't misunderstand me but the letter and all. . . .I feel sorry and should express my deepest condolences to you. . . . The note says 17 left, twice! I hereby request my resignation sir. . . . . ."

The warden and the assistant minister are both killed mysteriously within one week after those phone conversations. And the new warden hands a list of sixteen party members to be arrested to the chief of police before his formal transfer to the national penitentiary.

5

When he finally gets around his correspondence in the tumultuous and damp prison it is already about a year, a year of hardship, chaos, and a loss of connection and strict solitary life that has fed each and every one of them with loss of self-confidence and deep doubts about the future. At the peak of public activity is the army firing squads now eliminating pro and con, just the same. . . . Cyrus writes a card with a short message to be delivered to Salome at a reasonable yet bearable mood that she could enjoy feeling what he feels. The letter is passed from him to an inmate about to be released and from there to a connection whose identity is revealed to Cyrus during a prison visit as that visitor would somehow although secretly get it to the camp.

A massacre takes place about two months later. While the prison is now accommodating twice its normal capacity and no one knows yet how to hint the progress of status quo which is now interrupting the island life with sporadic shootings and covert government attacks against ordinary citizens who may or may not have had a hand in such dire political activities. Still, Cyrus does not know how long or why he has been imprisoned albeit it feels longer every time he considers his flaky sentence-this improvised crime! But this time the siege devastated the is;land as more than a couple of thousands are murdered and twice that number taken into custody. The bureaus abandon the nation uninformed and uncalled for setting doubts about the future. The ministry of information aiming to comply silently is out of control while the minister tries to live up to the legacy of his inherited military powerhouse, the general. Nevertheless, the rays of hope not only live on; instead, they reflect freely on the public opinion heating up the encounters between antis and supporters of the government of which the latter now grimly asserts a partisan conspiracy as the massacre becomes an international issue while silence perhaps being the only instrument used by the highest office of the island nation.

Salome has been suspected of foreplay and, at that, the mother of one-year-old Judah ever since she is detained and relocated to the women's national penitentiary after the massacre that costs the minister of information his life through retaliation. The woman yells and cries for hours uttering gibberish and whore talk while struggling to nurse her son. The guards are not aware but her visitors are quite familiar with the right hand over the left chest and nodding while they wait for the guards to let them through the multi-chamber corridors of the prison. They try to talk to Salome struggling to take her out of a trance and back to normality so she could say something to them that could be perhaps transmitted to the public assuring her well-being. *"His father is on the ship collecting relics and what have ya, but he won't like this apartment . . . .my child where you come from, do you know where you come from? I know your mamma . . . .mamma knows her child, but I know he won't like this apartment. . . . no way. . . . .the hell with the smell of piss. . . . his daddy knows best . . . . he'll move us to a bigger apartment when steps through that door. . . . where is your mamma child?"* Salome is the only surviving member of the camp aside from her son; the massacre has been triggered due to the correspondence Cyrus sends through the secret messenger, one of the inmates who is let go for good behavior but now he is working for the ministry and so they say although no one else has known about that postcard except him and his closest assistant who apparently turns bad while Cyrus is free but things change drastically once he is incarcerated again. With the sudden death of the minister the social arena is shaken by the power struggle giving way o petty espionage, bribery, prostitution, and just about any reconcilable way of escape in the bloody collapsing economy save for the party heads and most of the senators, the elite that support the traditional know-hows inherited from general himself.

Judah turns one at the woman's penitentiary far from the comfort of a house. He was born and raised in a clandestine training camp that held over five hundred members of which all died except. However, there are sixty activists from that camp forty of which have been imprisoned and twenty held for questioning, per say. They were molested, raped, and later court martialed. While the for horns go off sporadically for the incoming ships and decorate the harbor with a compatible voice of the maritime; that which brings young and old together in saving the day as an escape from the heating events.

The sole party of the island nation is ready for retaliation. At present, the executive branch holds a list of inductees to appear in front of the firing squad. They have been chosen from among the loyal members of the party. The end seems to be near for the eternal compromise between the leadership and the party. The death toll has more than tripled as the party does not seem any more promising than the altar of an undertaker or a graveyard. Mistrust sends rays of promise for deception through the already critical thresholds of the government filled with cynicism and horror. In its files, in infamy, one could search and find friends and lost ones like mothers, fathers, sons, daughters, and even grandparents or any derivative that links the members of the island community to one another; albeit, some still live on but to what end would such a guess hold truth would be as good as an idiot's. *The final moment is so common in its arrival. These days the nation, alas without forbearance or a last call to shield the mercy upon the life of, per say, homo sapiens.* As his file bears the last notice of his resilient presence and an unforgettable truth in which Cyrus confesses without being aware of rats; namely, the man who delivers this letter to the information ministry. Cyrus follows his steps carefully through a short lapse of freedom while, indeed, provoked by sexual tensity and yet a fraternal leap of faith in the future. It reads:

My dearest I have many times felt the pain as well as the sensual happiness of being amazed with an enthusiasm and anxiety that rarely happens to a prisoner, but this is a first time as there is a 'first' for everything, and I am trying to dig deeply into my humble and wary mind that has left me here in the middle of a prison song that hardly utters any love and is only for the guilty and hollow souls. Those moments and these hours although have begun to seem promising. However, I confess that my last imprisonment has survived the bad mood and the grey segments of confinement, and more, now I have you to think about. You the Jean d'Arc of the island nation and the queen of my heart and soul. Let me admit that our moments together taught me the reality of our dilemma and the present has never been more vivid than I could imagine. Omar has left us as a patriot of bondage and loyalty in my mind with respect to his dignity and mine. I have loved you every moment since yet to be your one and only admirer for ages to come. May justice serve us proper and free of prejudice, and allow us to hold hands again in leisure and real peace. My dearest I believe the boy should be able to say a few words by now, perhaps one year old or so. I don't believe there has been anything else aside from a forte of love and kisses that live on between us and those moments of pleasure will never escape my mind. I assure you that my only gift to you and for our precious moments of truth, warmth, and sympathy is in safe hands. I promise I will keep count of your whereabouts and I should now guarantee a bright future as I am pleased to say that my sole concern has been this island, in prison, in public, and in my mind as I have solemnly shared the truth with compatriots that remain behind these cold and senseless bars, some shorter and some of course longer. If I only knew how long I would be here or will I ever remain alive

Cyrus

The shield of resistance such as men like Cyrus and his cellmates or the contacts on the street are establishing a movement which is being shaped against oppression and betrayal of moral values. Among those messengers who have not deceived the rebellion there is now a big separation. On the other hand, the island is being sustained by a social order dependent on small acts of bribery, theft, and even human prostitution-men and women, rich or poor! Outbursts of cruelty and use of unnecessary force prevail in a dire manner while torture, to no useful pursuit, is used to threaten and create fear in different neighborhoods. Alas, the world should witness as there is no mercy or sign of relief even in the near future as the port has shut down and the only traffic is that of arms and ammunition that have piled up in the docks. Nevertheless, what the ships returned with does not matter; it reflected nothing upon the interest of the world outside as some well aware of the nature of this regime. They say that it is eating too much turtle yoke doing it to them. They shouldn't kill them; those creatures are harmless and they only crowd the sea and hardly the land-anyway the meat is too rich. Why go after them while they are always after each other? The rest of the world has no way of receiving inside news and the briefs are all about the ships that try to keep their smuggling missions a secret and solely reveal facts about the need for humanitarian aids that never end and are no more news. . . . !

Perhaps, the island nation's Olympic team is a sought after issue of interest. The ministry of information recruited the bulky forty-two-year-old messenger who has delivered Cyrus's note for Salome into the hands of that ministry and, later, his family is held hostage. This man was accompanied with a twenty-nine-year-old wrestler to represent the island nation in the most tragic manner through the Olympics in order to subside the turmoil both on the inside and out. However, the publicity would not last more than a few days into the competitions when disaster knocked on the door again and on its threshold steps a fatal tsunami that destroys the strongholds of the nation, among them the penitentiary that has collapsed as it stands without its barb wired walls for about one hundred yards that are shared with the sea. Cyrus is persuaded to flee among twenty-four other inmates that have mostly been serving sentences over two years or more. Cyrus, hesitant and cautious, is worried about the consequences but the hand of nature calls upon judgement as heart and soul are taken away by the breath of a brutal regime that deserves it. . . . "It's time to move on. . .!" They tell him, and he is left only the pain of sympathy and the strength to breath along the dire sequence of his beating pulse, cruelty, and the evil that knows no friend or calls no judge now that Lord has shown its power. They want him to help his people.

Cyrus is alone now with his comrades as they float, swim, and struggle about a few hundred yards or so away from the shore to reach safety at no avail and without any further help or a destination. The sighting of turtles is a sign of food, or perhaps a sanctuary but they push further from the shore holding on to scraps of wood and plastic containers that are used for garbage and food in the jail. They are now more than five hundred yards away from the surrounding rocks of the prison when they decide to go ashore. Exhaustion has taken them over; they open the seals of the prison containers although there could be anything in them, as they are used for any purpose around the penitentiary. Only two had food stored, and the other four garbage and blankets, as they used those to dry themselves. There is suddenly noise; it seemed to be coming from a distance away. Cyrus, still shivering, is finally able to dry himself and suggests that they should hit the waves again. He believes that is the only route to survival. The others, with questionable impressions and deep doubt, hesitate as two begin after turtles ostensibly to provide food. They are quiet in the dark as Cyrus carefully takes steps to front and back around their small camp trying to come up with a way to overcome the circumstance. They would be overpowered if accosted by the guards, but there is time as the penn is flooded and it would take at least half a day or more to get a posse together and probably longer to track them down. Cyrus begins to utter a few words through his teeth as he is the pride and spirit of the group; he is mad and disappointed but more grateful than a medicine man who would cure a member of a tribe and gets credit for it. . ..Cyrus tells them that they can assemble a vessel or two using the few containers by resealing them and using some wood, or anything they could find around that shore. It is almost dark. The waves, tumultuous and unpredictable, have reached the men who have fallen ten or so yards from the shore. Cyrus advises them to go deeper into the woods and begin search for anything, "time is scarce. . . . we have to move fast!!" The men, some to left and others to right, surround the beach clandestinely without looking at sea; they get farther and farther in the dark when suddenly they hear voices behind them. Behind the bushes and palm trees, they hide as the voices pass by. Praise the Lord! They are fishermen coming ashore. Two or three boats, small ones, coming to shore quietly as Cyrus signals them to bury themselves in the sand while the other group lurks with caution awaiting Cyrus's command. The fishermen, with loads of fish, step onto the dry white sand and chatter as they approach the bushes still about three quarters of a mile from the shelters-the village. The cellmates hold their breath and not a move! Hands fisted they think without a hunch while they are ready to fight for their lives. Without any weapons or other means to defend themselves they remain exhausted drawing the last breaths out of their consumed torsos that are merely lurking without a hope to win. Some of them with big arms and biceps yet for any man struggling to shore after swimming that distance, about a mile, floating and pushing through the waves, it would be hard to defeat those fishermen. There are twenty-five of them, somewhat bigger and not as wasted but Cyrus holds on until they get closer while checking their weapons, a few daggers, and two of them holding machetes. As the songs of prison still conquer the soul of the cellmates the real fight is about the strength to break free, occupy the free world, to show those fishermen that they meant no harm; that is what Cyrus had in his mind but it is getting too late and if any of them had a gun and shots went off it would be all over. . . Cyrus, breathing slowly with pure confidence and one life to live, covers for others shortly before the other group-due to tensity-jumps the fishermen but they are outnumbered and waiting with a promiscuous lapse of desire for survival because the fishermen do not act hostile at all notwithstanding the torn and savage look of the cellmates, and after a minute or less Cyrus shouts, "He has a gun. . . that one. . . in the white shirt. . . a gun!!!" He runs toward the man with white shirt and a shabby straw hat but he does not go for it. Cyrus runs fast and jumps on him. . . . "We know who you are! Calm down sir! Yes, we know who you are. . . . please. . . .!!" Cyrus freezes and stares at him; the two men eye to eye stand motionless. Finally, Cyrus raises his hand as a sign of seize-fire or peace toward his cellmates. He recognizes them, perhaps homo-sapiens, natives like his father was when he used to carry a gun mostly applied to signals or target shooting and never for selfdefense or harm. Cyrus learns fast and does knows how to use one, not only for target-shooting that he used to do in the backyard with the consensus of the neighbors but he kills two innocent turtles in two separate occasions hardly forgettable, it is the memory of the first kill, ending the life of an animal in plenty as all the boys roasted the damn turtle for grub. Cyrus spent days to learn to aim at targets and some days without the permission of his father who used to have a job and went fishing for sheer pleasure of accompanying friends and rum. He knows that an armed man could be going many ways and, most of the time, not on his own but by a temptation of his dignified rage or pride, or whatever. . . .but a warm gun could have a provocative grip in the hands of a dude, sometimes like sex or a perfectly fit suit! You would be someone else. Someone you always admire or feel a greed towards, a jealousy that creates an idol or a memory haunting you in the most sensitive moments of one's life.

He stands there, and brings his hand forward like in a handshake asking for the gun. "Give it to him man! Go ahead, pass him the damn gun! They are friends for all I know and you know that! Give it to him. . . ." As the two are standing silent and fragile like two statutes, the man with the white shirt pulls his gun off the holster and takes a glance at it. Then, he holds it for Cyrus with an eternal smile. Again, the two men look eye to eye until Cyrus takes the gun and turns to others. He wonders if anyone has any idea what has been going on squinting and shaking his head. The other fisherman steps toward him and, with desperate movements of his hands, he says, "You are in danger! They could be waiting for you in the village. This shore is the closest to the penitentiary! We were informed this morning. . . . you gotta go, come on! Hurry!!" Cyrus drops his head while scratching it.

"Where do we go!?"

"There is sea traffic. Perhaps you could hitch a boat or, maybe, something commercial. . .going to the village is useless!!!"

"Why don't we go with them? They need our help! Together we could sail faster. . . !!"

Everyone on the quiet and dark beach feels the blues during the magnificent ebbs and flows that adorn the amazed faces of those lost and hopeless men. A few go their way to bring a couple of more boats and to join them at sea later. The rest return to the water. It is a man and nature operation that promisingly plays the role of a scapegoat for the only safe haven that fifteen men could reach. A way to resist death or recapture, and the only way to persist and hope for something better through those turbulent waves of the wordless ocean. They all have homes and children whom they dearly love but the choice is not home now; it is freedom for the fear-stricken, half-alive cellmates and Cyrus-already identified by a few of the fishermen as the 'Preacher'! Half-an-hour later, the quiet sea begins to welcome the four small boats into its peaceful flow under a clear starry night. Some almost falling asleep to that soundless serenade and a few others quietly whispering. Two boats lead and two others follow while Cyrus, in the front, is sitting next to the watchman and the navigator while already about five miles away from the shore and still nothing in sight. The cellmates have not eaten all day and Cyrus can hear his stomach growl and tries to prevent a surrender to starvation. The watchman suggests raw fish; some of those they have caught earlier and brought with them. He offers his knife to Cyrus as a sign to others as Cyrus is the leader-so now it is conspicuous! He erects the gun briefly and then nods and takes the knife. He shows the wooden box which is his seat, and with a movement of his head and torso guides the fisherman to throw him one. He obeys and the fish lands by the box. Cyrus hurriedly dislocates the tail, head, and scrubs off its luminescent scales with the blunt edge of that knife. It is clean now. It takes him about a minute and then he raises the glittering beast with both hands clutching to it in front of his mouth while looking at the men in the other boats and pauses in hesitation ostensibly to show them how to eat it. Ayes are suddenly heard from all aboard and the fishermen begin to throw fish at the other boats like it was a net full of flying fish caught in the ocean. Thus, a few knives are passed around in the boats, and in a quick moment or so the cellmates and fishermen together are chowing down raw fish. Fresh and sincere describes the fish and the fishermen who lead in to persuade enjoyment and help soothe the burning appetite of those famished and ravenous fugitives. They all bite on the raw creatures with an immense avidity; a struggle to live and make it through these early hours of the morning and the time of relief comes subsequently when a couple of them jump out holding on to the boats and dump a load in the sea. The boats slowly, at a reachable distance without floating into each other as there is chatter going on between the men, pursue no direction except escaping the shores for the time being. Still, there is no set plan when, in the silence of the sea, during the predawn hours, a foghorn intrudes. *It must be a ship! What else?* As they are not close to any harbor, the fishermen insist that they are oaring away from the shore and not toward. This is a ship! It is headed for the island as now they can see a light far away. A dot, in their vision, perhaps it is about an half-an-hour away. *Have they seen a boat!?* It is not yet certain, but wouldn't it be better if they had since the sea could become hell through the next day-if they make it, two days!! They suddenly quarrel, discuss, shout, and beg for safety. Cyrus, in despair and an overcoming hunger, looks around as there is nowhere to go; a sea, and a horizon which is beginning to be seen differently in the early horrifying hours of that morning. He signals the rowers to change into that ship's direction. Without a compass there is no say where they are headed but the fishermen claimed it to be a freighter, a cargo.

The unidentified vessel is at last within threading distance of the boats. There is a familiar hauler of a sailor, and apparently the cargo ship begins anchoring while its sailors start to crowd the deck, about ten or more of them. No one thinks it would be necessary as they are looking at one another. They hesitate to make a move until finally the captain of the Seahide introduces himself through a bullhorn and gives permission for her to be boarded by the men in those boats. They seemed to be a bunch of hoodlums nothing short of lost and frightened by something or someone which happens to be of interest to the wary captain. Cyrus quickly hides his gun as they all prepare to climb the ladder rope once the ship becomes completely immobile. The other few hold on to their knives and follow Cyrus who jumps on the rope after the first couple of fishermen from the same boat and tries to hide behind them as much as possible to keep his small handgun hidden under his shirt. After five minutes or perhaps sooner they reach the deck. There is a sailor with a rifle pointing them towards the man with the bullhorn, the captain of the Seahide!

THE SIEGE

6

The rapprochement commenced when man thought it moral and intriguing to put forward the components of a pragmatic utopia and provocatively deceive the humanity that ruled the world of peace because it never filled each and every belly according to the pamphlets of the Maoists and Marxists and that well-heard repetitive rhapsody that soothed the innocent like a couple of overdue Aspirins. By and by, they would, the people, baptize their ideas and ideals in a flow of undermining theories like that of the left only to call it even: Equality for everyone! Will the system understand? Or there would be mayhem after, over and over, because they keep comforting us with invitations to the abyss having admonished a portrait to depict the future and not blame the past. So then, God and the system, as the proletariat is designed to be self-sufficient while man cries to be ruled by the system and have God's mercy upon him; a burden to sustain in retrospect while our confidence, individual morality, or anything of ours is bribed to choose God's direction, or the system's! Pamphlets, as a drawback and courtesy, point to the intellectuals as nearly as one could determine his destiny and stop out of the eternal circle, the one circle with birth and death both scribed in plaster.

The injection of life and death passes the sanctuaries of a national rite as it is apart from the latter a syringe full of deceitful blood that is all paid for by the elite, those puppeteers that overlook the turnarounds and cycles of freedom step-downs and always the last line remains with the child of duty while he creates fear with a new cycle: Pure freedom for all! The merchants of oligarchy, without leaving a trace, lead these lifespans. They dictate pain and insanity to the poor mothers sheerly obliged to give up on their infants, and to men, they present the pain of compromise and solemn social depression. Therefore, the steps of progress were overseen and the miraculous healers expanded their claim to a prodigal horizon surely like a daily dose of pain relievers which make forget and step down for the elite to step up and take away the bet. Posterity did not tell us about duty, yet duty would tell us about posterity and burdening notions of pain and poverty. While the miracle healers, Marxists, and the present fascists take the claim to future-the posterity.

Duty calls for an innocent and active sod to bring bread and not compromise, to hail honesty in using hands and spine to reach one's goal, to reach the utopia that only virtue describes as living and, thus, the foundation of the society lays its seeds for monuments, social centers, and finally the sought-after act of justice. But, paper is plenty and intellect has been deceived where, to a point, visionaries could see no more, and thinkers have forgotten about speculation and the entire body of rule makers has been converted, be it heresy in order to survive or a path to deception and blasphemy. "Lead us not, but let us see it once again. . ." Were the people created to be solely proud of birth and none else, to be prevailed by oligarchy and be bestowed without having a chance to their final moment of repent? "Brother confess to your sin so the guilt is not upon me. . . ." Then, government decides for people to when die or when to surrender to heresy and this impious path which has been chosen for them. Politics would not tick in a nation unless a gun is clicked. Thereon, the pamphlet givers, miracle healers, beggars, thieves, and tramps each play an orderly role between deep breaths of heat and flames that burn down the posture of a callous form of freedom never meant to touch the heart of the innocent class of individuals. Have they understood that the edge of the blade only gets sharper and more deadly as this system ages. The oligarchs age as well as anyone; they become more diabolical and sympathy escapes them as well as those breaths that signal the last of them when the new era begins.

Legend says that heroes are rare and reality is far more complicated yet justice always prevails and becomes one, in its familiar style, with the people-fair or ugly! The horizon becomes clear and nothing exists anymore while nature sings its solitary serenade to banish the blood of the innocent from the shores of a sea of pain and resentment. The system hails, "More for people. . ." and unequivocally supports the plans; those plans for the future of any nation. Yet, the time is short and casualty high. These are elements of intellect, and for some it is wit with which the miracle healers set a claim to resolve and progress forward if the conditions are met and promises delivered. Men and women follow the path, hungry for a cure from a myriad of pains and the grey world that surrounds them while the miracle becomes birth when a mother brings an infant into the society. This birth of an individual that works miracles, and even in millions it brings a zillion of miracles that still fall short of the final call. Heroes are a rarity, as devotion in this society, harsh and rude is a costly attempt upon one's life or yet again life and death! That is when the healer sits back and leaves you at your own risk! It is a very lethal game. Alas, the equality of proletariat and one-for-all and all-for-one sets the bar even lower when creating such a class is costly and its rules are cumbersome which leaves the worker in a crisis and a demise. The individual's burden becomes the whole's pain without any bread to feed his children.

And now, I tell you, government backs the entire entity and foundation of a society relaying its will to every base and segment of people, families, businesses, economy, and through any communication within the community. The obligation of a man of modern world is not only to the nature (life), but now it is directed too towards the progress of civilization while the two, especially the former, take shape in tragic patterns merely to raise deep emotions and a sense of sympathy which proves useless and futile in the quest for survival, the campaign that now embraces a poor nation in the present world. It being a global lack of protection or a familiar crisis of food and shelter or else, the tragedy lasts till the last drop of blood and sweat is inimically directed towards the hidden rulers who become rude and apparent having once obliged the people with a span of arrogant claims assigned to each and every economical, social, political, and financial contract. It is the formal obligations that ultimately kill a man, deprive a child, rape a fecund, and make slaves out of an innocent society.

In a past and certainly not future notwithstanding the thousand and one promises and oaths of office and all the prudence to be staged along with an honest posterior to bury any doubts, a government was baptized and from early on influenced the cradle, child, kins, family, homes, streets, and the market while exchange of news-a detail of government activity-began to mount the form and occurrence of events in nation's life. The home gained its own government and ministers, the elder ruled the younger no matter how bright the latter. . . ma and pa told it as it must have been told and thus an evolution undertook the society. It traced the activities of the system and evenly spreads it along the homes. "THE MINISTER OF FINANCE SEALED A DEAL!!" "DAD FINANCED A TELEVISION!!!" "THE MINISTRY OF COMMUNICATION CITED THE REQUIREMENTS FOR ADVANCE EDUCATION!!" Albeit there was no limit to the councilmen; all those representative that found it their duty to intervene and make life as the nation knew it. The elite took over, at the next stage, and we fell in the hands of the few, even more colorful; we were indeed in harmony with the outside world. There was no cutting slacks; left and right, pro and con, higher and lower were all in it. A framework shaped itself without any regards for a global scope of the issues while there was only one computer at the ministry of communication-the ultimate platform of connectivity for the entire island nation-operated by an illiterate commoner, a relay man, and other official gossipers. Homes carried the Cross. They believed and took the fall yet believing it was for the best of the community. The chaos spread now with men and women intertwined, oppressed, and tortured. And the first shot finally landed on a liaison officer as the dawn was subsiding in a soaking island nation.

Movement would not be movement without its virtuous endorsement of every piece of evidence and the life story of each of its forsaken participants, namely, because of how far they were to the right or the left. And left would have never been the left without its demands for equality. *And why? Why not?* The right had shown casualties but endorsed this movement. The nation came to a tragic and gravely unsustainable calamity when people and the movement, in their last effort to finalize their lives-life or death-looked within in search of clues; they knew there hid a notion of salvation in the eternity complaining about present which convinced others that this movement should stand! *Hail to the movement!* There were only a few relatively multi-story office buildings around the center of the capital, and alongside in the civic square. There were the ministry palaces that ran less than the fingers on one hand. Yet, before them, something strangely devastating had taken place which resembled the primary pattern of a movement in the eyes of the early morning sanitary workers as they were sweeping and smoking around the other ministries than that of the information.

The morning had dawned earlier where the passersby were in ones and twos and ostensibly going about their own business than minding someone else's. They knew, although not exactly, that the island had been ready for a while. The liaison officer was lying there a few or, perhaps, dozens of small steps from the fortress of the ministry of information without any regards paid by the sanitation workers as the shot had bore something familiar with it than just a gun fired. The scene was more like a foggy daydream that in the silence of men had dragged its grey posture through the early hours of that day.

"Promiseland thy promise shall have a seat on the green grass and peace shall prevail among men of one creed. . . ." His words had turned a nation and his crowd without fail. The man spoke to those ready to kill and banish the island. The infamous wrestling team captain at two hundred and ten pounds, all of it layers of undigested starch and pastry which were his favorites as he prepared for the competitions, listened but could not understand because acid reflux had already effected him without which it was hard to live while he had stayed away from those for almost a whole three month season in order to compete in the two-man wrestling team. This man, a familiar lad among the inmates and later was known to homo-sapiens whose ultimate intention in this movement had been shared among both masses-a union towards 'MOVEMENT'!! The guru, the trusted one, left the liaison with good words and those which worried them among all other elements of rebellion. The turmoil became such a consequence that one destiny stood between homes and guns; it was hidden from the innocent then blood ran through the alleys and saturated the gutters to paint the city with vengeance. Thereon, the rite of promising solidarity and dominance to one another among them became a 'moda nueva'. The wrestling team, of course, held a version of leadership as the symbol of longevity as island nation was turning old and rotten. Presently, all channels were contaminated with the smuggling and embezzlement of drugs specifically for illegal usage and, thus, passing the money to the elite of the desperate branches in its government.

Yes, the morning had passed its early hours when the island nation had to listen to a new voice on a national radio broadcast.

"PEOPLE OF THE ISLAND NATION THE NEW DEMOCRATIC LIBERATION MASS HAS TAKEN COMMAND AS OF THIS MORNING AND SHALL LEAD FURTHER AFFAIRS OF THE ISLAND THROUGH THE MINISTRY OF INFORMATION. BE STRONG, BE BRAVE, AND BE UNITED! THE NEXT BROADCAST WILL BE AIRED IN SIX HOURS. . . ."

As noon was approaching, the plaza was hot and humid although the surrounding palms were still dancing to an early wind. A cart that had a frier installed on it for the purpose of making turtle cocktails for the passersby carrying a handwritten sign which listed a price and the size of the handmade paper cones situated itself on the edge of southern lawn of plaza just the opposite side of the occupied ministry; it was being blocked by the army and the minimal crowd that stood behind it. The smell of garlic and wedges of lemon that accompanied each handful enticed the mind with a presence that yet had to witness the commonality of that placid plaza's daily business as the referrals had already stopped entering any of the buildings and continued populating the fortress which structured the plaza so uniquely that it took the carpool hours before they could take any positions through this duel. The crowd stared at the ministry in the hope that they would be given any sign of development and others in pursuit of a symbolic inquiry kept on hanging to their spots while not knowing what was to be happening until a bullhorn went off requesting that the onlookers disperse and go about their business.

It was the army that continued rushing into the plaza regardless of the bystanders. Avoiding any warnings they were fully aware that people might join up with the occupiers at some point pushing them aside they drove into the crowd. The transports turned out to be armament and machine guns were carried out and set up next to each vehicle as numbers of soldiers stood lining up face-to-face with the ministry. There had only been one shot fired having cost the life of a liaison officer; a government employee who was headed for work. This was a sign of the tenacious nature of the modus operandi.

As a national radio broadcast was due in about four hours to be aired by the liberators. . . the line-up almost in a circular form and in broken and lagging order held the contaminated soldiers with dark souls that patiently began to rap and chant patriotism expressed in words while beating on their guns, "I fight, one, my might, two, island nation, three, has my ration, four. . . . I fight, one. . . ." Their loud hurrahs having worried the impartial crowd kept the ministry in a breathtaking silence raising doubts about their resilience and the will to hold on. The lack of resistance would have been eventually measured at any moment whenever either side took the first step. The army and liberation went down in history as the present mass held their breath! The path to change had now gained a vanishing momentum; what was named as the movement of the handicapped as was the nation. This island of backward daily presence of poverty and illiteracy, these slave men suffering from hunger, and lowest ranks of living in the universe had raised its bruised torso to face the last punishment before earning its eternal and long-awaited freedom from decay. Blood, or the blood of this humanity, which the natural man vows for should have existed and it should have been found in the pages of its history, the island nation's. Any more than the killing of innocent and the surviving strength of the liberation it was time to put an end to the life, the fate, and the fault of the people. The preparations of the military were immense but the nation had suffered major losses of its patriots due to division and betrayal of duty by those homo-sapiens who took orders from the government no more and sought new ideologies. The civic plaza smelled of horror and resentment when people began to chatter without showing or demonstrating any banners; they were hanging on empty and grey insisting to decide who to go for, or run for their lives as the daily newspaper started to distribute around the hour past noon with a big word at the center of its headline:

"T A K E O V E R !!!"

The nation's only daily paper had the word "TAKEOVER!!!" as it headline and nothing else but its familiar logo. Indeed on this day the paper was blank; white pages of newsprint paper that extended to only one sheet with all four sides blank!

The ministry was not in shambles and the resulted siege had come calmly and easily while no one had meant to commit a crime beyond that of liberation-a democratic settlement. They stayed quietly on chairs away and under the windows exchanging short and raw sentences about the options that had left them not so many ways to choose from. They numbered at a small group that from the beginning had hoped for assistance and support while thinking that they were taking a chance and were to become united with those islanders who had agreed to participate and build this movement into its right direction, the way of people and the majority. The beating hearts resembled a tractor engine, in harmony and pure. Desperate but ready to fight, the chanting army that from behind those windows sounded like a different sign of power ready to charge, "We have the right to the last fight, this nation is our tonight!" This serious force now awaited them outside, unknown and unfamiliar to civilians; those women and children that felt for the men so much that island, that day, wanted them to live a new life starting there and then. The ministry had been picked for its ability to reach all. All those faultless whose fate had been devastated and suffered an epidemic of pain and still death. There was no way out but to put in what sweat they had wreaked and what hopes they had for victory. Thus, the target was now obvious. Only the army could withstand the push; and they had proven to be prepared to face that barrier. But in the ministry the pain of a scattered fear of unreachability and despair against hope was filling in between the walls of the aged structure and its distinguished gables. The soldiers had not yet made an announcement or send any warnings. They waited for the final command of the top and yet it wasn't clear who held that position or no one was anxious enough to know. It is that history that had hatched its long nested atrocity and had put man against man, and ready to shed blood against blood as the dusk had set its testimonial presence and no one had left the usually remote plaza. They could read the formations and the silent ongoing carpool that went on at the far back of the ever increasing barricades. The ministry used to be the command strategic communication headquarters as it took the military a few hours before they realized that they would have to plan a practical center to push ahead.

The ministry was in sweat and smoke; the strings of nerve had become numb while they worked on getting a message through on that sole computer of the island and without any success they waited only to see the honest animations of the PC insulting and ignoring them. The leader of the liberation group had taken his seat in front of the monitor with hopes that he could contact someone out there and ask for intervention and outside help but he even was not able to report this simple message. They had added up to over three or four thousand out there; men, women, civil and military all astonished at the fate of this TAKEOVER!

"We have our right to fight. . . . this nation is ours by tonight!"

They sang as their voices echoed through the plaza against the silence of the onlookers and the ajar windows of the ministry of information. They, the liberation, now had control of the computer. Apart from that, it was the daily paper that was going to be printed in about five or six hours, during the early hours of the morning. The liberation wanted the fastest way to test their position. Leaking the news beyond the shores of the island nation and sharing their hopes with the people of the island, with those that could fight, that wanted to fight-the wholesome majority! Now, the dusk was dark and heartbroken in its most somber alert that kept them awake in the rooms as they had divided and spread without any light except the occasional spark of a match to see one another or inhale nicotine. The point man was still on the computer. Their plan was to be injected into a network; they looked forward to other navies in the nearby seas or air power but perhaps far from reality or too soon to assume that it would ever happen. However, left only with the islanders, the liberation had begun to relay the original mission which was targeted through the computer of the ministry of information; it did not work. It only reached outside but who would take such messages seriously at that speed. The islanders' reputation bragging sheer illiteracy, high and far above the rest of a world that underscored internet as the food for the universal man. They finally had reached an immediate plan near the last hours of that night along the lapses of starvation and evidence of insomnia that were to take them into the morning. In silence, the army continued preparation for the dawn and there was no telling if they had decided to negotiate or create a massacre. The liberation had left one note unstated and that was the number of pros against cons and it happened to be all based on a whimsical assumption that the prodigy was hidden among those pros that would have, at a face-off, taken sides with the liberation. For them, it was the moment to request that assistance; they wanted to bring them onto the scene.

They had created a group of young fighters to act with the underground once they left the edifice during the early hours of the day as the army would have been doing logistics for reinforcement. The barriers had to be avoided. They had little time to set contacts and had to test the tumultuous flow of hostility. Nonetheless, that would determine the fate of the siege and, perhaps, turn back the pages of this lost history. Telephone, newspaper, shops, other organizations such as red cross and public health centers could have been duly approached, but with such a short time to spare this rigorous operation had to be performed by those ten or fifteen young hands who had no idea where to start taking these crucial steps and how to approach the underground. The island had a very potent and flaming underground network as they were yet in the theoretical stages of a marxist status. They had been playing with fire just like a child would have as liberation had to face its risks. The forbidden word was unity, indeed not ideology. The team had to trigger a powerful module to arouse interest and public opinion. They only had a day or two to do so. They believed it would at least stage a momentum within the island's communities until further help. No one had any idea who the liberation was. Those men and women, homo-sapiens, were the few that passed on the teachings of a courage and just spirit to that of the others.

Homo-sapiens were the men and women released from the penitentiary who had lived without living a life and remained ready for this day. The prison had been questioned by the military and was to be closely investigated under

97

strict orders from a top command. Its warden given advice as to his submission of resignation was nowhere to be found on the day of the siege while the liberation was counting on the powers of this man who had already ruled all colors of the system from top to bottom. The sole retaliatory act of government would have been this man's elimination which had been long due according to the opinions of the higher elements of the army. Liberation, however, had a hunch where to contact him in order to join in full force and support of all homo-sapiens hopefully to overturn the oligarchy. The siege did not occur to be unexpected in the circles of the ruling class; its initiation had long been observed with assurances that the generals were able to put out such blazing shows of vengeance when they came to it. Insofar the warden had been left to himself although incommunicado! The liberation had determined that by finding him they would have had enough time to reach all klans of the community in order to move the masses to one or another direction.

The army had started its approach in an unexpected direction by not nearing the building and shooting gas through the windows of the ministry. It had not been successful due to lack of strength and the difficulty in getting close to the ministry as the liberation remained relentless returning sporadic rounds of fire. The group of liberators that was to seek the underground had exited the building loosing two men in the bloody process and were still escaping the tight pursuit which continued outside the parameters of the civic plaza. They had to climb the houses at the rear of the ministry to escape through the rooftops and avoid using arms as far as they could to dodge any knowledge of their whereabouts. The army could not reach them in time as the two martyrs had been shooting at point blank to open way for the rest. God help them! They finally reached the street. There was no alleged point of contact. For them, it had to be a random search of all clans and immediate penetration into telephone and telegraph office along with the island nation's daily newspaper; however, these men did not have any idea what they were up to. The liberation knew the best bet was to appeal to brainpower as they had started after what remained of willing intellectuals.

7

The round window across the cabin from the bunk where I woke up to start another day seemed like a golden sun hidden under a mysterious and purple cloud with an identity similar to that of a real sun blazing over the late afternoon sea. My watch had been struggling without me inquiring about the correct time during the more familiar moments of a day and now it was suddenly five-thirty and I think that was in the afternoon! Because, I had only slept two hours since last I had checked my timepiece; it was three in the morning before I crashed into the bunk while the captain was just starting his shift after a bottle of gin between the two of us. All I remember was that someone had told us that we would be cruising those north and northeastern waves for a few days by a few knots at least for a few days until reaching the mid-oceanic shores of a new island republic that awaited its cargo of arms and food like all the other nations that we had sailed and would be in what amounted to a three month journey starting with the port that produced the fire power and the others which helped smuggle packaged chow not for people but only those that could pay the price of a regiment of decent meals. So the cargos were provided for notorious yet reputable channels at each and every stop around the center of this ocean.

The captain had long left his cabin and me. I had spent every day and night there merely energizing my late hours against those odd mornings getting the job done at each stop. The company had begun purifying its elements and missions as a sheerly elicit pattern to understand better its vast groups of clientele that aimed at sovereignty. I, well, I did part of the job by playing the transmitter; those piles of messages exchanged at every approach and delivery from location to location; docking, unloading, and finally departure consisted of the roots of the communications that I was there to provide. And I thought, always, to ask myself if God had been fair to me while this ship was rough and the cargo nothing less than entirely noisy and humiliating like a wild ass. No more did I fight the wars than being a retarded engineer, a specialist! I coded the transmissions and created roadmaps for each port to protect them from pirates and outsiders who tried to threaten or rob the shipments as our company had allegedly suspected it to initially be a danger to its relentless profitability and other desired forms of commercial security.

The smell of rust and tarpaulin, the searing filth, had begun to place me in a few places that I could think of in my past, yet every time I opened my eyes I still wanted one more bottle of gin and my share of salted ham and boiled fish fillet, courtesy of the staff of this floating dump. Seahide almost circled around the entire ocean to return to its port of origin. At ten or fifteen knots northbound, then ten or so knots westbound, then south, and finally full speed ahead towards north to refill, reload, and before anything have its crew hit the port's saloons and its popular brothel.

With his judgement and all the fairness God's creatures could afford they all would be sent back to the not so distant ocean. Based on that fairness and its deeming equality I had assumed the worst as an armed man; a hand pistol for a man from a third world nation that had held back from proliferation of ambitions and atrocities herself. It was rather easy to say that us engineers knew what the guns were for, or why now the ocean had turned into an armed zone. The nations along that route had become rebellious and weary of the outlook that kept stinging them like a wounded and frightened cobra. It was alarming that they would all change some day. For the better or worse, I found another bottle, and by six in the afternoon I was one-third closer to yet another empty quart. And, of course, per say, this drama continued within my contaminated mind that I didn't belong to the homeland, I had been away too long, and it was my spouse that was still a native but to no avail, and my company had provided everything including sufficient gallonage of gin fish. Yet, most important of all the silence of the sea which kept me company during my hibernations. The early evening hours filled the cabin with captain's high spirit without him there. The scent of crude tobacco was seeping through the ventilation and the airway under the cabin entry. In a few minutes I thought I had seen smoke aboard while staring at two sea doves entertaining me with bickering and pecking, like a distant machine gun behind a tall mountain; they were playing at the circular cabin window as a sheer twilight penetrated into that occupied space which now looked as though it was a tavern or such. I stood up rushing the doves away and peeped through while the deck was crowded and sailors were running to directions when I thought I heard one or two gunshots as the rumble sounded like harsh exchanges of curses and warnings. The sunset had already cheated me as it had occurred during the chaos about a half hour ago. I went for the light switch but suddenly something warned me that it would be dangerous when a rush of light filled the room and I could see two shadows, two men one pulling the other into that minimal cabin. I went for my gun as I was on the only side of this encounter that was exposed to light. So I could see that I was accosted by the figure pulling the other as that man's other hand rose toward me when I, hopelessly aiming, pulled the trigger and the figure fell. Now they were both on the ground. Captain was lifeless and, too, was the man that had carried his body to the cabin. I imagined he wanted the captain in his cabin hidden in order to keep his death a secret as a mutiny had undertaken the ship. The captain had mentioned about the boarding of a group of fugitives which he was planning to shelter and give them a haircut. He told me it was not officially an asylum and they would be disposed upon reaching shore. He told me that he had doubts about the identity of this group but it did not bother him as long as we were headed away from the island nation and not towards. These people did not matter because he could dump them at any harbor for labor. He mentioned that he kept them in an area near the engine room with minimal nutrition and bedding which would have kept them aware and ready for immediate disembarkation. The bodies lying next to one another taking up the narrow floor as smoke had filled the cabin like those port taverns that always kept the sailors and the porters busy the same intoxicating themselves with hand rolled cigars and rum like a thirsty cattle reaching the stream. All there was to do was to maintain my post as now I was drinking from the bottle breathing like a locomotive. The ship had become quiet; some running on the deck and then, again, silence took over but peace seemingly had been settled by the time I began feeling like I had inhaled a bale's worth of tobacco leaves.

Shortly, the wind cleared the smoke off the deck and the engine had died down when I heard noise in the hall by the bunkers. It was nearing the cabin; they sounded like they were inspecting the ship. By that moment I could not tell my friends from the enemies and would have not let go of my pistol pointing it at the door. I could not breath easily in that solitary cabin next to two dead bodies I had no reason to kill yet having done so otherwise. At least, I knew I killed one of them, and as for the other, he was a commoner more so a slave of slave women and gypsies of those parts he probably had visited. Damn the sea! Someday he would have died in that ocean; syphilis, AIDS, or any other addiction that best soothed an exhausted and melancholy captain to end his urge to constantly struggle to overcome his homelessness. A home he often mentioned and never was proud of. Captain was a rude man as his mature side merely talked about women and rum. Women from that ocean with different habits and that rum which made each more voluptuous. His temper was official, confident, and by the rules he happened to be overqualified for this job since its commencement. I stared at the wound on his belly; he seemed to have suffered for a while. Perhaps the other man was trying to keep him alive. That could be why he was carrying him back to the cabin.

The gin was not doing anything and now I was one-third away from the next bottle. Detecting the movement of shadows through that window while the reflection of that same light defined the deck through the passing hours of this long night. I trembled and could not tell wrong from right; I fell short of words to mumble like any other drunkard. More like commands to hide or stay quiet! Some of them in another lingo but for all that mattered it was still familiar to my bloodshot eyes. The smell of ocean had degraded anything and everything that had, insofar, happened to me; the familiar anthem, sound of the tumultuous and yet mute sea allowed men to run, and shout words of refuge on that mutinied vessel. Why was it so familiar to my warm and sweaty body? Only if I could have prayed and begged the Lord to remain my companion if it be the last moment of my life that had smothered me in a rusty cabin with two dead bodies, a few maps, a compass, and the remaining gin in a fingerprinted bottle that glowed dimly in the darkness of the captain's quarters. I was determined to live on, and to pull my gun on the first sod that came close to me; I had a share of it already and knew exactly where I was while the entrance to that tiny cabin could have been easily broken into. I held on to my gun pointing it toward the damn door while it sounded like there was some traffic in the corridor. The gunshots although few, two or three, had already stopped. The window reflected a circular shadow on the wall facing the bed which was right under it. Lord help me one last time! *What have I done!? I pray thee to save me from this mayhem and return me to land, a peaceful land.* Now my memory lived the past; not sure I could explain without any lights or the captain whom I thought I had shot in cold blood. But I only pulled the damn trigger once and heard only one shot go. . . Lord save my family who lived in a faraway land; a country I had not visited for over ten years, that would be more than a decade. My son should be over being a teen, a big man! I pray thee Lord that he should not and would not be a murderer. To kill his own kind, to shoot at people would be a demon. It was blasphemy that had taken me over.

I started to vomit on the bed. I could not stop because falling sick to my gut which was filled with gin, captain's favorite brand, Queen's brand as he visited the kingdom once a year to service his vessel. I looked through the window; it was about twenty or so years when the military took over my homeland after a coup that had kept me away in my second domicile. I had to surrender unlike this ship; I would live or would I? The sense of calm was becoming hideous and I could expect an explosion or gunshots to break the silence any time. No one was talking outside that cabin. I suspected they were all by the entrance but there was no one there. The corridor felt secluded. My bottle now empty I wanted to get up and look for a fresh one although they might have heard me tumbling. Could I keep my balance? Two bottles of it, a shooting, and Lord help me out, save me!

I had been away from my family for over twenty-five years and after my second homeland suffered an acute change of regimes due to uncounted votes during elections that resulted in a scuffle between parties and eventually a super power interacted and settled a puppet cabinet that yet rules the country of my last citizenship. I chose the sea. My profession required naval assignments to monitor interoceanic communication through a mother mega corporation. A shipping giant that had her share of the archipelago, among them island nation that had recently fell behind her import quotas and to speed things up they needed what I called deciphering the operations among this so called seaboard. I was on my way back only to return to the point departure and get on another vessel heading for the equatorial nations of the east.

I breathed quietly still spitting my bitter saliva until I felt my dry mouth. I began sucking my tongue. There were five bullets left in my pistol. There was never a need for it on a ship which carried a few armed sailors; it was more than what we needed and the cargo was ammunition, all that we might have needed to defend this ship. It never made sense to me why the Operations always sent me a memo to be armed with a hand gun, among all the liaison working in the same firm. Lord don't force me to use it again! I beg you! I wanted to see my son once more. I had sworn to him to never use a gun. It was almost midnight and I suspected everyone was hiding from something, but it was all a guess without knowing what the hell I was supposed to be doing. There were a couple of cigars by those maps on the small table. I lit one. I felt it was safe but the strike of the match was apparently witnessed by one of the sailors. The silence was terrorizing yet I was getting used to it sucking on the hand-rolled genuine tobacco leaves and doing my best to keep calm. My luminescent timepiece showed about a quarter of two when there was a knock on the door. "Cyrus open up!!" I quickly stepped toward the door and stood by the wall beside the door. Perhaps I could have held my gun at the back of the intruder once he attempted to enter the cabin. He would probably not even have a chance to turn around, I asserted.

"Are you there, Cyrus!?"

————————————

The engine room was crowded with sailors. The chatter was quiet but felt weary and worrisome; it sounded as though they were-everyone in peace-searching for a way to escape and flee from the promiscuous sea. It was lonely for them as they now stayed together and shared arms. It was frightening as they now looked for hope. They had killed all the engines and kept the ship floating without a destination yet. The words were conjugated carefully and the faces, bleak but hopeful, maintained a serious tone that had held this ship in limbo since the embarkation of a bunch of fishermen. . . . . . .

The would soon begin flickering as a dead engine would have not been able to charge the source of power in the ship. They were intimate without a cause for identity and the mutiny had ended. Each and everyone in that humid and nauseating chamber sought a unity that had been long due; they felt that a deep trust and a legitimate force was needed. Cyrus probably wanted it that way. *Hallelujah!* They wanted to explore the ocean as she had happened to become a domicile to those with the pride of pioneers who headed for the battle against the sea. They wanted to go back where they had come from, island nation. They all sensed their hearts' urgency to return home and change it.

The death of Cyrus which was blamed on the captain's aid brought forward a brief interrogation until they found out what happened as a sailor had witnessed that he wounded the captain and Cyrus, apparently a figurehead, wanted to take him to his cabin to save his life and the rest you already know. . . . The engineer after gaining consciousness, apparently had passed out after sitting and drinking for too damn long, explained what he was dong on that ship. But the bottom line the ship was without a captain and the refugees without a leader. They were trying to find out if any of those seamen could have led them to a harbor, especially island nation's. With all the ammo loaded on that ship an idea was growing larger and larger like a portrait of the future during the next couple of days. The island was half a day away from the dead vessel's parameters on the map. The stench of fuel and the blinking lights were becoming an issue and they had to turn the engine back on to charge the power cells which then would consume the fuel with about half a day left to carry her either way. The prisoners had to start talking sooner or later, and they did sooner than later before it had gone any further. They could not hide the loss of Cyrus and told the ship crew his story and how he was being watched and they had escaped prison. The sailors smoked, drank, sweated, and finally had the nerve to pledge their cooperation. The engine room smelled like a horrifying death chamber with all of them weary and only able to look at one another with an expression of approval.

The campaign had to be spontaneous as this journey was to be carefully safeguarded because none of those men knew what was to come after they had revved up the engines. The messages relaying the ships approach were to be sent under the new code, and the hungover engineer went on with the business confessing his deepest regrets. They had found him innocent and buried the two men along with a number of others, more sailors than prisoners, in the sea. The ship began its devastating rotation and the vessel trembled back into life around dawn. So the bottle of rum was passed from one hand to the other; they were trying to keep warm but sober, yet if alcohol had any use on a cargo ship best it had been used on a breakaway mission such as this. The sailors showed the cargo to the prisoners and told them all about the weapons. There was enough for a small force to enter combat and win it! A few enlisted sailors showed the men how to use the weapons; a few of them were semi-modern and unfamiliar. The sea was calm now on that hazy morning and waves peacefully brushed away from the ship while the conditions made the navigation very easy except to worry about the shore. The few close hands of Cyrus and the engineer remained in the engine room making plans as the noise forced them to talk loudly and use their hands to pass on some of the messages. They were getting somewhere; although the plan was simple and only if everything would have taken place accordingly. The engineer did not know their language quite well but understood it and relayed messages on the radio every fifteen minutes to keep that ship on the map. He had not specified the identity of the vessel but had explained that they were delivering food and basic necessities such as items of medical nature. Sailors kept telling him what to say! Island had not reacted as he was receiving the usual responses. The secret of the new coding was held only by him. He had told the authorities that the manifest of the ship was delivered to them a day ago by a cargo ship and he placed in its identification instead while making them think Seahide had harbored at destination and the log had been delivered to the port officers who permitted him to assist in conducting this journey both as a test and also as a commercial venture. The island port authorities had not suspected anything as they established communication through the new codifications.

The sea was the limit and turbulence still raised weariness among the souls of the men that had gathered on the ship to seek a destination; or perhaps, a point of no return that would have cost them their lives and doubts. The very essence of humanhood those men would not be able to deny by undermining the values that made them one. Around noon the ship was still about thirty miles away. Those prisoners were listless and rebellious to the point where life and death did not matter anymore but solely to serve a purpose because the life in their flesh belonged to the innocent, to their land, the island nation they all had fought for. Cyrus, during a speech, had confessed to his sins and adultery because he, for the first time, had been infatuated with a new honesty and fidelity that always overcame sin and promiscuity; he told his aides to follow and ignore stereotypes since time would not allow any limits to determination and the last words of the innocent. Cyrus had provoked struggle in his men and they now knew that there was no option but to defend the oppressed. Indeed, the island nation was awaiting the beats of a drum never pounded on, yet to be proclaimed as a cause for the minimal freedom of its patriots. The cargo was significant and the sailors had informed those fugitives that it would be enough to start a damn war, just what they wanted as the pain had reached the flesh and bones; just what the prisoners, the spirit of Cyrus's innocence and his fellow men, had predicted for the citizens of the island nation.

The messages relayed by the engineer were becoming scarce. He was running out of excuses and notions that would have, at least, allowed the ship to get closer without any suspicion of the port authorities. It was time to choose! The sailors and prisoners, in the engine room, had held on and finally decided to anchor about four or five miles from the shore. There would have been trouble awaiting them had they got any closer. So the engineer halted communication and the sailors released the rescue boats; there were about eight or nine of them each carrying about four to six men. This was what they wanted; only to be able to deliver arms for fifty or sixty men. The prisoners believed they could put together a posse only if they located their contacts on time. The engineer was told to kill time by explaining that the ship did not have enough fuel and it would have been better off by anchoring away from the port until the refueling was possible which meant a tanker should be delegated into a mission that would have led to battle. A battle that Seahide risked in order to remain awaiting her men and the prisoners.

This normal day, of all the island's moments, had taken an early toll into the adolescence of its importance and posture which always commenced at sea. The urge, and more, the renunciation of a fatal fate grew more for those men through a relentless voyage and yet into rebellion. Dead corpses of the martyrs and cries against oppression had reached the souls of those men. Alas, they were desperate to travel the path that Cyrus had already set forward. The group, armed with fresh ammunition, was now chasing a ghost as life meant less, and more so, it was instinct that had pushed it into this sail; it was said that civilization had come about in result of human guilt ; it was guilt that kept man standing. Still, they knew nothing about nothing except to share their treasure with the islanders in the hope of solace. It was about half a mile away from the port when they recognized the government boats and guards who had barricaded that harbor. It was obvious that something was happening and they knew it. The first lifeboat called for a halt and without crowding they decided to spread instead of heading for the port. There was no use fighting an early battle and getting wasted on those defenseless lifeboats. The first few boats headed for the far shore and signaled the others to go back. They had to set means of contact; and maybe, an easy way to get those guns into the right hands. Now they could use the hand radios without worrying about the port authorities since now they were out of sight by the farther shore. Those men did not know much about relaying their position to the Seahide so they let waves take them closer to the land and had decided to set contact in a couple of hours on the frequency that the engineer had given them, one different from the harbor's. And the man kept sending e-mail messages to the computer of the island. There was no response so he had told them that it was rather conspicuous but indeed safe to make a move because the ministry was probably closed or the computer was down which could have been good news or yet bad. If there had been anything unusual going on they could soon find out before making any moves. However, if the ministry had been closed, it meant they would have only dealt with the harbor officers. Nonetheless, the government boats seemed quite ready to charge and had assumed combat formation as far as the lifeboats could see. They reached the shore not a long way from the broken down prison where Cyrus and his companions had first escaped. The engineer was given their position and was told to inform the others about the whereabouts of that beach. They knew exactly where it was. Kind of hard to forget!

8

"Gentlemen, here we are a family. . . . And my tenure speaks for itself as well as you. . . the heads of our beloved nation. . . . !!Shaken, turbulent, a few dead, and the nation is alive; perhaps more real than ever such a day establishes the order of equality and freedom. When they see it change, and when they decide upon its affairs, and when equal morsels feed, albeit, equal men. Then, man rises upon the world and on top of it all the culmination of a humanitarian repeal and the integrity of mankind opens its wings and brings this nation under them like any other. But the heads of the state gather otherwise. It is not equality for all that is the aim but brutality and suppression by the ultimate force. Long live power! The iron hand that takes everything aside yet you ask what about justice!? The constitution, a paper tiger, never to be mentioned to the typical gangs of innocent bodies. They need blood to write, in red, the words of enforcement and implication of torture and death; a rundown alley full of flesh, a lesson for others." *Keep quiet! We bear arms that are loaded and aimed! Men and women of the island, retreat and obey!! Don't forget the past.*

The minister's rally puts into effect an armistice that should be broad and clear in the message. It will bring chain and leash law to the streets and under the palm trees that have not heard or seen, but have been colored white with words of oppression. They will locate the real enemy at any cost. Down with any revolution that takes away the hand rolled cigars and top bottled rum. Away with wisdom and wise words of outsiders! Claims a minister that his late model sedan was vandalized and it is indeed no matter of tolerance or procrastination! *Let rice flow in the hands of pros, and cons to be starved... What good do those slaves of strangers do for us? They have to ration the refined water and stop bringing bread to the streets. Starve them as intensely as it is possible in any human community. Let it be a reminder that the nation will sustain only the oligarchy that has kept it together!*

"Gentlemen, as I said. . . This is only to cause fraud! In our small family it is easy to see the facts that set aside tradition and history that accompany us until this day. This is a way that our nation has chosen to test its own powers. I raise a hand to renew my oath of duty with every one of you in the House to hold our majority rule once again and force this beast, the rebellion, to bow his head and stop this game of deception and blasphemy. These rumors, the events that have crowded the plaza, the takeover of the ministry, and this malevolent method our enemies have thereby implicated are all trivial notions citing the demands of petty citizens that can not even write what they want in simple words and that is perhaps why we have been left incommunicado. Ministers and representatives of the island nation know and have done better work throughout our prosperous territory. Needless to say, the history, the text books made available to our schools, the altars, and other social establishments all endorse our capability and those procedures we have put into effect for years to improve the living standards and it is us now, to once again prove to our constituents that we are here. . . as powerful as the twenty-first century man, and as determined as any government on the face of the earth!!"

The emergency session has not lasted over an hour yet when they all stand up and applaud by joining hands in unity and to put into effect the new plan. The ministers are to be in full alert and the representatives to inform their constituents. It is tomorrow that they would tighten all channels of communication and supplies, or perhaps as soon as it is possible! The ministries are ordered to close the port and to cut short the supplies of food and other everyday needs of the nation, all people, friend and enemy. It is to be noted that an intense economic crisis will be staged to result in desperate measures. The army is ordered to take to the streets, specifically around businesses and social centers, and therefore barricading all means of communication as quickly as possible.

The time is short and so is the breath of the fighters. They are many this time! They are slaves of a labor tracing an infamy. It is not the survival now, yet the question is the heap of faith; the eternity will be their witness once their nation is able to land on its two feet. Now their angels are crowding the street. *A call for detente! Will they ever learn that gunpowder would not last as long as the toll! The flesh and blood. . . . Read the blank pages and learn!* It is never too late to express the work of angels in words. Literally, the command is now lost. But man always prevails! And the dawn will yet be more powerful than ever. Angels will sing the "Come the Liberty!"

"Gentlemen, my family, the eternal heads of our nation. . . . the liberation's point man is a prisoner named Cyrus whom you probably know better from a few years ago. He was one of the defendants in a case involving his practice of law. He was taken to the court for claiming confidentiality against our request to reveal some names and that has put him in jail. His partner is dead now. There is a woman, the wife of his partner as we are told. Salome is having an affair with Cyrus in secret. Also, she is under treatment due to mental crisis; they are said to have a child that is no more under her care. The authorities have put the son in the care of an orphanage funded by the government. Cyrus has been the main axle to the movement's machine. We have been reported that his strong urge towards the liberation of our island has been rooted in him since his father's loss of his last wife, Cyrus's mother. Her death was an early call. She was only thirty-seven. I will get to the point!! He is a loose canon out there with an entire army of activists to back him up. His background is reason enough that he must be brought down and, as our enemy, neutralized at once!!! People like him have tried hard to make us look bad throughout the years. But gentlemen we are an establishment that has tolerated many a line of injustice, blasphemy, betrayal, and double-crossing never reaching their demonic purposes and have been dismantled through your noblest and most patriotic efforts toward our land, the island nation. . . . Let us not loose confidence and time! I demand each and everyone of you to be discreet, and without a notion of despair take action. Remember that our innocent nation awaits our final call as usual and there is no one to help her but the few that are present in this edifice. . . . !

The seats are warm and the breaths are warmer as blood rushes up instead of down. We live to free ourselves and yet freedom is waiting. The road is clear and nothing between us, eternity, and innocence. The marbles remain shining and blood still in the veins. . . . The road will be open and free of wrath yet vengeance will soon rule. We will come, yes. . . . we will come even closer than you know. The child of an endgame, not to be forgotten, adorned with petals of the spring bloom. We are all similar! Hands free but feet chained and kicking. Because the storm will free the soul. The shores will rise. The eggs are hatched and their offsprings would float with no aim, the turtles of the island are silent and never spoke! The streams will reside and fill our dark nature. It will end. It will fall again and again. We find the path to stand among them. And they will never be. That memory will be history although history oft lives on.

"Cyrus, our man, as a discretion could be compromised. . . . of course you, as heads of this nation know that there are ways to reach what is called a complete compromise! He is not said to be a strong man. Stubborn. . . . maybe! He's been back and forth to prison. We have done a few routines but nothing specific to bring an end to his persistence. He is educated and popular as we know now. Cyrus is powerful and at the top of this rebellion. People who surround him strongly believe in him. They are the ones who have long rooted with this man's ideology and now they are claiming that the horizon belong to them. Cyrus 'The Preacher' does not operate out of the prison or at least we think so. His contacts are a bunch of delinquents who are in and out of the prison frequently. Believe me gentlemen. . . . They have turned into a contagious disease and yet spreading. . . . These bastards are claiming a republic against us!!"

The blood streams of a rigid and chipping skeleton; and more, the rotten carcass that overshadows everything and everywhere in this nation has but surreptitiously decorated our community. All places including the ghettos and the only market that one day supplied the islanders, provided with minimal nutrition, at unaffordable prices. The moment is now and they dare to believe, for once out of those torturous times that have stolen their will to prevail and redeem their lives. This clandestine appointment is through a deep search of what is there to trigger the crisis into a more favorable circumstance, and put the people back on more tolerable seats. The clan heads would, amid the ebb and flow of the silent and alien shores of the island, go deep and try not to show their hands to the opposition. There will be many murders; it could turn into an assassin's carousel according to their speculations and what they find worthy of the innocent.

"Gentlemen. . . . I have kept one thing from you which now I would like to share with you and perhaps. . ." The longstanding minister of information proceeds to interrupt the echo and chatter among the few present as they expect him to single out the issues concerning the takeover.

"Until very recently we had Cyrus's father under guard and the fellow pointed out that he had some inheritance to leave him upon his death having already occurred. To be exact,. . . . he's been poured dirt on about three months ago, and to be kept secret his location, and the interrogation has not been confided until this very moment. Our preemptive lookout for possible links to the case and what men like Cyrus could do actually led us to believe that his father might be a head figure in his case of denial toward the government to access some files. The man is dead having buried all his anti-regime sentiments. Although Cyrus has an unclaimed inheritance that our factions have kept in the safe without informing him. We think we could lure him into cooperation by playing our game properly and by moving the pieces mannerly he might be willing to come into terms with us. His father leaves a house, the place of his birth which bears memories and deep affections for his mother. . . ."

The voices become loud and they face the minister with direct eye contacts and inquisitive faces. Then the room quickly turns quiet awaiting the weary minister to continue. This meeting could be, more than anything, decisive and is taking longer than expected but the clan's shock comes at the amount of information-that has never been told-piling up the confident minds of those present. Some now feel doubts about the honesty, legitimacy, and most of all are curious to know how deeply liberation has been watched and why the government has not detained these elements that indeed have been so conspicuous.

"Everyone. . . .listen please! I, for one, as the chief of the port operations and ministry of economics demand that by the end of this meeting the other respected presences lay everything on the table and explain why we were not informed earlier. . . . and yet why covert operations remain a secret until today!!? Who has made these decisions??"

The ventilation is clearing the sweat off their foreheads and keeps their damp palms dry just so much that each could reach and raise the glass of fruit punch to their mouth without thirst and enthusiasm to drink it. Insofar, this neurotic masquerade has been extended by the minister of information and his clan. He remains quiet just as he has been for many years. This meeting is forcing him to reveal through a merciful reach for help to save the seized ministry that for years has been the paper castle and record keeper in a partisanship although partial to chaos and terror.

"We are still in power gentlemen. . . . absolute power! I doubt that anyone including the minister of information could undermine the command that has been vindicated to stand a legacy of the rule of majority which we uphold as a golden harness to contain this stallion called liberation. I pity them and you minister. . . . for lacking the courage and discreet knowledge of the rules for this game!! I hope that the so called clandestine network of this ministry has been curtailed solely to our enemies. . . . and in this meeting we are all friends. . . .!"

The long list in possession of the minister of information is yet to be retained while the few strong men in the room feel a medieval burden of responsibility, due to their post, as those soldiers are feeling in the plaza of the city. But, before the apostle is to be compromised by this ostensible agenda for relief, the minister of information's life is taken by the hands of the chief of the army while the General, after stepping into the silent room and killing the minster, having overheard the citations insisting on a military rule to oversee the cabinet! They never find out who the apostle is and do not reach an agreement to set his fate. The days of the island nation are long and windy which brings to mind the rule of the elements besieging and making wander the helpless as time is now a need and the needless become eternal. A fantasy has so far pledged the real side of her for the sake of the innocent and, thereon, is acting her part for the armed and unarmed equally so the voice of the prodigal amphibians is now heard at every home or by every clown. The sea is generous and eternal, yet turbulence of its winds brush the streets anticipating the smoke of gunpowder as grey as sand. Each minister now shall live except information and each of them know there is a contact among the needless and ultimate power has prevailed moments ago witnessed by this, per say, secret gathering. Eyes are watchful, and focused upon them as one may ask the question, "What is government?" Although the government knows it is time as there is a need; the need to secure the gates of this Garden of Eden that has let boast the principles of an aristocratic society-this island nation is now at the mercy of its own vigilance. The wheels of the carriage that carries the flames of suppression turn slowly to directions, and it is the people who are not able and present according to the status quo closely graded by diplomacy and exploitation up to its highest ranks. The needless become eternal because the island nation suffers upon this vigil wrath of the seas.

Still a few drops of the sign of life, clear sweat, capriciously occupy chief's bare forehead. In fatigues, he takes the order into his hands presumptuously and free of shame. He sets his hat on the long conference table pretentiously facing the end table with staring eyes that seem to be ready to kill again as his smile is senseless and holding no hidden emotional flaws. He speaks slowly as he demands assurance in his familiar tone being heard carefully and taken seriously. He signals the two accompanying soldiers to close the entrance door and stay outside. His eyeballs hardly moved although there were some reactions toward his mimics of the legends and his contaminating deception in such a traditional dialogue as he struggles to be more intimate; he cites, "Gentlemen, the minister was going to roast and eventually blackmail each and every one of you. . . . . !!" The chief owes his tenure to those ministers present and the one lying breathless on the floor. The votes of the ministers have kept him in control of the army for the last few years without any questions asked about his, indeed, questionable loyalty and dignity. To them, he is armed and dangerous; nonetheless, he is the most powerful man on the island. As silence rules the secures room, the afternoon approaches its ending hours, yet reaching a decision has shaped into a new dilemma. Now this body of government, literally what governs the island nation now, sits breathless in a conference room as turmoil is teaching them the last lessons to be learned about trust and metaphysics of integrity which they find cumbersome and to be vindicated by each of them.

"He was after a compromise. . . . Hah!! I spit on that man with all the power invested in me! He was trying to help 'the Preacher' who is at large and has escaped the prison during the tsunami that hit us last week. . . Prime minister. . . that man is no species to be compromised! I promise you. . . .!!"

Remaining quiet and holding a puzzled gesture until now, the prime minster nods yet he raises his hand in negation, and then pointing at the dead man asks the chief about his act, as the wasting of an ally could be a felonious move that threatens others in the room including himself.

"Friend among friends, that's all sir! We have important decisions to make. . . a careful plan has to be laid out and there is no place for betrayal or espionage as you know sir. I, just as always, did my job. . . . !!!" His tone is serious yet arrogant as the chief seemingly places himself in the ultimate rank; that which endows him full control of the island. The ministers look at each other and then turn towards the prime minister while this oligarchy, in chaos, has to find a solution.

"Gentlemen, you are my family! A family with needs and wishes. . . ." Chief takes the first steps to replay the game of trust that he has never done so well. His record holds a lot of dark spots; from bribery to corruption, and consuming the allocations toward his private urges. He is confident that there is a need for his cooperation or else he can forcefully take the leadership away and make it his own. The ministers, now breathing in a faster pace and afraid to oppose or even interrupt him, leaning towards patience and tolerance as there is almost no time left. Army awaits them behind that door! As family they are as an immense condescension towards the poverty and the pains that bewilder the momentum of the winds. The mud houses embedded with half dressed children where refined water is unheard of and chlorine sounds like the name of an animal. Cold food, rotten pineapples, and all they do for it is trying to distill a low grade and spoiled bottle of rum for another family; perhaps, a rank higher yet still desperate in exchange for a sporadic ration of bread. A room bedding ten or more where husbands and wives sleep together with another couple or perhaps three or four pairs with children lying at their feet in those undesired midnight hours. The contrast is a twelve bedroom construction belonging to the minster of information, now dead, never to enter the island's dream mansion again. The mothers only breast feed their babies seldom now, and fathers can't bring home a proper ration to feed the household. Today family does not count for everything due to the rebellious body of young and also regretful aging natives that are not able to prevail warily hiding their pain under the eternal rays of the island's sun. The evidence set it straight; the kind of justice that has merely overlooked equality and public welfare, that is all! One wonders if God is still a witness. *There is a God!* One whose name is heard when a child is given birth in an alley. One whose name is cited when food passes the prime phases of digestion without nausea or poisoning. One whose name is heard when children play together one day, or when the elders are touched by a mood so tender. Indeed, island has a God; because his chores, aside from creating equal men, are to create bad as well as good or, perhaps, he only has done the good and it is the wrath of eternal flames that results in bad beings who want to rule the world (the island nation) forever. If we let God speak he would explain or come up with a dire solution not as grey as what now exists. Alas, they know there is a God, but whose side is he on!? And what comes after God?

———————————

He has one hand on his heart, and his left hand is invitingly pointed towards the ministers when the chief calls on the guards who still remain behind the closed door of the conference chamber. "Bring her in. . . !" The chief calmly moved his head from his right to the left eyeing each minister as though he has something very confidential and promiscuous to share with them, as they wait for the guards. His right hand on his heart obediently and holding a mysterious grin notwithstanding, the guards bring a woman in shabby clothes into the room shortly while approaching the end of the long table in order for all of them to be able to see her in clear. Pale and disillusioned, she looks the other way avoiding the chief and the ministers in a bitter impression that promises no further relief from the guards as they stand by her.

"Gentlemen, respected heads of this nation, confidantes. . . . you are looking at our gold reserve, this island's treasure. . .

an odyssey that will change our fate!!! Let me introduce Salome! This is a turning page in the history of the island nation and its desperate path! Some of you might well know her. . . ."

Suddenly, minister of justice jumps out of his seat throwing his hands forward as a sign of protest and disgust against chief's intention, although curiosity has already done the work as other minsters take a glance at him without any interest.

"Fellow ministers this is disgusting! I know her. . . we thought she is dead!! Chief do you have anything to say about that!?"

The chief stands up and steps off his chair approaching the schizophrenic Salome who seems to not know anyone and why they are all staring at her. Drowned in her prison melancholy, she tries to act natural by smiling in embarrassment.

"Listen to me when I tell you that a conspiracy has been awaiting you! Friends, I am here to save you as I have once already. . . . by putting an end to that bastards life. . . . Indeed, let our presence show what dignity hides behind every face at this table, and let us leave in oblivion a pest's attempt to destroy our country. . . He had plans to bring our motherland to its knees and conspire against each one present in this room! You sir,. . . respected Mr. minister of justice. . . you were to pay blood for your clandestine affairs with the daughter of our respected police chief!!! Or you sir. . . the island's sole genius of economics, one who has absolute command of this nation's commerce. . . you were to pay ransom to that bastard for manipulating the tax

documentations and tipping from our annual budget. . .
and the rest, all of us were the targets that he was about
to strike one by one, and then to take advantage of this
innocent woman who has done nothing but living her life
in peace until the blasphemous minister of information
took custody of her and her child, Cyrus's son, and secretly
arranged for her detention! He took away their son to exploit
and condemn those two and thus dictate his evil plans into
the affairs of the island nation! Yes,. . . I had to do what I
did. . .!!"

Chief then confesses to the summons he has received
from the dead minister to show up and contain this
secret conference, and thereon, negotiate their way into
the unilateral leadership of the country. The army would
follow and the supporters of Cyrus would therefore join once
they return his son to Salome; therefore, the movement is
brought under control and there would be no obstacles on
their way. A dead man can not talk; hereon, it is the chief
who promises himself the leadership by confessing to the
sins that, according to the bunch present at the meeting, do
not make a difference in the status quo. This barricade, the
issue at hand requires careful review and discreet attention
of all present yet the chief continues to baptize himself with
an unworthy pride blaming the divine justice for what is
happening. Chief reveals everything and introduces Salome
solely because he has promised them that his intentions are
radical and yet perhaps irrational; he raises the anxiety to the
point that ministers are baffled and shocked by this man's
strange honesty which insofar is nothing better than a total
sham. The chief proceeds to introduce his plan although
he leaves the negotiations for last, and shares its initiatives
with the tribune. He names it Operation Tribune as a totally

peaceful platform at the civic plaza is to be crowded by journalists and the intellectuals closest to the government to speak about future, welfare, solutions, and an invitation to a community effort for progress and anything else that they could muster to weaken the deep-rooted division. The chief brings up the tsunami and that part of the population affected by it, and advises the ministers to provide a camp, tents and food, for them. The group, devastated, stands up and hails his arrogance still striving to understand this animosity and the cause behind his acts. Yet, he seems to have his mind set. He, again, places his right hand on his heart and with the left hand he invites others to do the same. Salome is standing in confusion and a lapse of autistic disorientation. She is quietly weeping due to excitement as she observes this ritual that puts in effect indications of an heinous account of the government's activities she is familiar with but unable to put a stop to it. She wipes her tears with her forearm and mumbles, "Go baby, go baby, mamma go. . . . !!!"

Operation Tribune is named so because it would be guarded by the army, and will be in effect taking place next day. Chief requested the cabinet to put a posse together in order to trigger this operation and advised them to do so accordingly based on what has been discussed in the meeting, and that he personally, after assuming the supreme tenure of the ministry of information, will edit the blueprint of this operation. He cites that it should be 'in tune with the horizon of modernity'!

9

The puddle smelled of spoiled dung, black as char; it is what the tsunami leaves behind among other more significant damages that are yet not mended. The flattened shacks, masses of unattended garbage and rotten foodstuff that clogs the still unsettled sewage structure. And the mutt is looking more like a Rottweiler than any other, skinny on some backbone which shows how they keep him starving to remain alert and protect the entrance of the garage against unexpected visitors. The white circular plastic clock on its torn down and cracked cement facade tells it to be almost five to four in that humid and boiling afternoon; the place is crowded with junks of all kinds as the latest would be a forty-year-old model mostly sitting to be rebuilt again and again for those who could afford it as others have left it because they have given up on the useless carcass. The entrance is crowded with one mechanic who only does the oil changes and the tune-ups with the prices written in large and handwritten yellow and white paint on the facade's rough cement. They would be done on Fridays which is far more time than needed, those being a once-in-a-lifetime dedication to auto care around the island, one in a lifetime. In the back room the parts depot is where the liberation has nested. Among the water pumps, radiator, spark plugs, and etc. there is a table where the decisions are made and the old man has started again as usual. There is something different about his pallid and trembling face. He knows something is wrong but who would take his word as they always complain about his bickering and jiberish. They all sit there by the refurbished radiators and broken fans having a discussion when he begins to go against it and they stay patient and tolerant towards a procrastination that never ends and, now, has overtaken them. The old man is wary and he does not want anything to go wrong. It is just everything else that worries him, and the lives of his comrades, like his own sons and daughters. He believes the discrimination should end and suddenly shouts through the silence as if taken by rum; he pleads innocence like a preyer that could be heard by the man outside working on a car. The depot smells of used engine oil sunk in burned rubber. He carries on with his merciful repentance for he says he would not do it again and leave the island to the angels. The two younger men are busy writing and whispering for a while as they try hard to create some peace and be able to think of ideas. Somebody has to come up with a plan. The dilemma is that of terror and he seemingly can not obey the silence. They have been sitting around that worktable since morning. No news is not good news; they do not know what to do or how to do anything if it came to that. He shouts again in broken words and through his missing front teeth overusing his extended lips. He believes that Cyrus is on his way. . . . but why is he late? He has the explanation in plain truth as the early visitor describes that he is contemplating, and, he takes a few cigars with him as the old man always keeps a pocket full. Denial of the actions taken by the army is unusual but they need a man count as the messenger has explained in a few words hurriedly. The plea is clear as the young ones explain to him that 'The Preacher' is thinking big and he is ready to put an end to it. The old man pours himself some coffee as usual while it seems to be around noon time, and picks up a sheet of paper and, with his reading glasses, scans the page looking warily concerned and lost. Those manners are not strange to the other two ostensibly because after these few hours along with the morning news they happen to come to a compromise with the old man's hunches. He points out the ministry and denies the messenger as he cites that they do have a small force standing by but the message has been that they should wait until the final word is given. He tells them that 'The Preacher' is considering something major and he is willing to stand by it by any means; however, much ammunition and arms are needed to pull it through. *Really!!* They are flabbergasted but knowing that Cyrus always hides something under his sleeve, they believe the pretentious messenger.

The three remain seated waiting for a word from the plaza when the old man points out Cyrus's father and how they have investigated his health and death. He has known that family for many years. "That boy has felt the pressure. . . and that's why he is waiting!!! Something must be bothering him right now. . . . ! I hope he is safe because the last thing that warden wants is to see him exposed! Or maybe he wants things to die down a bit. . . .I don't know! I just think it's a little unusual to sit back and not do anything. . . .!"

The three are in charge of relaying messages to someone out there, someone who would help; a powerful force to step in and save the day. They hoped that with a message from Cyrus things would change, yet that has happened and, still, there is no way out. The older one wonders how long they could hold on to the ministry. He makes a call as his disappointed tone explains the situation bringing fear into the remote auto part depot. Now, he knows that the ministry should be maintained under control at least for another couple of days while it has been barricaded for a little more than a day. They are told that the army has been reinforced while surrounding the building, and they would move in anytime to take it back. There has been no shooting after those couple of warning shots during the first day around morning. He bangs his fist on the worn down work table as the the two young comrades suddenly turn towards him. He knows that the body count is what is needed. So he picks the phone again and dials a number. His nephew is a high school teacher as he explains that he wants to contact his school and gets that number from his wife. Thus, he immediately calls the school while they tell him that classes are held and he is teaching. They assured him that he would be asked to call back as the old man passed on the number of garage; of course, not the phone on the table, but the garage's number for the public. The two visits that day did not bring much hope to those three. The other young man explains that he has some friends that have been keeping up with the liberation indirectly, and would be interested to help; he said he will go there. He assured the other two that they might even have guns but that he would have to explain everything, and it would not be clear how many people, or specifically how many guns!

The posse from the plaza has taken a car to be able to cover a wide area for help even knocking on everyone's door, those they would think useful or cooperative. This day filled the chronicles of the liberation's activities in a very different way. There is no sign of a predictable action which shows that it is merely an ambition, the occupation of the ministry without a set plan, because the posse has reported that they smell a rat and they would not want to waste any time. The takeover had to be laid out as soon as possible without any words exchanged outside the circle of operatives. The posse has headed toward the mayor's house to find his son who has secretly supported the liberation and they hoped that he would come to their aid by introducing new parties into the movement, or perhaps use influence to open some doors that could assist the progress of this takeover.

The phone rings and the old man waits three ringtones and then picks it up. It is his nephew nervously introducing himself in a whisper. He might be watched and apparently has a hunch as to the cause for the old man's call. The old man starts fresh with him, he calls him a hero and the nation a teenager who needs to grow up by getting all philosophical like he respected his nephew's profession, a teacher! This day becomes more important as he adds that everyone has to make a move to make it work.

"She is still cruising at sixteen and has never acted any more mature than that. . . . A few popular songs and that soda drink and chocolates that make her stand on her two feet, and beg them ship captains to contaminate her with that garbage more and more!! You agree with me that today we could take the right direction and help her to grow up out of this epidemic infancy. . . . It has now taken too long!! And it can't get worse. . . . Now give me the good news!!?"

The party on the other end says that it would take at least a day to get his team together; perhaps about twenty or thirty, or forty if he was lucky because the word has gotten around and they are scared that the army might begin to use their guns. He mentions ammunition too if they could provide them it for at least a few of them. The old man exclaims that it is possible the arms will reach him the next day as they are expecting some to come in through Cyrus's team as his nephew has heard about him.

"I sent a member of the posse along with the contact sent by Cyrus who promised there will be guns and ammo. Nephew do you feel ready!?. . . I mean. . . are we just ready or you think we are on the right path? You know. . . I knew his father; the man was always looking devastated and one day he explained that it is his son that frightens him! He is reading too much he says!! 'What he reads has become a great concern to me' he says! 'It scares me every time I have to buy a book for him!' The salesman would look at him like he is asking for too much. Those books, you know, could not be overlooked; the salesman would then wonder who wanted them! And his friends, the other students whom he associates with were all kins of the elite.. . . No wonder he got himself into trouble! 'It was a dilemma buying books for him!!' The bookstore would never forget him! Cyrus has done his education in dignity and has worked hard. . . What do you think . . . my nephew!? You are educated as well. . . What is your opinion?"

The man on the other end of the line whispers, "I don't know, but you are right, so you said there will be guns; then, should my guys join them or will they bring them to us? Where are they, uncle? Maybe we could directly head over there and begin the armament and then pair up with them in the plaza. . . !!" The old man rubs his short and moderately trimmed beard then looks around the garage warily. He thoughtfully reconsiders his posture and then, frowning, says, "He said some small community near the broken down prison, but I couldn't imagine where the supplies are coming from! Perhaps he will plan a mission so all of us could follow. . . .that would be the best option. In order for us to unify, we must assemble a force however small; the next step would be to appeal to the masses!!!" The two begin to sink in silence; so sympathetic that it brings some tears in the old man's eyes and he assures his nephew that he will have an answer by midday tomorrow. The young teacher wishes him luck as he hurriedly asks if there is anything else that he could do for him and the two hang up.

The word is nihilism in a crossword puzzle that is sitting beside the cup of coffee that remains cold, old, and worthless to the taste as he feels something, in a sweat, with a deep-rooted guess and an islandish behavior that can cause it to echo into those mechanical shelves and eventually the entire garage, and combine with the dog's mundane barking at an approaching car. The opening to the outside of the building into the alley and towards the main road usually makes it easy for the attendants to start the paperwork and even, with blind eyes, listen to the outreaching sound of the shoddy engines to elaborate on the fees, and maintain their reputation by, perhaps, putting a fair price on the repairs as each one is typically one needy client. Most of their clientele, these days, often end up at the garage because they also have to make money through taxi-ing passengers from spots around the inner city to the short and suburban distances with these aged vehicles mostly during afternoons that traditionally mark the end of the day around this capital.

A cool breeze keeps him free of perspiration while he coughs continuously until there is blood. Mercy! And this mercy unlike the last breath of Socrates, as in doubt and terror leaves him helpless and yet dependent on a horrifying wisdom that interprets the fate of a man! His handkerchief shows the drops of blood, and he only retreats to the chair as the phone rings again, without any attention by the young man and the other promising the client and swearing his best service and long life for the sacred vehicle, and the old man picks up the receiver and says hello with no vital tone in his voice. He is pale and paler, even blue and grey as one could detect the vein traces on his temples now while he intends still to merely keep it a secret. The young man across the table from him is jotting down names and numbers, for parts and prices as the other swears to God and his family outside by the window. It is just on time by looking at the old man's impression that he receives a message he has been waiting for. He bangs his hand on the table and the crossword puzzle, cut out, halfway worked through, a piece of paper however philosophical to a novice or an apostle. He yells in exuberance with a conspicuous tone; enough that the young man notices blood as he is struggling to remain on the chair but too dizzy, too weak; he spits some blood and, thereon, he falls. He rushes to help him but the young man only can call the other one who is now done with swearing and greets the client that has to make it back on foot. He decides that the persuasion and price are both too high compared to the city's present demand for carpool. *All the fuss that government has raised seems to never end!* The two rush towards a van to load him into the vehicle for transport to a proper sanctuary, a doctor or the hospital. Suddenly the old man insists that there are doubts that Cyrus will be safe. He acknowledges having a hemorrhage and can barely see. He tells them that the last call is help and the one before is probably trouble while the meticulous persistence of his nephew proves to be a brief inquiry into the whereabouts of Cyrus. He insists and requests that either of the two to go to his hiding and inform Cyrus before they find him, and for the other to plan out the reinforcements as it is what the last phone call is about.

At eighteen and if they were rich and desperate enough to find Marx and become pupils who study hard trying to understand the basics that he brings up to create change, and later they discover the history with Lenin replaced by Stalin who brings bread and tells the world that man can be tough so be it comrades in arms. . . . You begin to defend and establish your family, one, two, or three, and more. Luck does not have anything to do with it, my God! How was Hitler created!? He comes into the scene unprepared without a hint of sensible Marxism; thereon, he becomes the opposite pole while all men are equal and are believed to be perfect specimens under the red flag. This logic of proletariat wins again without remorse. The times of Guevara and Castro and their bout into a senseless phase that humankind finds not only intoxicating but a lavishing forte into purities of real freedom while one begins to hold the book harder and justly confess to the ingenious ways of division and corruption of change, and then you become a teacher, and then a spy. Fate paints humankind in black as well as white. 'A sheer mode of combustion and turbulence as a way to show us means of living miraculous as well as mischievous. . .

He lays on the floor of ruinous garage and the hungry dog barks relentlessly as the good guard of secret chamber of the liberation just as the old man leaves this world with that trusted grin on his lips.

Public. . . public. . . if ever existed, is the scene of this drama even in the midst of peaceful zones, the central corners of exchange of ideas and peace! It is a pity trusting the death of many as the aforementioned because revolution solely becomes the redistribution of the privileges of aristocracy. Death counts but in nature. Bullets count but when they find out who paid for them, and so on. Others are dying too, some from cancer, strokes, and even hemorrhoids, and some from filth, Cholera, Syphilis, infections so unfamiliar and helpless that the formers becomes an agreeable fate. The old man grins because he knows that he would not remain unlisted in the statistics and what else he has predicted through his aged yet limited mind that unlike communists always crowding the parties to push the numbers, and blame the economy; albeit, no one knows what comes next. He has wasted his last breath to bury the kingdom of hypocrisy haphazardly yet with wishes that are understood but have to wait their turn. . .

Time never stops for the innocent as she much less gives man the opportunity to measure his moves and then she is or becomes the lover of those who are courageous enough to bury her just like before social emancipation, or for that matter as a heap into courtship, not the one after a brief release of urine, a dose of viagra, and sinking in champagne dreams but the one ending with one's own life yet with a lack that is identified with late in life. The time when this circus pays the old man dearly as a young man, null ideology; and promotes him within the framework of cannibalism and cynical release of self once he dives into a zone where time supposedly is dead. But we know how it is when time plays dead or, according to Kant could be undertaken by the sublime where she is subjugated by an act. Forgiveness, blessing, emotional, beauty, romantic, or if it mattered an oblivious misgiving that can change a man. He tries the carousel with children around him where innocence, in this foreign land where he collegiately educated his mind solely to help others become better, interfered with his views about the infants, juveniles, adolescents, and all that could create a lapse in progress where time plays dead. He last bids farewell to return to island nation with strong assertions of the future but knows that time could play the role of a hypocrite. *And this is certain!* The path, as shaky as it looks, is only a promise to stop the time in his country. Those shores filled with palm trees and the waves brushing them in a mood of deception and struggle like a prostitute who goes as deep and sweet as one's own significant other to earn her living. This cycle dismantles the will of its men and the island's outlook. He waits years in solitude like others who had nothing to do but raise their right hand and rest it on their heart and let go. *It is them!* They come for you and leave you with the turtles, by the sea, until you come to your senses and cooperate. This does not happen to the timid inhabitants but those with a will, alive and well-aimed, that counted for only a few at one time. The phone rings just as the van is put into motion carrying his corpse away to some unidentified spot by the sea and the young man standing on the street watching it go decides to go back in and answer it. The tone is familiar. It is them. This is easy to guess. They know where they are and soon would come. The call is probably to identify with the members of the liberation or to investigate the size of this group.

The children grow into mature forms and create families of their own in time to pass the torch of wisdom to their children with pride and a familiar heritage that is said to pay to the community, playgrounds, schools, and to other members less privileged. But this goes on and on in the island nation as these absent causes have left the majority bewildered; the people who are denied that side of the coin which shows them the comfort and logic behind traveling to this world through a cradle embracing a mother's warm bosom. The land is no more ready than an oblivion divided among the victims of the tsunami and those have been without the necessities of a poor life, and dread to admit they are present and alive. That phone call remains unanswered and the young man collects the papers and maps heading for a hideout.

The island's death toll, in the last few days as this incident rises beyond geographical and climatical norms, is now a tragedy within a revolution. The government, the few now would decide to request aid from neighboring nations. Within the dying men and women lays traces of new willpower, the hands of a revolution so unknown to these humble and innocently backward inhabitants. *The force be with you!* The time is right as normal means of transportation are limited to the government and there is nothing left for the residents. It is turtle meat feeding these victims and the coastal villages and it too will soon become scarce. The forecast unknown to most of the people is not promising as fog has covered the shores and most of the island still penetrating into the ghettos and roads the same-in a march towards the inferno. The shops, most of them, have not been opened since the takeover. At least, they are trying to demonstrate awareness and support while the army is far from logistically ready. The van reaches the community to find the prisoners armed and ready without a trace of Cyrus. They finally bury the old man with all due respects and prayers for a martyr. He accounts for the cars in the garage and assures them that transportation is available notwithstanding all that has happened claiming that there is still time. The young man believes it would take the authorities at least half a day to locate, reach, and confiscate the stock of cars and parts in the garage, and persuades them to load up the guns and ammo as soon as possible. The fishermen and prisoners quickly join and load the old van and shove in as much as they could, and hop in on top of the arms. Some of them hanging by the doors, and a few others climb to the top of the vehicle making it look like a bus ride to the city. It would be driven back shortly while the few that are left behind sail out to the Seahide to load another small cargo of arms for the shore. A radio unit has been given to the driver. Thereafter, they load two or more on the boats heading for the coast.

As the computer in the ministry of information sits there helplessly, and that is literally true. This single unit has been useless as no one had any idea how to operate it. They felt it to be some rightist plot to shelter these nonhuman mechanisms as it has occurred to be an uncelebrated act on the island, and the others smell the iron man to be hidden in the machine to doom solidarity among innocent well wishers that only look after the future generation as the only proxy in demand. But how left matters over right or the other way happens in the middle of a familiar feud, and it answers the curiosity of the intelligence, however minuscule, that still exists in the island nation. Why brother kills brother? Why innocent men and women are doomed? Perhaps, time has something to do with it as she allows for injustice as well as feeding one in a famine, or answers the basic questions in a maze of complexity and doubt extending to further eras! There are some fundaments that bring upon a nation atrocities which formulate freedom in a shape that would be an asset to island nation, and that is the devil's advocate disguised in many characters as one is called proletariat or any other name that claims we are all brothers, and not even a difference of opinion could leave us apart. When a child steps into this world he learns the basics of survival through the family and those close to him and surely not by the principles of a thesis or ideology. The island nation's dilemma of separation is beginning to face a question as every bit of progress upholds separation as an endorsement to its revolt. It does not, however, need another Napoleon or Kant with his complexity of logical notes to elate them-intelligence-to the point of outburst. Island nation knows she is small and pure yet stricken of its basic needs; she finds the end game as a step in history where logic takes too long and morale would not survive it. The backstabbers crowd the government without remorse and there is no power in sight that underscores a position of equality or social welfare. Indeed, the government relaxes feeding on metal and fresh forces over hungry, betrayed, and homeless that never know anything about security until they die! Now the steps are heavier, as in mine fields; there are a few although faithful to each other still away from the trustful elements that normally allow for the formation of unity. They are warned by misconduct, falsehood, and conspiracy as the liberation takes careful steps forward more cautiously than before by controlling the intensity that has overtaken their hungry souls. They decide to move on! The garage is crowded again with the passengers of the van and it looks like no one has been there. They start to look for car keys of the cars on the lot; it is not clear which one would work and which would not. It seems that they might have been examined by the government forces while nobody was there. The telephone, strangely, still works and the warehouse is intact. The leader, one of Cyrus's close friends who has escaped with him from the tsunami stricken prison, dictates that no one could use that telephone and, thereon, only the radios should be used. The young man who has driven them back to the garage begins to help them crank the cars. How much time do they have!? It is not clear, not much, because the garage seems suspiciously spotted. The last call has yet kept the mechanic thinking as he drove to the seaside to join Cyrus. While they search for more keys the driver wonders where his young comrade is. He is not in the garage and the worktable is naked as a sanctuary once accommodating insects. He informs others to remain alert and quickly unload the guns and load them into the cars when a bullhorn went off nearby, "You are surrounded! In the name of island nation drop your guns and. . . . . ."

10

God could not be existing now that the poignant side of religion denies him; the islanders' faith in fetish which is worshipped in vain and by will of the conscious yet illiterate in a time scarcely comprehended and not yet delivered into the right hands; those who see the truth but can not understand could only ask for discretion from what high power, that which determines all life and is believed to be righteous. The abyss of poverty plays a role in the act of Gods that are not in existence when the prodigal and native can not see beyond palms, hills, and no further than the sand on the beaches of island nation. The rite of passage into the future and beyond solely is in the hands of God. Yet is he not!? He is not to see the turtles silent, hidden, slow like the desperate life on this island. He comes once and for all. God is the shaking hands of the liberation; the papers which are now at the cellar in the minister's house, those plans that might bring a presence to aid the poor sods of this nation that know nothing but fetishism and oligarchy as another way to freedom and welfare.

The mechanic, vomiting and trembling in that cellar, has many things to say after that encounter with the enemy he has looked forward to face again. Him and the minister's son, *one of us,* look through the papers with faith and assurance- the scenario of final stage. *They will have God!* The vomiting young man wants to talk; he can see now after escaping for his life; after seeing the real enemy; the one among friends, that one which has nothing to lose except his prey! He wants to comfort his wounds and broken heart. He explains what kind of danger would be awaiting the others at the garage but is hopeful; blessing his companions with the wishes of his starving mind. That how we see God, he blames years of fetish and filth; that they will have their share of a peaceful life. He hopes that future is near like he feels exclaiming it with inner pulses of courage. His brave eyes have now seen the injured in a hospital with beds, surgeons, doctors, nurses; those that cure them, and heal these wounds that yet remain being an indigenous mark in the island's heritage. Children vaccinated and elders comforted with medicine. The majority vote has taken the house of representatives by its free and sheltered constituents that vote freely and not under duress. The army, across the island, setting down construction projects to build new and equipped houses. Those that accommodate families: men, women, and children. Community playgrounds and fields of green grass for the youth to build up and become agile and capable of competition-an evolution into healthy physical forms. The constitution to protect the islanders with basic rights of man. The island to reach ultimate meaningfulness and a modern society that advocates equality and security for all. He mutters, but only his wishes, tired and exhausted by the constant wrath and blasphemous beats of inferiority through the drums of poverty and injustice. He wants his fresh vision to materialize while tenaciously and partially dreams the unseen; he delves into the promised heaven wishing by his excited heart and vomits. He smiles and, again, pursues his raucous testimony of desire and hope which keeps him breathing easier. This hatred that puts love in its familiar form letting him feel the truth and what has led him into what he is now. They both, motionless and frightened, share this moment with a different kind of compromise; one that is rare and seldom seen on this soil. He spits his vomit and nobly confesses to his lapse of melancholy still holding his head up just like any fighter, any of them who would sacrifice his life for others. Indeed to sacrifice a hand so the other hand could embrace, and give an eye, so the other could see the heaven; that heaven which would rule this nation in harmony one day. Overcoming the iron bars that hold it back in misery. He exclaims that he now sees the freedom. *Isn't it fear that gives man courage and the will to act?* It is not fetish he insists as he conquers the hour weary of his fellow liberators; that army which never is; that army which will take up the assignment to give this vision and this earth within the shores of the island nation the promised life. The days that will see the people singing one song and seeing one picture, that of green grass, blue sea, and a society of honor. The two cannot hold these drops of tear.

The army now holds the plaza according to the minister's son when he answers the phone and Operation Tribune has already started commencing with a chosen group of educated ranks within the press and government. He tells his nauseated companion that they still hold the ministry of information, and there has been no shooting while the presentations are a portrait of deception and the usual promises uttered by the *intelligencia of a private nation!* They have started the campaign since a couple of hours after dawn while he reports from his brief conversation on the phone.

After a night without sleep the two men, the minister's son and the young man from the garage, begin now to search for more help. They believe they must persist as this Operation Tribune could become an effective campaign to stop the liberation. The panel, per say, is promising a new constitution and creation of jobs in an effort to build the island into an ideal country with new housing for everyone, hospitals, and more schools; soon illiteracy is taken out of the way and the inhabitants rendered useful in the new society.

Win or lose, the two men, more content than rebellious notwithstanding the taunting seclusion, become convinced that something has tilted the government; the liberation perhaps has established a clear line of fire provoking the officials to resist. *Good news?* For that they should be rewarded as the liberation seeks the people's cooperation and the two find themselves at the center while such information solely raises the chaos they are against. The hours are intensified with horror; that feeling, so familiar, that has taken the island by the throat through an ostensible and, per say, a ritual process that always settles in fear and desperation. That, for comrades, are these moments of liberation. The conversation soon becomes a monotony of handicap, illiteracy, and an awareness that mainly explains the shortcomings to the two that sat helpless through every conversation in sweaty short sleeves and white linen pants, the common apparel around the island which is a proxy of class and profession. The son of the minister is politely searching solutions after less than a minute into the conversation as generally the other party on the line complains and expresses hesitations because of safety for his family. The other now over with his nausea only applies partisanship and coherence to provoke a sense of life and death by drawing a picture of what future could be to both of them. This item of luxury shows how capable and suited the callers are compared with those who yet have no knowledge of wired transmission of dialogue, telephone! So the two are hoping for the poor, needy, and destitute to join and pray that it will soon happen when the cell phone of the minister's son interrupts them beginning to ring. It must be important that this instrument is only in the hands of a few. He waits for the third and fourth ring and takes a look at his hallucinating and weary companion who suddenly becomes silent and entirely forgets who he is talking to on the land line. And finally, as the ringer persists, he picks up his mobile and slowly utters a few words of greeting. This call unlike others throughout the day must be from the liberation whom have been given the number and who only hold a cellular phone. They reservedly hold back staring at each other as yet the caller has not said a word, at least not immediately. The moment, not so solidly in anticipation suddenly retains a sepulchral tempo due to the impression of the son. They are distracted from the radio as he suddenly directs, with his eyes, the attention of the other to the receiver pointing his bulging eyeballs at the cellular. The son, independent since his graduation from college that he has completed overseas finds it hard to characterize this dire lapse of events. Most likely he, along with the other feel the importance; or yet, the trigger that their useful presence could ignite due to their position, but the voice on the other side of the line spells danger as he greeted him again. . . .

"It is such an honor to hear your voice! My father is away at this time, or perhaps a bit preoccupied." He answers.

Oh. . . me? Certainly, yes!?" He answers.

After a minute he answers again.

"Gladly, it would be an honor and my privilege to serve the country. Anything I could help!"

After a minute he answers again.

"Sure chief! Please send me the necessary papers. . . thank you. . . I will be there!"

He hangs up and turns to the young man from the garage.

"It's Operation Tribune! What he is up to! He just asked me to participate!!"

The radio voice phases into an urgent news announcement!

"Just an hour ago, there was a deadly fire at a remote garage around the outskirts of the city. . . . allegedly the liberation has assumed responsibility for the fire! No reported fatalities as of yet as we resume this program on the hour, every hour!"

The two now breathing the air warily in devastation remain wordless; however, there is always a solution to where they might start, or how the son of the minister should go about giving a speech at the Tribune in the civic plaza. He had to begin somewhere, but the momentum, to him, could be shifted as he shares his drama with his young and now unbalanced companion who is worried about those who are supposed to mobilize the liberation with those cars at the garage. He begins to doubt his hearing and vision bursting into an heartfelt temerity to return to the garage. Although it is obvious there is going to be aerial surveillance as it

149

might have already started. They do not want anything to leak.

———————————————

He decides to take the alley ways through his ride in the city driving in rusted, obsolete, pickup that is more common than any other mode of transportation, it being a car, bike, or a motorcycle, the latter being the most popular. He is worried that the owner might locate him. His desperate flight from the garage would spare him any time to take something better. His idea of refuge has changed during the last forty-eight hours and now he is determined to find Cyrus and others so he could share all the new information and events of his short escape to the house of the minister and his son. What politics dictate to him at the time shapes as an endgame and a portrait of a final hour. The government is intentionally sealing all options and he is worried that the next attempt would be at Cyrus's life and his men. He drives average speed to avoid discernibility and frequently checks the cracked rear view mirror. The afternoon heat is remote and humid, yet the horror of another attack is building up in his gut that he is trying to find others risking his own life. He is certain once he sets contact they would be able plan out a new roadmap, while a life of turbulence and fright continues to sting his sweating flesh. Truth leaves him as a candle burning on both sides; he hopes that the son of the minister would not eventually cooperate with the government, and, more, that Cyrus and others survive the leaks taking further action before they get their hands on them. The good news is that they are armed, at this point he knows that his path will end in spilling blood, just a new phase in the act of rebellion; he feels this as the truck is heating up and almost out of the city limits. . . . His intense belief in what he is doing brings a wonder within his shattered memory when he suspects that there might be an encounter between the government and his friends still going on, or ever has occurred so he, almost about a mile or so from that fishing community and a few miles from the prison, drives carefully off the bumpy road and pulls into the surrounding brush hiding the rusty monster behind the off-road, aged, fruitless palms, and resumes on foot towards that beach community swallowing his breath that now starts to feel cool through the sea breeze. He naturally hurries but unconscious of the hour as he has not reached a human in almost two miles, and a couple more to go where a ricochet wakes him from imbalance and fear. He jumps for cover, a safe one at that, where he is protected by the brush and trees as the latter can not do the job of a barrier and the former can not stop bullet from hitting him. He lays flat on his chest with his head up scanning the range. The shooting continues but not in his direction when he realizes the clash of the two sides has been taking place for hours. *But who is who!!?* Henceforth he finds an empty barrel a distance away and rushes for it as the shooting seems sporadic and has almost discontinued. The deeply stained barrel moves before he gets close enough. He stops and falls on his knees carefully scrutinizing further movements of the rusted barrel. He quits crouching and dives forward with his agile figure soundlessly landing a couple of steps from the barrel as it stops to move.

"Come out with your hands up, or I'll shoot!! Before you do that throw out your weapon, hurry or I'll. . . ."

The barrel moves slightly, and there is a man, a fisherman dressed in white linen and a straw hat with his hands upward stepping over the barrel and looking around inquisitively.

The young mechanic watches him carefully and patiently maintains his hiding until there are a couple of shots; not in their direction but it scares the fisherman who jumps for his life flat on the ground.

"Here, pssst. . . ., here. . ."

The youth utters quietly as the man finally sees him and crawls towards him.

"Who are you?" A voice inquires.

"I come in peace. . . ." Answers the other.

"GOD: ABSENT OR INVISIBLE? The officials skipped the simple questions yesterday and got to the point while the army allegedly could not hold its position. A divided army and a bully official completed a day in the works of a banishing government. . . ."

The morning brings with it not only the newspaper but shooting erupts around ten o'clock. The two men join the liberation in the village as the midnight hours have drawn a quiet siege against the stormy shore that has recently seen so many deaths due to the bloody tsunami that topples the jail. Indeed, the silence takes the fighters by surprise as they plan to consume more ammunition and earn the first victory of the campaign, but no. . . the bullets are not directed toward them. They are aimed closer, almost sounding like point blanks as they remain hidden in the holes waiting for the army to yet make a move. No one has been shot and there has been no casualties from the night before while the young man from the garage explains what is happening and he points out the Operation Tribune, and more, the first lesson is taught which mainly cites the need for human force as, by now, they realize that they are in possession of sufficient amount of arms on the vessel at sea, Seahide. Their resistance against the army by the shore is a strong indication that there is a good chance of victory while the shooting continues until noon at the army trenches when finally a white flag marks the earliest hour of the blazing afternoon. *Help us understand what is going on!* While the liberation has been scrutinizing the barrage, they discover the reason behind the surrender, and send a volunteer to the other side responding to the raising of the white flag; minutes pass as the man walks back to the liberation front followed by a number of soldiers and officers. Something, not so vividly, becomes visible through this interaction while the fishermen and the prisoners do not feel quite alone as they once did! The day has almost stepped into its last quarter, the evening of the first victory that could have been otherwise; perhaps a blood bath at the dawn of the movement-yet it is not. The men shake hands and the women, mostly wives and daughters of the fishermen, bring rum and foodstuff for men to celebrate the arrival of the evening after. Alas, work is more important as, perhaps, is fate; they spend the night hours now to draw conclusions as the rum in this island always paints an earnest picture in the minds of its inhabitants. They await the arrival of the newspaper which usually comes in around the earliest hours of the morning, about two hours after dawn if everything goes accordingly. They want to learn about Operation Tribune; the minister's son would be among the lineup which appears at the platform and this means that the fate of liberation is duly in the hands of its participants now and not the

government. Now, as many other occasions, is what holds
the divine providence, the time becomes a heart-sensitive
flow of dreams and aspirations of those who have tolerated
pain and ruthlessness; the time is now, and they well know
that the decisions should be subtle and nonrandom. Target
is inly steps away from its end. *But are they so near?* Soldiers
in green and prisoners in blue, fishermen in white have
started the elaborate stage of decentralization, and thus, they
have to recruit to spread the huge share of their God-given
ammunition, that is the only way. Four radios, more than
fifty thousand rounds of ammo, four hundred weapons,
and most important of all they were left twenty cargo trucks
from the face-off with the army.

The three hundred and sixty strong men now have raised,
per say, the faith and, indeed, have now become a reason to
persist as the camp is gaining some mode of peace while they
occupy the grounds preparing and awaiting the higher ranks
and the prisoners to draw a plan to keep the momentum
focused at the target. The camp soon gains sound and color;
the sun brings a momentary heat into the hearts and souls
of those men. The humidity is on its lower levels, the air is
almost dry and the fishermen promise food in the coming
hours. The army men gradually become oriented with the
liberation, each man squatting next to the other passing the
word around, a sort of communication sounding like a bunch
of gossipers whispering in the ears of others taking turns.
In the short span of these promised hours the fishermen
produce grub, bread and stew fresh from the cottages and
to their surprise there was plenty enough of turtle, palm
root recipe, and fresh bread for everyone. Surely, it seems
that this union remains impregnated with oncoming similar
occasions as the friendship turns out faithfully and deep

in the heart and soul of all present. The leaders now talk about bringing things to order and the camp is busy eating readily prepared rations with a horrendous appetite. The bread warm as it is explained that the women of the small community had hours before begun baking it regardless of the outcome of that shootout. The soldiers are calm, and, some, mention casualties as they are the first of this newly initiated dawn of rebellion. There will be injuries, and there are a few, one or two. No one now hopes for more. The planners discuss the peaceful methods and curiously seek solutions. The young mechanic finds out that Cyrus is dead; this being relayed to him through a prisoner who used to be one of his closest aids. And he mentions that his father has left him a house-inheritance. The sorrow is no more disappointing as the young man sighs while eyeing the camp with a thoughtful impression. "They are a power on the island! There is hope!" He exclaims.

"The first thing is our ability to reach them. . . I am afraid without a plan there is no hope for us in this. . . ."

"You mentioned the bus depot and stations where there are gatherings!?"

"Yes, but it could be dangerous. . . we could be outdone as we speak!! It is important that we take the government intelligence serious! We should spread and watch their moves if there was any. . . The main thing is to avoid being set up!!!"

"With the army men we do have a better chance. . . ."

Interrupts the other!

"That will come later, they are not ready. . . we should keep them here. . .ready to strike, but our operation is to be handled by our men only!!! One more thing.. the ministry posse should be directed back to the city plaza, and accompanied by enough arms, ammunition, and more men! They need our help and the sooner we help them the better our position will be at the heat of the capital! Oh, by the way. . . we should send them a radio! All radios are to be distributed among this force!!!! Communication is an imperative to our future in this struggle. . . !!!"

"We have quite a few that army brought in.. .but. . . .how are we going to get them there!? I mean the ministry of information!?"

"Simple! Those army trucks in our possession could be used as cover, and at that,. . .we can wear army uniforms and pick out a few soldiers to help us out through the checkpoints!!"

"Harlot. . . you are a genius but I think you better stay with us! We need you here. . ." Said the other.

"I better go with them and set up a plan while they are still surviving. . . I say we put together two trucks each with about twenty men and that will hold us at least for a day or maybe two at the worst! They tell me the army has not started shooting, it's important that we take advantage of this before they commence fire!"

Harlot, about 27, has little affection for himself; he now knows that his life, for the third time in two days is on the line while he changes into an officer's uniform that the real officer loyally hands to him. They are the men who plead for freedom of the island nation in the shadow of death. Army surely would step forward soon! The ministry has been under siege at least for four days. Anything is possible, even reinforcement, which would look more like a massacre of the liberation at the plaza. Yet, before long, Harlot and about three dozen others load the trucks and mount up heading for the civic plaza where they would reroute through the opposite entrance of the plaza that is absolutely in harm's way; it is on the same side of the plaza as the ministry of information. They knew that they have to stay barricaded yet Harlot, the young man from the garage, sets early radio contact with the army by playing a messenger and informs the crouching commanders of the force at the plaza that there will be two trucks approaching the target by noon, and it will be a quiet operation to dismantle the liberation's shield of arms through a sabotage of the barricades at close range they could reach under circumstances. Harlot advises the commanders not to fire yet and await an order that would be given once they penetrate the ministry in the name of the chief.

The army's long stand at the plaza now is overlooked by people, and the center of the plaza is occupied by a podium guarded with a group of soldiers. The commander relays his approval to Harlot, but insists that they should rush the plan since people are starting protests, and that the ministry has already been occupied for too long!

"It's a bad influence. . . you understand sir,. . . over!!!"

Harlot coughs and clears his voice. He responds.

"Leave everything to me commander! Over and out!!!"

11

A group of guards protecting the platform stayed motionless and plenty alert as the mood around the plaza resembled one race horse's face breathing large gulps of air and releasing with a sound like a human cleaning his nose into a napkin. The horse ready to race further would then be speeding up with due aggression and animal arrogance. The sound echoed through the plaza and everyone within one or two mile radius could hear what was said very clearly. Salome still, bipolar and melancholic, realized where she was; she spoke her words without help but pretension was limitless yet some understood why!

"Our country, now more than ever, is one nation and living citizens strive together and enjoy the welfare that is provided by our respectful government. . ."

In the ministry of information they were listening and Casino, with a gun guarding the window, murmured words each time Salome paused to go on to the next sentence. He was melancholic, but with an undaunted attention toward where he was hating to think that, at any time, the guards might begin shooting. Salome went on. . . . .

"I have met the heads of our nation! They are kind, aware, and now ready to help like always. . . ."

Casino raised his voice but still as if mumbling with haste yet weary.

"They sent troops to kill us, of course, ready to help,. . . . tell me about it!!"

She continues. "We discussed the status quo. . . the storm. . . .and the economy! People. . . ."

Casino inside the ministry murmurs, "Oh yeah!? Discussing what, what economy. . . .?! Forty percent of the wealth goes to the top half a percent!!!. . . .Woman. . . . what have they done to you. . . . . .!!?" As though he was being heard, Casino was fearless pressing his fingers against his weapon. He yells:

"We must do something!! She is not herself!! She is brainwashed. . . . They have planned this!!!"

That room in the ministry was quiet and others were listening to the loudspeakers that kept a constant echo through the plaza and the vicinity.

"People of island nation remain united today! They are safe, healthy, and secure from political hazards. . . ." Salome went on.

"There are over two hundred thousand starving! Sick, and threatened by those bastards. . . . .Come on Salome are you doped. . . .??" Casino responded quietly, and raging by looking at others crouching about the big room in the ministry! The big crowd in the plaza was astonishingly silent. It laid a blanket of worry over the face of the army that stood guard in the plaza.

Yet, that post-marxist, maoist, or what colored the plaza in dots of red and white, blue or green; the pretension that freedom still existed among the palm trees and the tents full of hungry and injured, and the nation waiting like a starving and naive boy where a neo-capitalist or a face-off between lies and tyranny ruled those hours of hope. Salome spoke her dedicated words of advice but not hoping for surrender as she still remembered that behind those large windows of the ministry of information God had helped settle a bloody platoon or two which were the last scene in the eyes of the island nation that described anything closest to a hope-a sparkle of liberation!

"We are grateful now that our country is helping the homeless and shelters them. . . and feeds the hungry in this moment of despair and more than ever respects our nationalist values. . . ." She is interrupted as everyone began to whistle cynically and comically at an amputated man on a wheelchair approaching the podium with the help of two guards, "Where did you get that Elohim. . . is that your car!!?" Someone yelled. Another whistled, "What you got to say boy!!? Now you can march with the guards old man. . . . ain't ya!!?" "Check him out. . . a new set of wheels and all that!!!!" Some whistled!

Elohim, the old man with a full head of white snowy hair, and a tan skin who was on his two amputated feet and walked with the help of his hands, approached the podium and, as a part of the Tribune coughed and cleared his voice while the guards lowered the microphones! Casino, in cold sweat, began to yell, "They couldn't leave him alone, not even him. . . . what's next you pigs. . . . !!?" The room in the ministry was quiet except the episodes of Casino's responses that kept them preoccupied.

"There will not be any shooting,. . . . and that is it! It is an order!!! If I have to put it that way!!!!" Harlot yelled.

The signs and the surface of this Tribune revealed a lot about what really had happened as the liberation looked upon the podium and now had to tolerate such hypocrisy with patience, or even trying to find a way about this move. Elohim had begun to speak in the microphones. His broken language and scratchy voice kept the crowd in attention as he was a well-known islander around the parts of the city where reality ruled with its impostures imposing on the lives of others for whom there were no miracles.

"Citizens and friends. . . . ! You know that I come from the urban districts where I assure you change is already in place!!! It even has effected my life as most of you know, I. . . ." A member of the crowd makes a nasty noise, that only comes from the backside of a man, with his mouth. . .

"Buddy they sure paid you off!!!"

"Elohim! Who are they? Why don't you tell the truth!?"

"Hey old man how much!!?"

The crowd went on as the old man's face dryly held an unnatural smile that hinted the reality of this callous effort. Elohim continued.

"Young and old must join hands, share their pains as well as the good news which is the new campaign of our government against poverty and towards the creation of welfare for all, and I would say that I am a good example of. . . . ." He is interrupted by a bystander.

"Hey buddy. . . .what's it to you? Why don't you tell us how much. . . ." He began whistling and some howled like wolves; like wolves that lurk and then attack to kill their prey; like the bites of pride that once stood erect among the people of the island nation. "The man is a good example of the direction our government is heading towards. . . . it's simple. . .they are doing whatever they can. . .!!!" Casino whispered holding his gun with both hands and still crouching by a window steps away from the other where Harlot and two others were squatting and observing the Operation Tribune take place. The crowd, now more aware, had begun booing Elohim on that wheelchair and it all started to spread seeds of hope in the hearts of the members of the liberation. While those men in the ministry of information wanted to see resentment, they were also in search of signs that people might join them; their assignment would be settled once there appeared notions that the crowd would be turning to the other side for help and it was happening when Elohim was brought down and the platform became available for the next member of the so-called volunteers to deliver his message.

The vibration of the speakers and the anti forces had insofar proven deceitful; the air was filled with a desperate manner of telling the other side to get lost. People stood up to the false endorsements of the chosen members of the Tribune and the day went on in pursuit of standards of betrayal and other rotten evidence that showed the government was willing to go deep! "They are willing to do anything,. . . bastards!"

Harlot said. He remembered, bewildered and wary, the young man remembered his companion in the garage; indeed, he was invited to join the Tribune by the chief himself. Although there was something he wanted to know! What would the chief do to him afterwards? He wanted to know. The building being under scrutiny be the guards; it was impossible for him to use the phone. So Harlot got on the radio and set contact with the center, and they told him that minster's son had already contacted them while Harlot had explained to the others about their escape from that garage. He wanted to help and was carefully awaiting the liberation to lead the way. Harlot had sensed hope; this young man had come from an educated family in the capital and had finished college overseas while his education, after returning to the island nation, helped him immensely to see how different he was from others and how to help them. He was close to the minister's son as both were college graduates and aware of the cruelty that was imposed on the people of the motherland. "He will be at the plaza Tribune the day after tomorrow!" Explained the man on the other end of the radio contact.

Harlot left his post and rushed to the center of the room while he yelled, "We need a

C.O.U.! He would would be on the podium helping us if we are smart enough to take advantage. . . .It is our chance! And more, we need to start recruiting!! Crank the damn radio and start talking! Everyone should talk. . . think of something and say it!! We have to hold on to our post. . . and.. that. . . is the one and only national radio of the island nation! They know it too! It's all a plan to dismantle us and keep us where we are. . . Besides, you guys already ran a message promising further broadcast. . . then for God's sake go for it!!! But we still need a C.O.U.(Code of Unity) and I know just the person. Bring the radio here and keep low so they can't see us!! I wouldn't be surprised if they began shooting. . . . ."

The podium, now quiet, Operation Tribune was taking a new direction. An apparent setup that was a stage for the puppet show was planned before a few more journalists would have taken over the microphone. It took about an hour or so to set up a small curtain and the artists took their places behind the satin curtain that carried a pattern of yellow and torcuoise blue flowers and looked more petite and comic than anything dramatic as the crowd thought it to be a funny act. It started with a man and a woman on the opposite sides of the small stage. The puppets approached each other and the woman asked,

"My dear husband how was the sea today!?"

"I don't know. . . perhaps as usual. . . a dozen or so fish! How is my dear son!!?"

The animated tones of the man and the woman were broadcast through the loudspeakers which echoed over the flabbergasted crowd at the plaza. The liberation listened. People watched and some giggled.

"He is as usual studying, but he wants to get out of the house and go to the playground and play like other children!"

"He knows how much his father loves him and has the best wishes for his future. . . ."

"Yes! But he is tired and exhausted. . . . I've done everything I could, and so has he!"

"But he knows. . . ." Interrupted.

"Yes, yes. . . . I have explained everything but he insists that he shall use his cane. . .and everything will be fine!!"

"What about the future!!? He always says he wants to be a scientist. . . I am more than willing to help him with school if I could!! He knows we both love him!"

"He knows that, and he has made us proud by achieving best results in school!" Agreed the mother.

"So what could be wrong?"

"He is depressed! He wants to play like the other boys. . . ." Father interrupted.

"But what could we do!?"

"I don't know dear, but there must be something we could do! The principal of school came by today and congratulated us for our son's exceptional achievements. . . He finds him and his future very promising!"

"He knows how proud I am of him and would do anything to make him happy. . . ."

"And now it is time to prepare dinner!"

"I have left a nice and meaty fish in the kitchen. . . !"

The mother steps out of the room(stage). And the father begins to speak to himself. . . .

"God. . . what could I do for him? He is handicapped, but has one of the brightest minds I have ever known. Me and his mother have done everything we could for him! He should be grateful yet everyday he complains that he is inferior to other kids and he wants to do what they do. . . . play ball, run, swim, or be like other kids! Help me help him!! Guide me to the right direction! I am getting old and soon he will be a man and then he will have to make a living. . . . God help us help him!! I don't want his mother to be sad. . . She is proud of him too, but his loss is not our fault; it is a lapse of nature!! What could we do!!?"

The voice behind the stage begins to speak.

"You are a fisherman. You are good at your trade and you work hard and you sell fish at the market for a good price! Everyone respects you and your family. . . Your on feels let down and there is a way!! There is a healer of all pains and ills. . . .but you need to obey by his rules! You have to be loyal to the land and his kingdom. . . ."

The wife steps into the stage.

"The dinner is ready my dear. . ."

"I am suddenly not hungry! Pardon me! But I am going out for some fresh air! And don't tell our son anything. . . .I will be back soon!!!"

Another voice behind the curtain announces.

"A day passes!"

The husband suddenly steps into the stage.

"Good day honey! How is our son!?"

"Where have you been? I was worried sick all night. . . . and what are you wearing!!? Is that a uniform!!?"

"My dear wife. . . I officially joined the army this morning!!"

"But you never believed in the king's army. . . . what has changed your mind all of a sudden!?"

"I will go to war like a man! I will be loyal to our king. . . . let us drink the rum and celebrate!! I have to leave soon!!!"

"What happens to us. . . . me, your son, the house!!?"

"The king will take care of you too! I have to go now!! I will win the war and make our country proud!!!"

"Goodbye my dear, so long!!!"

The second voice announces the time again.

"One month passes. . . ."

The wife, alone on the stage, hears a doorbell and responds.

"Come in!!!"

There is a man in the suit; he steps onto the stage. The wife exclaims.

"Hi, Mr. Principal! What can I do for you? You seem shaken and excited!! Is everything OK!!?"

"It is about your son. . . he suddenly started walking this morning!!! He is healed! It is a miracle!!! I don't know any better way to explain it. . . . He is completely cured and does not need the help of canes no more!!!"

"Oh principal. . . is it true!!? How could that be? God help us!! I wish his father was here!!! Where is he now!!?"

"He is playing with his classmates in the schoolyard!!" The principal explains. Suddenly there is a knock on the door. . . .

"Who is it?" The wife asks.

"I am from the army and I need to talk to the head of the house!"

"Come in. . . ., please!!" The wife responds. A soldier walks onto the stage.

"What can I do for you?"

"Ma'am your husband has been given a medal of honor for his courage and loyalty,. . . I am sorry to say that as his inheritor you are to receive this medal! We are very proud of him; he was a good soldier!"

Presently, after the closure of the curtain, there was silence and whispers that echoed like a loud humming sound, and words of scattered nature that held no other meaning than pure insult, criticism, and negative and neutral opinions expressing the crowd's fear of renewed yet uncelebrated neo-patriotism. The puppet show even triggered the liberation to activate the radio as they shortly began a talk show as an opening for future contact with the people; the people whom liberation thought would be available and, more precisely, useful in the interests of a movement which yet were unclear. More, liberation now avoided further provocative actions as they were concerned that people of the island nation would support the government after that rhetorical show had pushed them to a favorable partisanship. This masquerade had begun vowing for the scene in which the journalists and, not the army, persuasively minted their partial exclamations in a silence more frightening than the soothing image yet expected by the heads of the government. A long line of fruit crates-wooden boxes that are nailed together in the haste of picking season to pack and send-were stacked seemingly to stand noticably taller than the crowd whose presence was turning into a decisive act in the fate of this incident. Harlot got up and ran towards the broadcast cabin located near the back entrance of the hall; the lobby of the ministry where the liberation had lurked under cover. He turned on the transmitter and began adjusting the volumes and setting the microphone reasonably close to his mouth. "Look Harlot they are up to something. . . look those women are pregnant!!!" Casino yelled hiding by the window.

One to fourteen, the numbers that had decorated the frontal bulges of these women; fourteen of them that each carried an unborn child soon to be delivered. Fourteen, the number of the constitutional covenants, meant much more to the islanders. It is a reminder of the day when island nation became independent and had freed herself from the colonial rule. The Covenants of the Dawn were delivered through the speech of a head of the independence cabinet. "The Dawn" is another word for independence. The island had been enduring colonialism for over forty years after its tribal existence gave up against the bribery and the commercial interests of the colonists at the time. Fourteen pregnant women stood on top of the crates in a line facing one direction; that of the ministry and began singing the national anthem! What brought people to an applause was not the act of propaganda but the effort those women made at getting up the platform and singing what might be called an improvised and out-of-key version of the anthem! The pestering and joking yet continued into the hours of the dark and eyes turning to liberation fighters at the ministry who now had started their first broadcast in three days after the takeover. This, in turn, would bring some kind of hope to those awaiting a sign on the part of liberation that seemed flabbergasted due to callous and comical intentions of the government at this so-called art of propaganda and fascism.

The port was shut down. Any passage except for military and duty carriers was out of question. A half or more of the islanders were without shelter yet most of them received the news through their transistor radios. Food was scarce. The balance was hanging by a very thin thread, and it seemed that what was an end to the world, according to the elders, was nearing during that somber evening that marked the beginning of the winter.

The hardbacks of the island would soon begin marking their mates as another year steps into its aimless fertility to be taken away by the mad sea. The humidity and current of the torrential climate, now tragic due to an early attack of an hurricane, would sustain a new air in the lungs of the islanders for whom the wind would bring nothing but the news of ocean and its familiar turbulence.

"Here. . . . let us celebrate the Dawn another time! A moment that dignifies and too washes our commitments to our country with holy drops of sacrifice and bravery. . . . This moment shows us all the fluid future of the island nation,. . . Ladies and gentlemen! These women carry the future of our homeland like many other fertile women of the island, and since the Dawn this government has taken upon its burden the responsibility of raising the newborns into our community and teaching them the right from wrong!! People of my island. . . the Covenants of Dawn yet make it hard to pity this heaven. . . this escapade which shelters each honest man and feeds each hungry soul with justice and security! Your welfare. . . .islanders. . . .is in the safe and powerful hands of this government and has been for many years. . . .Rise to unity and a powerful island nation once and for all to show the foreign elements and those who seek refuge from justice that we are one and we will resist traitors! People! It is these moments that underline the golden pages in the history of our nation with the blood of our soldiers and those who fought for independence!! Long live islanders who have led us and will direct us to an everlasting independence and away from colonialism and leftist commonwealths!!!"

———————————

Smelling the sinful sweat that familiarly painted the house alas like nights in that shack with only two rooms and keeping six while the guest did his business and the head of the house counting them carnal bills making him feel like a king just as the few other times during the week which meant run and pills. These people lived and let go chewing rotten bananas and instead throwing the peels into a warped skillet that could accommodate the minimal meal feeding

six ended up in having over them newcomers, strangers-
the newly freed. He sipped his rum and shot his saliva all
around the entry but his impression let out the detail; that
ongoing rendezvous and a little more money to keep them
still under those palms passing the days and being grateful!!
The sound of urine hitting the floor in the toilette behind
a hanging rag like a serenade of conclusion to the festive
and prospering exchange of flesh and coins killing the joy
in him as he prepared himself for the whipping. He had to
do something to convince the children and himself that
they recognized and saw, and they could do better if they
wanted instead of surrender to easy dough and walking
out like they are somebody he wasn't. He blamed her every
night in the sweaty room with four children, always hungry,
half naked, fed in the neighbor's or off the garbage and
littering of the passing traffic. Sometimes he had to step
inside in the middle of the business to rid of the flies and
the strongly penetrating smells of the gutter. . . .Yet he
laughed and planned to start going for twice a day next week
after like usual, but she was weak and he had to feed her
too so she could take care of the four little ones that were
hardly around. He also got a couple of hand-rolled ones. So
he lit up one with the client's lighter relaxing with a loyal
impression; that one impression that undertook others like
him. . . ! The clouds might have turned to pour and wash off
the sidewalks and ease the carbon intake and, perhaps, rain
could have helped the produce because there was a woman
next door who had planted vegetables. They sporadically
got some for helping her with the gardening or carrying her
stuff to the house. Too, he got the news from her because
she had a small radio and shared the news with most of the
nearby neighbors although he kept everything to himself.
The others, women and children, had no right to the news.

Why should they know? They could not understand why there was medicine. For the truck brought a load of them small white boxes with writings on them. He knew because he had to take medicine one time for VD and he knew it made you heal, but he wouldn't bother to tell his wife or children. They never get sick!!! Only the head of the house did since he had to do all the work. The medicine could have cured the neighborhood of VD so they wouldn't be irritated when they urinated or wouldn't release liquid through the day staining their rags. Nonetheless, he was learning when the truck came and left; it was not the chief's because these guys were young and they wrote something again and again with black markers on those small white boxes. They looked different. They looked at them differently and hardly trying to scare them. They spoke unlike chief's men and wore no uniforms so they must have been from the doctor's office.

In the yard, she kneeled by the bushes of tomato and mint as he stepped in without a noise; he wasn't called for but he carried his ration of small white boxes ceremoniously and tauntingly flabbergasted with his conspicuous illiteracy that always made him run to her without a knock; she knew his need well enough but not to get boiled up about. She knew how to read and write. He set them down carefully in a polite distance to avoid any distraction and stepped away, "Medicine. . . . !!!" The sun was blazing in the mist. In its core the day seemed short but heading towards a peaceful and dry night as it strangely enforced the songs that birds sang in those days and began equivocally discussing the climate and the traffic tweeting and balancing on the stems of the taller branches in her yard. But she forgot them completely and picked up one of them and said a few words of prayer. She looked up to him standing up.

She pointed toward his house and her other hand showing the medicine, "For your wife!. . . . For the children!!" She stood and nodded with dismal approval while her pupils still remained surprised; she scrutinized him for possibility of theft. He denied shaking his head and pointed a full length of his hand towards the street, "Call me a lier but they are giving away medicine!!!" She headed for the entrance to the backyard while tolerating his pursuit as she was carrying a box of that medicine!

"A=10??. . . A=10? What does it mean. . . . Who wrote that on the box!?? We gotta find out!! It might be the dosage. . . but wait a minute!!! There is one printed under the directions. . . ."

They were all gone. There was no trace of the truck or anyone else. So the neighbor and him asked others and found other medicine boxes with 'A=10' written on them. Those were Penicillin to be exact. She returned to the house with him and took a box. She let him take the rest to his wife and children. The whole neighborhood remained quiet that night. The old neighbor spent the night by her radio. She knew there would be some notion of the truck or trucks. There might be a broadcast some time soon!

There was nothing that night and I was carefully listening with the radio on all night on the Seahide. I had done my best throughout the blessed moves of the liberation. No one would have turned down needed medicine especially on the island. Most of them knew they required medicine to last and face their pains. They told me to lay out a code. What Casino explained was the Code of Unity through the wireless. I, too, had it ready among all the designs I had created for the port authorities until we finally got the code they were presently using for government communication. This one was the so-called civilian version that could have been used for script messages and I knew that was what they were looking for. However, no one could have done better in such short notice; while A rotates into 11, 12, 13, 14, and so the rest of the alphabet follow accordingly, i.e. if A was 12, B would be 13, and C would be 14, etc. These words in a sentence would have made it ideal for short messages which was what they wanted at the ministry of information. But, here on the Seahide, we now had a new cargo although not yet reported; close to a quarter of a ton, and I quote, of heroin ready to hit the market while it was being shipped to island nation. It was to be delivered to no one but the chief through the commanding ambassador of his cabinet. The crew had stopped them ten or so miles away from the port hoping to find food and friends as they had been doing everything to assemble a force-men ready to fight against chief and the sea. They had found the ambassador and his beautiful wife in the cargo boat with the stuff. We were to hold it until they passed the message that the liberation wanted a dialogue. And, of course, the sooner they agreed the earlier I could return to my family.

When the ambassador and wife were sent to the shore the message was clear which meant that the liberation would not have tolerated anything except a positive response; otherwise the truth was to be revealed. Not only that, the quarter of a ton would have been put to good use and the route traced to the point of origin and publicized as well!

"THE WEEKEND EDITION!!!

The holdup at the plaza continues to occupy the nation's attention while the alleged liberation has not made any statements as an explanation for this act of solidarity. The government led by the chief of forces has proceeded to curtail the activities of the liberation by tracing the latter's leadership according to the sources remaining to be anonymous. The takeover, now into its first week, has been peaceful while no exchange of fire has been reported. The chief is expected to outline his agenda next week in order to put an end to this crisis and the details would probably explain how the liberation and the government would reach a compromise. The Tribune, a peaceful operation initiated by the government of the chief, begins its fourth day of procession with many members of the government and various other professions continuing their participation. This class action is believed to be an ideal way to demonstrate the intentions of the nation's democratic regime and allegedly put an end to the standoff. Also, the occupation of the ministry of information has delayed all international and domestic affairs of the government directly dependent on this office. . . .

12

"Embargo. . . . !!"

"Embargo. . . . !???"

Come times, but not for an eternal high like them sailors always getting on with stories about the ghosts of ocean or some other ghost that, if friendly, should have buzzed them the hell as rambunctiously as any human being except that they dealt with the water, mostly salty, and you don't even have to be thirsty to know that; just as good and clear because the chief always hosted it especially. If not thirsty go on full blast ahead, the last of the cargo that was to be shipped through the presently disabled port. Alas, the shipments always found their way through some wrong hands; for that reason he had no hand in freighting or charging those cargos save for the main one coming in led by the sole proprietor council. The one and only ambassador who strictly believed in the Covenants, The Covenants of Dawn! One who, nothing on his way, arranged and bossed around every single sailor and portman according to direct orders from the top. The best guesthouse, super escorts to the mansion, and all the beauties he could swallow while away from his wife who was much less one of a kind and dear to the chief's luscious passions as they were transported in separate motorcades; one escorted and the woman not in a private vehicle driven by a uniformed liaison who rushed her late in the afternoon knowing that the ambassador had tended afternoon tea and other affairs after having been overseas for duty for quite a long time.

"What embargo!? Speak clearly! You know I am busy colonel. . . I have already spoken to all of my contacts personally, and the cargo will be ready in two or three days as expected. . . You do your part as usu. . . ." He is interrupted.

"Impossible!! I know they need them. . . that's nonsense"

"Ah. . . about the Tribune. . . . my best regards no matter what happens! And do order to fire after the minister's son does his part. . . . Yes, yes, everything remains quiet until he finishes his speech. . . . What!? No? Listen to me!! Only after he does his turn you can fire if necessary. . . . I don't want this thing to get complicated. . . you understand!? Yes! Yeah? Lead her to the library when she arrives and the usual!!! The new code should change everything, the boats should remain guarded and under my direct command! You understand? I am sure! Let the cargos into the new ones. . . those boats are anchored at my command!! Yes, keep me updated through the port code and I want every detail reported to me! You understand colonel!!? No! No more reinforcement at the plaza!! It would attract too much attention. . . . we have enough. . . . Not yet! Heavy artillery is going to be too much! Keep me informed. . . and the reception tomorrow to be cancelled as I mentioned earlier!! I am seeing the ambassador. . . OK! OK! Contact me on my library line!"

The colonel hung up and dialed a number as he was fingering her official note and told his lower rank to hold fire yet for two more days; because the minister's son was to give his speech to the public at the plaza. He hung up again and called again ordering a driver to pick up the wife of the newly arriving ambassador. They had arrived at the island since two days ago. He undid the two folds in up and down directions and set the short and alarming letter in front of him. There had not been a word said about the content which left it confidential between the colonel and the signer.

A letter not typically long yet when it happened to be long the writer would be literate and have written it on his own, or her, or their, whatever! If somebody had written it for the signer, it would not have been a long one. Only literate, but the officer could care less as he was sure and certain about who had written it as it did matter. *Yet not!*

"To the officers responsible for classification and rendition of the affairs of the nation (our nation):"

However, when Salome wrote it must have been important, perhaps comically or with hideous notions of melancholy which happened to not leave her alone and no more reason for abandoning home to cross the ocean. Once and for all, and hopefully the affairs would have taken a toll and come to an end. When everyone was free then she would return!

"For reasons yet to be sorted and signified there remains no cause for pursuit of life. . ."

But the colonel had his doubts as he was investigating other aspects of the circumstances at the time. He was thinking two days ahead when the guards would have had to keep the minister's son safe behind the podium. Why he would symbolize something this nation had not yet seen? He would be the target of the liberation than the people whom by then-pros and cons-would have reacted. What he would have said did not matter much to the army except that he was classified an intellectual. Colonel, determined to keep the letter a secret, called for the guards at the gate and reported that the special guest of the chief would soon be arriving. Area around the palace was quiet and fresh from the newly mowed grass. Maintained daily and guarded minutely, the palace had its usual mood familiar to the colonel in charge of its protection and management who walked out to the palm garden overshadowing the rear area of the palace, and lit a cigar deep in thought. It took about fifteen minutes before a guard stepped close and reported the arrival of the escorted vehicle as he had expected it. Colonel ordered for the guest to be directed to the library and snapped the burning ash with the opposite index finger off the aromatic hand-rolled cigar holding onto it as he walked back inside. He back stepped two steps toward his swivel chair falling seated and looked over his table and then slowly placed the cold cigar in the ash tray. He grabbed the letter again, more collected; he opened it and read it one more time. *What are you up to woman!!?* Doubt and fear caused laughter and in a second's moment the cool air his sentiments that always entertained the colonel, the man in charge of fear, stage, and top secrets! *What he does we know! What he wants to do. . . . ?* The ink, the rolodex, the chair, the desk, the books on the shelves, the map, the cabinets, the files, the telephone, the intercom, the white phone, the phone to the army, the gramophone, the globe, and the laughter echoed through the room, through everything he could set his eyes on except the hand-rolled one he had put out moments ago, where it became the past for the present question! That was funny. Chief thought but was *he* laughing.

We are the center of sarcasm and, facing the island breeze, we see the father of the Covenants of Dawn with his cain twaddling through the corridors, unheard and not frightening but pallid and noticeably dead, that justice has gone, to home, and away from the gardens, the halls, and all the rooms including library. . . Last I saw it! He is image size and real size and present size like he aged and I would see them in robes measuring the length of the halls accompanied by the servers and the guards wouldn't dare approach when he laughed at every move he made heinously. It was egregious; he left out a line then threw meat at them all around the pool house. The cigar told a story and chief was not laughing but had to see his guest.

The colonel examined his boots and poured a drink, but walked again. Perhaps, better on foot rather than being asleep. Indeed, how many amendments, Covenants' items to the Dawn!? Or would he be acknowledgeable when he hung his cain echoing in the hallways!!? That was the way he dreamt of fidelity, to subdue the intellect which washed off pain and pride bringing him normalcy through the powers of inferiority in his soul. Once he had it, they said, there was no telling him from a beast. Expected to survive a dose that killed him before he knew the plan; his plan was made at sea! Colonel threw the cigar back in the ashtray and raised the receiver also laughing. *It is an order!*

Chief had recently pardoned a few prisoners. So what is wrong with that! But Salome was Top Secret-and with no doubt-a part of the plan. The hemisphere being crowded suddenly there was a knock on his door that slightly echoed through his hemispheric room. He was meditating on his decision which happened to be a national issue, Top Secret, but hemispherically it would have had lengthy consequences. Yet he knew that a discreet logic curtailed pursuit and induced partial views towards the current situation. *Who's who? The remainder of the afternoon was entitled "Romance in the Shell."* The dusk was near when he stepped to the door and opened it quietly. *Yes?* The chief's rhetoric laughter would not have worried him because of the occasion ever so less than traumatic, and yet, fear which came with every big decision. Nothing asked, nothing mentioned, nothing leaked, nothing harmful, he closed the door once he was finished with the guard and called the officer in charge of 'his plan'. The chief administrative clerk of the palace immediately relayed the command to the secret service and put the letter of permission to leave in the hands of the sergeant guard!

A visa was to be issued to the nation of interest, and Salome, to be escorted to the transport of embarkation. Complete dedication to Cyrus, alas the theme was familiar yet it was and would be significant under the status quo. Consequently a plan was laid to accommodate members of the Section 2 (Top Secret) in the nation of destination to detect solely her contacts with liberation; if any, Cyrus!

The gleaming sun prepared to descend and the lambs crowded the fortress unrestive and forced to force the other to a direction to obey the shepherd. The guest was completely tanned with a crack at her skirt that had gone all the way near her element of femininity; being under a glamour to the fancy of every guard and including the colonel who browsed her over at the fountain plaza by the palace entrance. The car drove around the fountain on its way out and the brunette with those large green eyes and the 34-25-35 story that always said all for chief softly entered the lobby. Chief's laughter echoed informing the rest of the palace that he welcome a guest yet already known to the guards and officers on duty. Like usual, they headed for the library, and without a pause, the door shut, and it would be at least half an hour before he requested any type of service!

The colonel gayly sipped his rum. He had assumed a major operation and ordered it into operation, but without a doubt he expected feedback, reports to the top. From espionage to sabotage, and from there, perhaps, his promotion!! He called the administrative wing again, he told the officer that the letter should be handed in quietly and without a sniff of red tape. . . . *Looking natural! Being open to suggestions! Making friends!!* The dilemma was not existence, but let us overcome the obstacles and he was certain. Chief would have approved, but before he knew, the colonel would have had an answer. He felt cordial at best for the good of the nation and determined to file a full report once the masks fell which would be the first time after the prison had collapsed.

The echo of the first shot trembled everything in the hallway and his window too when he rushed out to inquire. It was the last and was a blast not a gunshot. He ran to the entrance to his office area and into the hallway while swiftly pulling his gun out of holster. It happened to be a grenade blast. Shouting "Library! Library. . !!" the colonel hurried towards the library. It took him about a minute to make it from his office or maybe more! Guards must have been shooting into the air because it all sounded like a gunfight to him. Smoke was blowing out through the entrance making the library look like a giant oven with a tray full of burning meat. In heavens must be! Where the soul separated from the body and ejaculation died forever, and pulse disappeared yet leaving the body in cold blood all solidifying. Was an autopsy possible? Every soldier would have asked knowing the grenade and its type of sequential action of shrapnel. Colonel hesitated until a couple of guards got out of the smoke and back to the hallway then he stepped in; he had a hunch. What he saw. . . Grace of God, he had pictured! Still scattered flames filled the room and they worked the extinguishers relentlessly with extra care so colonel could investigate, scrutinize the factual evidence for the last time because everyone knew that no one should have known. They realized that colonel already knew that as well.

Heavens in front of his eyes and the enemy at his back, he promised the Mother of Covenants that she should rule and bless the souls of whomever and whatever that had participated and collaborated in this uncalled for action.

The purpose was plenty, doomed with immense determination of his sensual instincts he promptly recorded the hindsight and a flashback with chief's wife blaming him as though sending a message which only he grasped. He interpreted it as a likely retaliation for whatever that had gone on earlier that day. Section 2! He froze at the center of the library eyeing all that was left and called a guard as his breathing slowed down until one of them responded and saluted in confirmation, ready to obey his order. The inside man had an instinct like chief's who was apparently dead! They had to move things around to discover any corpses or at least any portions that could present live evidence supporting any reasonable doubt that bore the least notion of backstabbing, conspiracy, sabotage, treason, or any other natural act of betrayal. He stood still with sweat covering his forehead and soaking his uniform. Another guard came near and showed him an automatic pistol. "Chief's sir!" He walked away as the guard followed him carrying the handgun, and both exited the library. They walked back to his office as he finally grabbed the pistol from the wary guard. The guard was relieved as he showed him the door. Colonel set it on his desk. *What's going to happen now? Alas, heaven is awaiting all of us. . . .*

They could do anything they would have wanted regardless if the country had resisted or even compromised the immunity and welfare of its innocent citizens. Archangel still facing them had granted its last testimony with those role of a leader's wife and nation's mother that only had her cain to point to her will and tolerated no remorse. The bells chimed through the palace this time with a new bell that rattled the nerves of this force and she stood with an awe that had never been familiar to a soldier unless he asked and then there was not much he could understand and do. Only obedience prevailed and, only that, stood prevalently as the sole and irrevocable message that found its way through the palace and the guards. So he won't be no more but who will?

They wanted to get away when colonel called the administrative clerk and told him to escort Salome to the port when she was ready; then contact the ministers as soon as he got a chance. . . "Oh, by the way, call the ambassador on a secure line and request backup for the palace!! Do not, by no means, allow a word to leak out of here!!" He sat down and stared at the letter. It meant, confounded with irony, that power is reluctant yet with any sanctimony or a grey act of mercy and fate what remains is a countdown. *So if we lived we would keep our hands stretched and eyes open to leave unnoticed those obstacles that divide and pursue in apolitical and ecclesiastical forms the touching excuse and reason why we should believe as we believe in reincarnation but not yet the wheel that turns to deep plough the mind and soul in search of facts back and forth. If said, albeit with a sheer testimony that awakes our soil from the outskirts of the palace up to the boats carrying the nutrition to feed the inhabitants at this cultivated domain of the liberation on one side and the numerous men in our army on the other, for young and old to further be nursed and once again to survive the numerous lapses of toleration and repent. And Detente have never existed!!*

He was the powerhouse and all of them knew; colonel had stepped it up without any compromise with insecurity. A lonely knight that would have soon found himself at the court, a soldier that would not have willingly assumed his new duty found within him as the outer orbit had deeply abstained and morality could have been a distant bet. Without a superior this island was a short lived bonfire that made no sense to a warrior who meant warfare and not merely revenge and vigilance since notwithstanding the lack of credible opposition, the two sides would have been at a deadlock only if he could reach his ends and outs, now!

As the poor colonel remained in charge to pick a pen and write his faith, or alas narrow everything to a pleasant and without-a-motive faith that could luridly prevail in the future, the supreme devotion and the queen supreme found it suspicious that his role was so flawlessly laid out and delivered to him without any contention. Come on what now while the books had burnt and guards knew and had found pieces of *Capsiular ligament,* and other *Atlanto-axials, Inferior Maxillary bones, Forearm Superficial muscles, Supinator brevis, Extensor longus pollicis, partial heart,* identified *popliteal artery: attached, Thyroid cartilage, mediastinum, uriniferous tubes* or what was collected, *sorotum, metacarpals,* other ligament and duly an endless search for the chief who was said to be at large. *But that's it!!!*

He was shaking his manhood in the latrine when he started thinking what would happen if the public was rather consulted than compromised. Only a fool would have said that he thought. He remembered the days and those endless orders that dragged him out of bed and into a jeep for an early morning session of torture dealing with an intoxicated chief who smelled like another latrine. However, public was now to be compromised and so was the ambassador.

Her jewelry, the only explanation given, was the mere proof that she'd been there. *And done that!* Colonel had ordered his dinner; the imported pheasants with palm roots pickled in sweet wine and sipping his limited edition rum that only the blessed late chief and his close hands could drink. He glanced at his family's picture, his wife and three sons, and a little daughter that would be turning three weeks from then. He reconsidered, pursued, contemplated, and, finally syndicating his last thought, was determined to lay out as it had happened and tell the ambassador the truth as he had developed an appetite for the seizure of this regime hopefully with the help of a disillusioned and paranoid ambassador whose only choice would have been to mourn his wife's death and hide behind the power of the army. Ego had penetrated into colonel's mind, at a degree which he speculated dominating the misplaced and contained cabinet-the ministers! Hail to the few! Power to the people! God bless the chosen! Let us live now because heaven is quiet and far! Come next week the turtles were at the beach again and doing their business.

My queen will you accept me and, without the notion of a doubt hold my hand through the phases of eternal kingdom because he will never die and I'll be a ventriloquist. . . . hold me tight and I will feed my children, all of them, in Royal style. He would not leave the room; staring at the telephone until about eight or nine to receive more information, but no more. They now had enough evidence showing that the explosives were brought in. They were small ones but enough to kill two. Conspiracy did not quite seem to be the motive for some reason although colonel began to explain it as adultery and betrayal, or whatever the ambassador wanted it called. He called his driver thinking exactly what he would tell the ambassador. There was little gone off his dinner plate as the car was ready. They headed for his compound not too far away as the palace remained under investigation until further notice of the command.

––––––––––––––

In a pinstripe double-breasted soft and silky linen suit, the ambassador was escorted out of the compound into the second vehicle of the motorcade. There was no escorts, only two SUVs due to the attraction that might have ensued. The suited man seemed unshaken and discreet, but colonel was seemingly in a hurry to find answers to many questions that loitered on his still devastated mind. The motorcade left the compound in less than ten minutes while he did not bother to ask any questions. *He knew!* The brought him to the solitaries on the acres of the palace and took his handcuffs; then, they led him into a cell of which there were only three without any exposure to light or the other. Colonel returned to his office and put his uniform back on having taken it off for this short trip to stay hidden from the watchful eyes of the members of the opposition force, the liberation. So were the guards and drivers of the motorcade out of uniform. He drank a shot of rum in a shot glass and downed it with a sip of water; then he picked up the phone and dialed the palace security command to prepare for interrogation. As he began his short walk to the cells he was convinced in his prevalence and undertaking of the imperatives that could have led to leadership, like this act of custody and many more that he was reminded of or had personally imagined that they would mint his steps to supremacy. However, power would have done every man the good of dominance and intolerance of tolerance and patience. Colonel was one now, an Apostle that so grew so swiftly into a Lucipher's bastard without a second's hesitation for empathy and degradation of his long lost will. He performed, now, albeit at no remorse or it might have been called condescension of the principles of his past. The day, being his day of reincarnation, *the Coronation of the Son*! He was pleased with his act and felt the strength as any other man could feel it when he reaches the peak of a lost heaven. Yes! He could too rule and practice those attached forms of justice as he had accused the ambassador whom he faced with a hint of mercy, conspiracy, and had explicitly described that day's earlier incident to him at no options for a pardon while reading him his last tale of the living life! Ambassador, pallid and calm, listened without a notion of surprise as he demonstrated an impression beholding natural stipulations that he knew and always knew, but never thought it might be unnatural for a husband to tolerate his wife's acts of infidelity and forgive in order to live on as in the island as anywhere else abroad. Like many others, men and women, husbands and wifes, he preferred peace in time and had responded to colonel. "What would you do? You're a married man. . . . .!!" He was wordless but sunk in wrath and, mindless of who and how important the man in the white suit was to his country at a time of such immensity in diplomatic, sociological, and political upheaval that had brought those tow men together in that cell. The ambassador knew him well but colonel was helpless with manners except that he announced his final decision to court martial him for premeditated acts that could have and would have altered the fate of the nation. In the truculent encounter of the two which later resulted in an slap in the face and a kick at the abdomen, the ambassador held on to confess that he had never seen the well-mannered officers of the palace being so disloyal, impolite, and sanctified beneath the lowest grades of manhood! He was ready to die and believed in his wife's solemn oath of love for both of them, or else, why would she conspire and end the life of such powerful lover. The evidence all told him without a doubt that she was tired, hopeless, and perhaps afraid to breach their vows as it was almost a cinematic drama, merciless, to him as a man who had served all classifications of government and had dealt with poor and rich, religious and atheist, pro and con, good and bad, weak and strong, loyal and infidel, civilian and soldier, and hollow or dignified as colonel seemed to be while he shared his strong speculations with the ambassador claiming that he was connected with the liberation, no doubt!!!

An accusation not far from the testimony that God had performed and blessed the two men while one offered good rum and the other cried heartlessly without regrets that he knew what had taken place in the library among those bookshelves. His long-bought wife had always played the patron and the conqueror of hearts even with the liberation. He drank rum and cried not answering colonel's questions regarding a conspiracy or an affair among the three of them.

"How did your wife find herself in the hands of chief? And wasn't that obvious enough!? At least to you? God bless fidelity and the island!! But where would it end without a haste or waste of human affection as the rise of promiscuity among the wives of the higher echelon, elite, that one day they would have to answer questions and duly punished in the hands of a righteous judge!?"

Ambassador's tears had not stopped while he drank shot after shot with no shame toward colonel. He, then, began and explained his woman. His intellectual abilities far outdid her simple and earthly beauty; a woman good for any man if she wanted! There, they stopped while the guard reported a telephone call for colonel. Everything secretively outlasted the evening into the early hours of the morning. *Man what should I do to live?* This bloodbath would pursue the next when the next step would have been taken when the willing colonel decided on the life of ambassador then and there in that dark cell. "Feed him, keep him clean, and most important of all. . . .watch him carefully!! He is ours!" *Competent men ever in such a short history all did one thing and only one thing, looking history in the back and next they looked back at history but did it make them more tolerant or boisterous didn't matter, the clause of antiquity had served a sentence before jury was ever selected; a justice with a vision that saw through and through deeper than any other power it allowed its existence, but why men strive or sacrifice face and flesh to play puppets and let go of logic senselessly like a handful of rocks. This stone age infuriates those women who are skeptical, with the power of charm and the attraction to materialism, and a patch of narcissism. . . History, then, wouldn't tell the tale as a woman knew it and that's the wit that persuades her inner instinct; those savage items that fall over human nature like a black curtain and lead to notoriety and a flawless segment that neither would correct a wrong nor bless a soul!*

The ambassador had to have contact with the outside; they had assumed, but to him, he was better off secluded and under arrest. Since, for him, there was no telling what colonel was looking for. And he had a lot on his plate! So, now, both men found themselves on one side looking up to the quiet dawn that would spread its miraculous beams over the island slowly and peacefully.

"MORNING EDITION:

The government will unveil the nation's new plan to resist terrorism upon the arrival of the ambassador today. He will be meeting with the cabinet for an exchange of ideas and further planning the future of the nation's diplomatic ties towards its allies during his visit. . ."

13

There was a changing mood; something in the form or way guards moved, and even reinforcements who had shortly arrived. People looked on, some just had joined others and obviously not working and some had stayed in the plaza all night, and some even for days. The next Tribune spokesperson, the son of a minister, was almost ready and his impression as bleak as that of the duel between the liberation and the army of island nation. The noise running through the plaza was loud but weary and, for the most parts quiet at such a time in the morning where some had to work and some wondered if there was any work in the future. The announcer quietly reaches for the microphone as there was a short screech and a loud whistle that provoked reaching for their earlobes as the crowd, retarded, reacted and then with apologies he invited the next spokesperson to the podium who was easy to recognize for most of the onlookers.

He approached the platform looking up at the building of the ministry of information across the plaza facing him where he was on his feet and, perhaps, ready to stand against those who had been in that building for too long; those who knew him still had pointed their guns at his direction. Casino had been to school with him when both had earned collegiate credentials, and he knew Harlot and maybe a couple of others who had barricaded that ministry. The sky was covered with sad and pale tropical clouds as a thundershower was expected to pour around the time of the day to find a escape route for the sun and after the eruption of light its caustic heat put more lines on the foreheads of those already aged inhabitants who now were wondering what the point of all that was. Where the government was going with it no one knew, but the orders were to start up the army right after his speech. Chief always thought that if someone from the elite went up there, it would have persuaded the people and something right would happen. A lot of people knew him aside from those in the liberation lurking in the ministry. They, too, were ready to listen while the young man raised his hand and waved to the crowd; then he crossed his chest resting his hand on his heart. . . . .

"People of the island I wish we could rest at home and pass the appearing heat of the sun while resting in a cool and quiet home! Island is grey now and it doesn't have to be! Since we all know the truth is that a hurdle is upon us that is to be passed! It is to be passed justly and truthfully. . . There are the heads of this nation who work day and night to ease these circumstances and provide yet prevail. . . They are still there while we are proud and free to choose them over any enemy that might jeopardize our wellbeing. This is not a curfew!! The guards are here to protect and keep in order our respectful citizens that have taken over that building (pointing)!!! Those people should listen thoroughly and understand where we are through the golden pages of our history! The takeover of the ministry and our radio station is somewhat unjust. . . There has to be a cause for every human action and now is the time to explain! It is because of our unity and harmony of actions that I am here, and I would like to pay my due respects to the minister and chief. . . ."

There was tropical downpour that suddenly moved the crowd and they began to sing the national anthem interrupting the speaker. Some raised their hands holding transistor radios. There seemingly was broadcast as they had waited more than a week to hear their much valued and famous news broadcasts once again; the only activity in the island that kept people in peace and entertained. They began waving the radios when the speaker gradually realized that it might be liberation having relayed a message so he, with a change of tone, louder, continued his speech; he went on with his soft, higher class, educated, and spoiled kid style trying to reach everyone and break through the noise that had begun to worry the guards who looked ready to shoot awaiting a command. This last nobleman was now lost, but washed from guilt recollecting the bias that undertook him once in that old stinking garage. He remembered all the phases that filled him with due vengeance already and a collision with God that for him only existed for those in the palace and the uptown. As for others it was a whole loaf of bread, a bucket of ice cream, bananas, or pineapples. The sequence was strange and the feeling was foreign; he had a feeling that he, alas, never rehearsed or prepared as he was told to only greet the spectators with good words as rain said otherwise while the devil began to defeat the train of resistance by a distant measure. It was the breathless audience who had started the golden message making him aware of himself, nothing short of a Messiah!!! He was given a spot and a tragic role in the life of his life's struggle for freedom. This moment would live to repeat and color the pages of the island's paper as the photographers had been banned from participation! There was no logic except that the plaza was soaking from rain and something had disappeared. Then, another began to bloom like an opportunity for sacrifice. To give one's life seemed like a choice; a glimmer of hope tickled the abandoned ego of the islander! Bamboozled by the crowd, now he used a different tone after the broadcast. The crowd showed little interest and paid no attention to the man behind the microphone as suddenly he had begun louder and stronger. He was yelling; madly, with a unique passion, anger, a melancholy that did not care what would happen to him, sometimes with tears, insisting, sometimes swearing; he finally discharged in insult and the rhetoric of the antis, the true words which had remained rotting in his head. He was outspoken until he started swearing at the guards. Shortly, the crowd became quiet and listened as something more significant had been boisterously taking the center, and the rain continued. Some pulled their shirts over their heads, and others just got wet and kept on listening.

"Casino, Harlot, my brothers in arm. . . . . . .I am now grateful without a doubt in my out-washed exhausted mind that the news on the radio is real news that once again our nation is struggling to stand on her feet!! Watching over us the generations who brought us together here to draw a picture that would become a future for young and old to be proud of!! I beseech the regime and chief to lay down their arms and surrender to the demands of the liberation who insofar have been standing side by side with justice and are deeply dignified and loyal to the island nation. . . . . .You heroes over there hear me now as I was given a voice today that I could not use loudly, but as the sins are washed off me I could no more procrastinate! There is no more a place for deceiving the rightful! There is no more time for a broken promise. . . . And there is no more tolerance for those who step on us and treat humans like beasts! People are listening now, I could feel it,. . . . I hear it in this moment of leap and silent attention. . . . And unequivocally invite everyone to help those in that building. . . . Let us remember the good days and be sure to look up to many more.. . . A future for our children that we could be proud of and once and for all sow the seeds of knowledge, justice, and welfare of all the islanders. . . ."

The crowd started walking slowly towards the guards and the podium. The circle became tighter and some others started throwing whatever they could find at the soldiers. Closer and closer, they approached and surrounded them. Still getting closer, some pulled away their weapons and began beating up the hesitant army soldiers. He stood at the podium observing this siege and went on. . . .

"Casino! Do not become violent if unnecessary, because we know our destination is only a short distance away and numbers are telling the story. . . . We don't need to be hostile! People listen to your liberators and be proud as they are proud of you today!!! A dose of that friendship was given away around the island and you have seen and remember how far we are away from victory!!! Now our efforts are as vivid as the rising sun. Follow the messages on your radios, those are now absolutely important! Keep your medicines and read the instructions. . .The letters would explain our positions and means and ends to our unified efforts to besiege the resistance. . . . Listen carefully because my comrades are strong and aware!! Let it be a lesson for. . . . ."

A shot was fired at the minister's son behind the podium putting him down and the crowd went into a stampede over the army who began to back away. Some got behind the barricades and started shooting at close range when suddenly more shots were heard at the opposite wing of the plaza. The liberation was relentless and a few of them stepped out of the building and followed the crowd who was now completely entangled with the army. The liberation continued shooting and the crowd finally reached the shooter who had killed the minister's son and began to hit him with fists and kicks, even stones and sticks until he was off his feet spread on the ground in a puddle of blood.

The fear factor, always an element of survival if implemented based on pursuit of a better consequence, undertook the scene with the two sides seemingly hungry for blood which was not true as this fight would not have lasted when the soldiers, or some of them, let go of the weapons and politely gave them away one after the other. Behind the barricades, the shooting stopped and the army began to come forward in peace. They dropped their weapons and surrendered, indeed, after two or three of them were killed. The main entry of the ministry of information which had not been opened for at least a week opened as soon as the occupiers observed the surrender. They rushed out including Casino who stepped onto the podium. Apparently, two of them stayed inside to keep control of the radio station and another three continued guarding the building. Casino checked the microphone. He, then, began reading a message they had already sent on air.

"Our efforts are endless, our wills strong, our hearts are with you. . . Stay alert and continue listening to emergency broadcasts!! Long live Island Nation! 221823. 2415. 10162718. . . . . .Tomorrow will be the day! It will see you through fire and rain! Believe in victory and believe me! The end is near. . . . .Tomorrow!!"

(A=10, B=11, C=12, D=13, E=14,. . . . . .W=32, X=33, Y=34, Z=35!!)

Partly overshadowed by and lost in ambition, the few left in the ministry including Harlot resume communication through the radio. The items on their agenda varied; apart from immense emotions and sharing the news about this long awaited scene in the plaza, they were all about the next takeover which had to be sooner than later. It might have cost lives. The message was clear until the other party informed Harlot about the drug cargo and the ambassador being at large. It was too late to change plans but why!? What could be done!? And why had the ambassador not contacted regarding their plan? I was informed by Harlot, personally, to keep a watchful eye like everyone else on Seahide because if he had cheated us it would mean our lives were in danger. The communication added up to a reluctance, a frenzy that could be causeless as an abyss, a pointless move that would ever push the revolution to the edge. But they knew it would take a strike of a match or a minimal amount of explosive to set the cargo on fire and completely destroy it. Would chief risk his next incoming suitcase of mulla for such a ridiculous reason such as an overthrow. No? Yes? They would play it by the ear. . . . The communication preceded onto an evaluation of available force, and they discussed the amount of arms on hand. They were to be loaded and transported by early morning to back the attack set for next day. They relayed a need for more arms which Harlot promised to look into. How many fighters? Harlot had informed his men that they should be on alert as this phase of the movement was a vital stage of it all. They now had to prove themselves that they could do it! Their ability to go through it pressed questions of fidelity as before; a cacophony that, as unpleasant as the rainy days of winter on the island, undertook our logic thoughts like every other member of the liberation. The elements of espionage were intangible, there was almost no sign of it, but liberation was concerned how the force and the two sides encountered each other. If there had been a spy among us or the code had leaked, it mattered, however, it could never have stopped the liberation. Harlot had brought it up while on the air and he was preparing a script (Jotting down items) for a one-hour broadcast which he meant to pursue for, at least, the next week or so to get closer to the islanders and, more so, to take advantage of the opportunity to become the voice of the island while the island's only other organ, the newspaper, had completely fallen into the hands of the government. What if a few educated members of the community decided to take the code to the army or the thugs!? I had mentioned that while relaying the code to the shore but the fact was that having something on hand was better than no contact at all! Besides, as they were distributing medicine, the liberation was cautious so they chose neighborhoods liable to be lifeless and far below the suspicions of the government. It mattered and would move all people closer. I thought this code could have been deciphered by anyone older than than a sixteen year old. It was made flexible so we could change it at the spare of a short time. Harlot suggested that he would pass the message during his daily announcements and, perhaps, create a temporary post to lead a cover operation. The main item on the agenda was strategy and the liberation was no strategist since those hardy bulk literatures only interpreted philosophy or covered communal sermons that merely provoked the revolutionary yet putting to sleep a fighter!

Casino was examining the mobile phone hurriedly. He had found it on the minister's son dead and covered with a torn shirt. He knew that it actually stored the callers' numbers and remembered his conversation with chief in the garage on that afternoon a week or so ago. The sea breeze usually got to the plaza late in the day comforting the passersby, being news to the elders, and smelling like a new life had just started. The mist was a token of the island's generous climate that had astonished locals as well as the visitors since the beginning of time. Casino, still, hoping for something he didn't know, but realized that phone had only been in the hands of the island's elite and other influentials as his late friend who actually happened to be among the higher class. Casino put the phone in his pocket and pulled the son's torso to an army lory that had been left by the podium. He, with the help of others, placed it in the trunk along with a few others. The dead did not count more than five!! He, staring at the crowd and the soldiers who had surrendered, finally signaled them to huddle and listen. Now, it did not matter who was who; they were all ready to fight along with the liberation as Casino commanded them to get into the trucks and follow him to that village by the seashore.

It was almost dawn. Had it all gone accordingly, the next takeover would have taken place around noon. The liberation, now a body of fighters and soldiers, had begun to deal more officially with the situation. They went on by the book; a good reason to be asked more questions! They inquired about the position of the army in different strongholds already starting to jot down notes and safekeeping every map they had found while they studied them. The spirit was high and morale as strong as it could have been. The motorcade underscored a historical day, not only, as it had taught them some lessons among which was the tired and disappointed faces of those soldiers that was a glimmer of victory. It explained why they had given up so easily meaning most of them were willing to give up the same. A simple sketch had been drawn in the minds of the liberation telling them that the enemy was not exactly the army or at least not yet. The man in charge at the village had everything in order before the motorcade had arrived. Everyone had been given a weapon and ammo; indeed, warned to shoot only if absolutely necessary. He had sent the cargos of medicine and village bread to the bus station and the ramshackle train station that nowadays hardly had any populous arrivals but any passengers still counted and the liberation needed them. The villagers had been making bread and placing a small piece of paper with the code written on it in the dough. It was, they thought, still necessary to distribute the code to let the people understand that there was a common ground. Unity and free spirit had to be the mainstream of this operation. The hardest part was to deal with the regime's elite force. They had decided to carry on with the broadcasts which would frequently cite the codes and messages and it was another way to recruit. Liberation was sure that people would soon enough understand their methods and trust them for what they were. Liberation was determined to announce the importance of their actions and explain why they would have consequently needed men ready to give up their lives. It was although a line of duty that had to be passed from one man to another. The liberation hoped for explicit regrouping and an upheaval among the community who yet were to be clarified in regards to the intensity of this movement.

The only boat allowed in the restricted port belonged to an importer freight that had brought in small items, newspapers, and legit brands of liquor, of course for rich women of the island latest fashion apparel that would have sold for three or four times of their real value. However, what they were worth did not matter for the rich were entertained solely by having a connection with the outside. A gift would have kept the women happy and men proud that showed, at least, there was a token of the outer world over which they could have reached a compromise. The newspaper, that day, which actually belonged to a week ago had announced,

"FIASCO IN THE WATERMELON PARALLEL."

Although a vague message, it was all the foreign media could do at the time. A brief message that something unimportant and intangible was happening somewhere! Anyhow, the newspapers are always like that; they wouldn't have wanted to wreak havoc if it really wasn't global. It would have scared the readers! The armed forces on the parallel were very limited and there had to be a good reason for them to mediate in any sort of crisis. But, also, island had to be an important strategic locale for anyone to worry about, and perhaps something about the island that smelled like wealth which it wasn't. More, the cargo that the ambassador was hauling to the island was mainly serving a similar purpose. It was to buy friendship and dependable neighbors for the watermelon parallel. It, albeit, did not happen that way and no telling where he was. I was too worried after having seen the shipment of paper and other nicknacks that passed us by peacefully. One thing was clear and that was the news had to be leaking from the top because neither I nor the liberation would have informed the outsiders; we anted to keep the conflict small and easy to contain, since the palace was the last resort with sufficient communication capabilities to inform the foreign media. I assumed that the ambassador's visit had something to do with it. Indeed, it was hazardous that they might have attacked Seahide to get the dope back, and it was possibly a hazard that a foreign force might have intervened, but this was not yet part of the liberation's agenda. Although it would soon become so once they saw those newspapers. However, all was for the good of this nation and I thought I keep it a secret.

At last a commentary, as a version of the generality of this chaos, acted out as if a revolution really was taking place by taking its position along a short line in history where we were exposed to strange forces that would have no use but pester and become obsolete; but why not shoot the bullet at a torso instead of a lifeless and remote target. Why not subscribe to hell and count the sins that overshadow anywhere between murder, sodomy, and other diabolic forms of human act as hell is near!? And hell now was the destination as the revolution wanted to step in badly forgetting those unimportant bodies of flesh and blood. Without further due, the enemy was to be deviated from the press and to solidify into a form of mediation, one that took so long to appreciate the peacetime and, thus, sought blood to an overwhelming persuasion. *What they would see in island nation is beyond wisdom!* Virtue stood out of line and yet hell became where one did not want to arrive at. Perhaps they were aiming at hell as the liberation had considered requesting outside help on that night of peace before fascism saw the last of its generation beyond the shores of an abyss. That low-life inhumane fascism proved worthless and the aim for a new morning was in line with any thematic dream that sowed the seeds of welfare and well-being; human conditions that had agelessly remained below poverty. "Hell is that place that one avoids!"

Hell includes a surgery room or a graveyard just as island nation, so why would have a foreign force wanted to interfere? There was one chance in a million they would have turned against the government, yet a chance in a million they would have backed the liberation. To them or others, there was no liberation. *Had they gone that far!!* No one knew where they were led to or how much more of this they had tolerated, but they had sensed hell; that twilight that came after sin although for some it was itself easier than the *original sin.* In the midst of it all the liberation was yet gaining a form, that of a striking force. Because the pioneers of this power remained breathless over its sudden leap to existence, all the island now knew about this movement, and a phase that took human labor to share it by spreading the truth.

Among the incomers in the bus station, on the inbound routes, the port, the farms, the ghettos, schools and shops there was presence and a promise to pass arms if one was willing to fight. . . The second ministry was to be seized in the morning next day, and this was the only road to victory left for liberation to choose. The few army tucks in the hands of liberation were being loaded at the village with arms and bread. The messages were hidden in the loaves baked by fisherman's wives and children as a single effort to distribute the code; it was to be deciphered by midday. People were to receive and understand those messages. Before dawn, a few trucks would take their positions around the ministry of agriculture to arm the crowd already there. Other loaded vehicles were destined to spread around the capital's populated locations to evaluate the ability and preparedness of the volunteers provoking cooperation and transporting them to the ministry hoping for another victory as bloodless as possible. The liberation had already determined that the army would give up easily if the primary push was strong enough. The chance in hell was the possibility of a sudden impact as army was to be backed up by an outsider or a stringent plan operated by the special guards led by the palace. Hell, the twilight of uncertainty, promised the first act in this dramatic segment of sacrifice and carnage. It seemed it belonged to no one, or anyone with a license to loose his life with his gun where he did not want to go; it was to be the last hell! They wanted a takeover without the battle. The trucks were to be operated quietly with minimum radio contact. The liberation was to convince grassroots intelligently and brief the common islander to volunteer.

A warfare that would hold the peace yet allow for imperatives to be taken over in the daylight. The liberation did not believe the volunteers could fight in the dark. Hell is hate and love island so I know code that free them from night mist a mystery as victory from within a portion of war and there are so that truth be murdered and steps will show the way while it was people who guns were given at the port a mission turned and the turtle eggs through the dark clouds and the moving image the moon rising stop the fear hell is near trolly comes at a nearby low of chill stopping the color of hell the counting contrast a prelude or people again trial was away with chilling champion of choosing a note and find free a sound without a flag that parts with pride and prisoners would two more days the wind over turtles begins rum a bloody water that bring home and so soldiers yell to fall along the shells wherever we decided a falling corridor without those bombs and they are a part and freedom an unabashed dignified passed on another full-proof detriment which around away from the blood and time and pulse stop them when among a few were the courage and grateful winning became the aid pouring rain or dawn forever believe it or not about descent feverishly hand them and these never drops no blood with few more the life the free soldiers hell is where I hate to go!

BOOM, BOOM, BOOM, BOOBOOBOOBOOBOO BOOBOOM. . . BOOM. . . . . . .

Through the pothole, it was tangible to see or to see a tangible part of the orange floater airplane circling over Seahide that early morning, and it was easy to pick up the transmissions with a nearby island about a full day's sail. A day, island had its own; eight o'clock in the morning while the fog still had settled to remain blocking the view around the island and even the central district of the capital was adorned with nothing but smog. The plane continued circling the parameters of the Seahide and a bit later headed for the island. We had already set communication on a new wavelength employing the three radios the liberation had taken away from the army as prize money. Counting the transmitter of Seahide there were four radios in operation; they were in dependable hands. The one at the fishing village was actually being operated by an army communication officer after having surrendered to the liberation. The one by the ministry was used by Casino and the second one by the ministry was also operated by an army officer now helping the liberation to win its second battle. Four lorries were unloading and distributing guns and loaves of bread as the volunteers sporadically appeared;

most of them carried transistor radios that morning. A sign of awareness was filling the streets without the ministry's guards knowing what was gong on. This day marked the arrival of the liberation into officialdom. Radio station at the ministry of information constantly kept up its provocation announcements and the broadcast was all about invitation and codified messages that were to be passed to the people. The fresh loaves were from the village with a small piece of paper in each of them bearing the Code of Unity, A=10. This code was to remain until further notice. The ministry, from a few blocks away, seemed to proceed to its relatively normal routine yet with a heavier security. There was to be no shooting unless absolutely necessary. The liberation informed every comrade to stay calm and remain attached to their weapons. Most importantly, they were to keep themselves carefully barricaded. The commencement of the siege would be signaled with two air shots which was the responsibility of the commander of the nearest lorry to the ministry of agriculture who was no one else but Casino. As the clock in the radio station at the ministry of information showed ten Harlot began a new broadcast by flipping through the pages of island's history and then beseeched the ministers to compromise with the dictator to come to an agreement and surrender. It was a long shot but these programs were to create proper morale and energize the spirit of comradery.

The orange old plane crossed the island's capital and it must've run out of fuel because around ten o'clock it was outbound, indeed, to its landing point. I had reported the sighting to Harlot and Casino had also justified the cranky flight of that floater plane overhead.

The area around the ministry became suspiciously quiet while the armed comrades stayed hidden and watchful awaiting the signal as the street located in front of the building was guarded at both ends without the knowing of the guards. When there was an escorted car approaching the ministry Casino signaled his men to stop them. And what do you know!!? It was the minister going to work. The guards resisted and shot a liberation man. So they shot back while outnumbering the motorcade and took over immediately. Casino detained the driver and sat behind the wheel. He, then, drove the vehicle to the next block where an army truck was parked and ordered his men to handle the minister. The ministry guards had heard the shooting and begun firing at random as they killed two armed liberation men. Yet Casino had not produced a signal. He wanted to have the building completely surrounded while waiting to see if there were more arrivals at the ministry. He finally raised his rifle in the air and shot twice.

14

".........and prison leaves a man with his desire to fly over the free white pillows of cloud. He wonders constantly about the cell bars that become meaningless after a span of years and then the prisoner is a new man; a man without much sense. He moves on two feet the same directions every day and best he could do is count them steps like a child!" Casino concluded two hours ago.

"Where is my husband. . . . !??" She asked. "Sir! Where is my husband???" She repeated.

The former call had come through the cell phone Casino had hidden for the right opportunity. The latter was the wife, minister of agriculture's longtime spouse who did not know colonel too well and did not even know anything about what was going on presently. Colonel, not a man supportive of human lives, or at least for the time being; it would not have been the right choice since the heat was on him. Along with those disgruntled ministers they argued about the future and speculated upon the status quo; the army did not fight and would not carry on the orders from the top. What had astonished him was he had known so differently; he believed they could stop the liberation at any point of the encounter if they wanted to. But the actual scene of the protests had proven otherwise. The ministers hesitated in compromising with the palace, they wanted peace and whatever came with it. Colonel was afraid to pass the power into the hands of those who were hard of leadership and believed that they might turn back against him. The ministers' vote of confidence lacked unity and there was no telling how much power they had in their hands. They could, however, choose to cooperate and that was the target that colonel kept aiming at. The vote among them was not unanimous. Unlike the others, the ministers of agriculture and information found no use holding his side. They saw fit to join the people as best they could. Colonel was harshly criticized for leading a clumsy and milk-fed army, yet he would have argued otherwise promising that the real force was yet to take the scene once he implemented his special guards who were trained and prepared to kill any thing in sight, and highly skilled in armed combat. Ministers believed that there was no need for killing, but it seemed that colonel himself was waiting for something as he frivolously concluded his discussions without reaching any resolutions. His absentmindedness was questioned and the ministers decided on a collective solution that would be humanly relayed to the liberation forces. It is said that the minister of agriculture, apparently volunteering to deliver the message, decided to go to work in the hopes of reaching the liberation alive in order to negotiate. As during that morning of his arrest by the liberation his car was heavily guarded yet when stopped he signaled them to surrender like most of the army, insofar.

"Mrs. Minister your husband. . . . is available!! He is safe. . . . please control yourself!!" He responded while interrupting himself still thinking of Casino who had commenced on that cellular phone saying a thing or two about himself or, thought colonel, about whom he might address to a higher philosophical ground. . . .

"Who is this? You must know chief. . . . you must know better!!! A separatist! A separatist which suffers no end to pain and no beginning to his relentless misery by living and floating in an aborted city or indeed in smoke. . . . without having any contact or any links with the outside. . . .you understand!? Yet able in a frenzy of solitude to see the truth. . . . ! He lives long and sees everything just as eternally as the Noah's Ark, tattooed on his most beloved part seen every time he says his name to forgive. . . . He learns presently! He sees others next to his puddle of smoke imprisoned between the last of tobacco and the filter and they never break until the innocent see his tattoo and free him. . . Dump the cigarette and let him out!! But you know Chief. . . it takes him a long time to forgive the others because he is raised a separatist and something holds him back from asserting his kind even if he knew it!! Until learning that logically he is still a portion of tar!!! The separatist is given one wish to hope that it will all end in his favor when time stops. . . but that is when the tar is already used and the blood that runs through the veins is a taste of separation. . . that is when the society shows its ominous figure as though separated into space. . . . !! Chief you have to agree that we count!!" Casino pauses waiting for an answer.

Minister's attempt to expose himself had come from nowhere. His intimate rapport with the others (ministers) did not quite explain anything except that colonel had brought up the possibility of a cabinet meeting while they wondered why chief had been against it since the start of this conflict. The wife persisted to get answers and colonel was speechless until finally interrupting her with a sigh he promised to look into the loss of the minister as soon as possible. He promised her that nothing would happen to him. He apologized that he had to go and take care of some matters at hand. Among them the abduction of the minster of agriculture! Although he held high hopes for something. Something that would happen soon as he stepped into the hallway of the palace heading for the communication room where there was a computer, a few phones, radio transmitter, a satellite television, and a number of other broadcast equipments. Also, direct lines to the radio station, the island nation newspaper, and the army headquarters. He sat down with a piece of paper in front of him and began writing a few words when he picked up the palace inbound phone and inquired the administration officer about the ambassador. He was fine yet still under suicide watch. Colonel, now helpless, hung up and without moving his eyes thought about the man from liberation-Casino. In truth, they didn't know each other as Casino believed the cellular phone was holding chief's number on dial and colonel still wondered how and why he had been called on chief's private number, and who was Casino who had not introduced himself. For him, the moment pressed like the urge for a shot of rum!! The thirst for victory and to end the misery that now built itself like the eternal spider web. *Where were they going? What was the liberation getting at?* He finally stood up pacing the room in quiet and counted his steps in search for escape from this unwanted demeanor of his country, or was it!!? Was island nation escaping herself or the soldiers just fancied to give up like the scattered clouds flying over this hole in the sea. He had to ask, but he had done his best insofar as he could finger through his greying hair and absently bite his upset stomach sipping his rum he had poured from the privately labeled palace's bottles kept locked at the communication center for the top echelon. Looking through the half-opened window he observed the changing of the guards that was still done meticulously using a borrowed discipline from the colonists with imported fatigues and guns not fully paid for yet. In Watermelon Parallel army (military) was an inheritance like most newly independent nations around the world who remained short of trained forces during the aftermath of assuming the rule. The either bought it or were granted a temporary army. Professional soldiers, mercenaries, and a minimal number of draftees made up every army the colonists set up throughout the Watermelon Parallel-only a few degrees from the developed nations on the world map.

"We don't make decisions! We only claim what must be. . . by now. . our right to freedom!!! We hold sides with the poor and illiterate!!! What sustains the majority desire. . . . Chief. . . we are persuaded by the movements of the natural population into real life. . . ! Those rights that are denied. . . and those privileges that are hidden away make up for the reason that makes us fight! We are not intentionally taking lives. . . . And any more of this resistance. . . it could cost us and you many a generation to make up for it!!!. . . . About him! We will hold him in a cell as we deserved according to you. . . until our demands are met!! We would remain in pursuit of compromise or whatever that would replace it by virtue or an act of man. . . or whatever left of us by then! One thing chief. . . . do not try to bring us down because you think you find us hostile!!!! Believe me we are not left any other option save for what is being done and the way it is done!! Our prisoner even agrees with us completely and. . . . he claimed to be helpless towards the regime!!!!

So. . . I have confidence. . . at least for now. . . in you to follow the path of wisdom and observe this situation with utmost care weighing your choices!! Time is short and we are ready to give up lives if necessary. . . and so are the people of Island Nation!!!!!! As for the minister. . . prison leaves a man with his desire to fly over. . . ." Casino continued as quoted earlier.

"You cannot do this!!! You know you haven't seen the real impact of our army. . . . you know you will loose!!! What do you want!?? This is a tragedy which at the end will only be a loss to you. . . . The righteous people of this island know this very well!! I want a solution as well as you. . . but you are making it harder to find one. . . . !!" Colonel answered and the call is over.

THE MIRAGE

15

Promiscuity undertakes the task so that individual freedom extends its limits into no mandom blistering the sore toes of the spirit of freedom that now walks its destiny into the nights. The streets are all occupied by panhandlers and other stuffs related to this freedom they called "freedom". On that street the old ministry sits so elegantly that the locals familiarly compare it to the ultimate architectural masterpieces of the world although the site is a modest command center of the pre-independence colonists. It is older than twenty years bearing no tangible history except that the minister always pays the beggars or waves hands for the prostitutes, that yet hold the 'moral ground' in the capital, before entering this building. It is hard to turn around their lives, teach them literacy and hygiene, and to bring them to an honest and fruitful family life! Alas, what they do doesn't pay much!! The ministry now is scrutinized regularly inside and out; it stands among a dozen or so government facilities and probably is among the top five in the island for its size and significance.

It is the headquarter of the Democratic Liberation People's Party.

Men in half-uniforms, untucked and black with large buttoned pockets, are guarding the streets in isolation rather than in uniformity like an army or a police force. They are a new force with laws and a discipline that draws a picture of revolution never-taken-place! The Liberation presents itself in an abysmal method. To oppose, stand up, impose, and it strives to regulate the veins of this shattered island. They are the armed children of the history which attests their justice, and are those who bring peace any way they can. Now and then, a small altercation or a minor issue of ideological nature occurs to be their business as they would generously react based on the new protocol. They look like an army acting harmoniously although without a military discipline yet purely political. Black fatigues without ranks or identity, they are covered under a new shield with an old exposure. They are the power that would bring people under one umbrella, the power that would feed people and serve them truthful promises of the coming glory, the days of an everlasting immunity.

We come to you and your kins without blood or revenge standing against the winds of the ocean, with loyalty to brothers and we'll join, we'll unite, we'll stand falling through the reality by a few distances away from ideals. But they would never gain color or form when guns shape the silence where there is no rule but fundamentalism. Perhaps, we start from the basics and feed them on to bring men and women together for a phase or two as our children would live and blood would baptize the society with dignity and justice through humane rights compensating for a loss forgiven if there is any power left to sustain it.

Armed and yet indigenous to elections the People's army guard the party headquarters like turtles guard their nests; not so loyally but obedient to nature and natural process and ongoings on the streets. The force is quiet; the capital sings the song short of joyful prayers and apart form the war that brought Liberation to party-dom. These days mark the recaption of the revolutionary Liberation and cooperation with the government who is yet ruling the Island Nation. The agreement for a new cabinet and placement of the LIberation into a party has been established after the peace treaty to put an end to the atrocities and possibility of domestic war. The army has accommodated them little by little allowing them into the system just like an old sea turtle carrying a bait on his bite. The form of this placement, as planned, is designed so the pro-Liberations are quieted as they have persisted with protests and distribution of propaganda. They have held a stronger fighting face than the government and as they became a party, the third in the Island Nation, it led them to expand their wings across the island further out of only the capital. The rule of leadership, majority, is presently not the focus of LIberation. What moves them is autonomy; a magnetic power to absorb the people-as many of them as possible. The concessions to Liberation's legalization come as a long shot that it might, as it has, bring peace to this island, and it is the election that would lay down a shift of power. They feel that the end to suppression has come, although it is not yet clear what kind of majority they would earn during the upcoming circumstantial elections. *How important is it!?*

Casino has already begun, as the lead party member, to set his administration in order and raise a hand in freeing the political prisoners. For one, he requested the search for Salome and, thus, her absolute freedom. The red tape would significantly blur the picture as for a lot of other prisoners; the government sometimes denies the existence of some of them due to a taciturn administration. The Liberation Party, in need of endorsements, is headed into elections with minimal support of the government and backing of the poor as well as the revolutionaries and most of the small intellectual society of the Island Nation. They have been doing what they can to get to the center where the votes are which means a lot insofar as gaining as many seats in the legislation as possible.

Salome has raised eyebrows during the historical standoff and, among the protestors, she is an important member of the island's concerned citizens. To Casino, she is an endorsement of the old school intellectuals that have once provoked the father of the movement, Cyrus. These crucial days, as history calls the shots, have puzzled the party, the Liberation guards have calmed the streets and districts under their control, but the aim for Casino is to free as many political prisoners as possible, especially those who have contributed to the earlier stages of the uprising. He believes this can enhance the morale even further to create a strong sense of pride among the dismayed and mystified who now are about to have a choice! The Liberation is in denial about the votes which curtails them to bureaucracy that focuses on the attempts of the army to yet create another burden upon them. The army stands strong but in a compromise; people matter yet what prevails is a call to mediocrity. It bewilders the officers to see they stand side by side along a bunch of amateur guards with those grotesque partial uniforms they are quickly becoming a rhetoric issue and much joked about. However, the strength of the guards once proven is a significant factor in the future elections. Votes would not explain anything it is thought and public opinion in the island, at its all time low, compares to a model system proven to be ineffective. The two sides quietly play according to the other's rule as a show of peaceful and bilateral trust. *What could keep people from disappointment and give them hope?* The hungry and illiterate hold a majority in this coming election and it is reason enough why Liberation tries to play by the cabinet's rules at least until they could direct and manage part of that cabinet, hopefully, in a near future.

Coalition, Center-Left, and the new party, The Democratic Liberation People's Party ostensibly conclude the political vision of this government through the status quo at the Island Nation. But the dimension of functions and the workload of each forsee the elements that at this point would be overwhelming as the will to manipulate each other greatly takes advantage of shares that have to be assigned to each party after the votes are casted. Coalition, synonymous with the army is in control of the nation and would be until the rolling of the new votes. The ministers participate in its functions and they are as always the same usual command of the army and all governmental operations that have anything to do with manipulation and tampering of the budget, directly or indirectly, while Center-Left is a paper tiger only standing against the Coalition at times of critical nature-when they could find no excuse for an absurd act or political wrongdoing. Center-Left plays a safety valve in the channels of this small government. They are apparently to crowd the elections with new candidates decorating the ballots and the arena of Island Nation's politics through liberal notions of individual freedom and all the rights to participate in one's government, indeed. Alas, this has triggered the sentiments of the people, the majority lower class that now has begun to relay discreet messages about rights, freedom, and most important of all the welfare that Liberation has already started to deal with. Its leadership, although, has focussed primarily on the release of the political prisoners; according to the Democratic People's Liberation Party there is to be no political elements remaining in jail-those who have had a hand in the revolution and have participated risking their lives.

The desk covers a good portion of the room at the headquarters, office of the principal director, protected by armed Liberation soldiers who guard not only the building but their own lives and police the capital as an auxiliary operation too in order to control a share of the security arrangements. The government of the Coalition Party, namely, as it is referred to by the media, is the decoy that covers the operations of the cabinet yet they are worried that it all may not last after the elections so they have lined up a proposal and Casino has to make a decision. For them, Casino and Harlot who have strong intentions to reach the leadership of the Island Nation plans like this are boisterous attempts at containing the order. It is obvious that the pallid pages of this proposal are, at no cost, another manner in which Coalition Party would enforce itself. Casino, astonished at the speed with which these papers and pages have built up, sits face to face with Harlot as the two men have come a long way to this conditional autonomy that is hoped to finally meet their expectations. Casino pleads for renewing their ties with the force, but Harlot admits that they would have trouble gaining complete control.

Coalition's proposal regarding the nationalization of tobacco and bringing the cigar industry under the command of the government consists of a multi-dimensional nature that keeps the two men at their seats for a few hours before they can understand why it has been provided for ratification of the Liberation Party. It is, perhaps, too early for this sort of bureaucracy; and more, Liberation does expect to have some answers to their own proposals. Casino claims that the bargaining table has become too crowded with demands that are not related to the issues at hand!! He has been having doubts about the real nature of the Center-Left that has strangely stayed quiet up until then. They should have some dialogue ready by now, he mentions to Harlot. He tells Casino that they should create an assembly as soon as possible. It is Harlot who is worried about the verbatim chaos that poses at the horizon of the future political scene. They don't appear quite satisfied with nationalization of this industry as cigars are hand rolled and the rollers are in a moderate satisfactory status hoping for higher profits after the new government is elected. . . Coalition's hope is reelection and maintaining force but at what cost!!? No one knows!! There is also a proposal to build an airport which catches the two men's attention as it is to be funded mostly through sales of tobacco, especially cigars. Casino remembers the Seahide and notes that the drug cargo is still under possession of the Liberation yet the government has been unusually quiet about retaining it. They are feeling guilty about holding up, and are interested in finding out more about the ongoings that have shaped the present government's strategy.

As it is a humid summer afternoon at degrees of temperature above a normal and friendly weather, Casino decides to set contact with the man in control of the powers of this government. He requests a secured line to the head of the army; he is expecting this call!!!

"Dear applicant:

Concerning your request for permission to exit Island Nation for abroad, the commission has found it unacceptable and not commensurate with the policies of this office. You are presently under the care of the ministry and will remain so until further action is taken to prove it void. Perhaps, you could make a new request at a later date for reconsideration. This office further finds in your discretion to fully cooperate and peacefully surrender to its purpose as a respectful citizen of our Island Nation.

Cordially,

Ministry of Foreign Affairs"

Before she can refold this letter the few officers at the room show her the way out. Her relocation now makes sense to her and she finds herself jeopardized but no idea where they would take her. Before she can step into the vehicle a distant soldier, among the group escorting her, would salute her by clapping his heals and approaching her without the others having a chance to react he bends and kisses her hand. He, then, steps back as she gets in the vehicle. The motorcade starts its short trip to an unknown location without any further due. The explosion is loud as one could hear the glass hitting the houses. The vehicle turns into a ball of fire not over two minutes into its route. Then the plan to relocate a deceased detainee continues for the purpose of bargaining. Colonel has plans and so do the cabinet to commence a new phase of cooperation with the biased army that is being trained by the ex-colonists-reliving the history. The devastation is not reported on the radio as the relocation is top secret. The car at the end of the motorcade is immediately redirected and the front vehicle of the bunch follows the former's zigzags. The flaming frame of Salome's ride remains in the middle of the remote street as the smell of burning gasoline spreads over the filthy stink of the contaminated sewers of that district. She holds on for months before she would reveal her whereabouts to the government in the hopes of an exile. She is dead; a dead prisoner, to be exiled or not! Her attention, short of normal, contains the elements of an uprising as she has delivered her figure callously to the wind. Would colonel attempt on the lives of his own men? A setup!!? It is clear the explosives are planted by an expert, but how many experts are there on the island!? This incident could easily be investigated and resolved. Later on, the paper, media, and the government would draw their own conclusions burying her in another conspiracy. Yet the smoke brings attention through blocks and blocks away from that neighborhood which seemed it has seen nothing but pain and oppression.

According to a recent attending echelon of philanthropists from a sponsoring major power half a globe away the Island Nation is claimed to be in a state of disaster. The head of this group has promised to meet the members of the parties especially the Liberation to measure the extent of which they would be able to aid and, perhaps, set up a base on the island in order to assist these people who have suffered from so much terror. He is interviewed by one of the officers of government from the communication ministry to be published in the island's daily. The chances that there would be a future opportunity in investments is quite attractive but the philanthropists seemingly prefer their charities to raise money rather than looking like a bunch of hungry entrepreneurs looking for gold. Liberation, Coalition, and

Center-Left accordingly have requested to be able to make their acquaintances with the head of this group who is a philosopher as well as a philanthropist in his seventies said to be holding strong ties with the higher classes of his home nation particularly those who have a hand in manipulating the world order in one way or another-the privileged class. The general idea is not promising in lieu of the fact that, now, Island Nation would be a serious target for the outsiders yet complexities would appear when the three parties creating obstacles decide to host this group in the uncelebrated presence of representatives of a ruling military regime. More or less, a double-jeopardy that accidentally creates a police action over these scavengers that see more in this island than what actually meets the eye. The island's recent days demonstrate resources; more resources than ever during the early stages of the electoral campaigns.

"BY THE EDITOR:

THE SEA QUEEN FESTIVAL TOOK PLACE IN THE MIDST OF A TURBULENT NATIONAL CRISIS WITH MANY COLORS PAINTING A MYSTERIOUS PORTRAIT OF PEOPLE IN ACTION UNDER AN UNFAMILIAR ORDER-GOVERNMENT. IT ACTUALLY CREATED A SHADE OF BLUNT WHITE OVER THESE COLORS EXPOSING THEM TO RAYS OF A SUN UNSEEN BY THIS PLANET. . . . ."

People are quiet; the festival is in full tilt, and the outsiders, on the verge of penetration, are seeking assistance to seal a point of contact for reasons of profiteering that has never stopped on this sea nest since the beginning of time. The outsiders, namely the Coalition, are in search of endorsements that would safe vouch improvements in the condition of middle-class (the rare layer of this community) who are capable of turning around the vote of the ruling class due to its intellectuals' influence, and nationalistic superiority that has always stood at the center of the Island Nation's culture and public opinion. Alas, the Sea Queen is decorated in fresh palm leaves, and colors that are indigenous to sea life with glitters of enormous attraction; it devastates the nation once a year with so many followers and participants, more than any other event on this piece of earth in the middle of the ocean and yet so strange to those who could command a ship safely to a destination. Island Nation has opened its doors to the world, or at least so much of that world as they could see. Philanthropists, technicians for the port, communications, health, and infrastructure; the army mercenaries and training teams, and on the other hand, the exports which yet have to be broadened into international dimensions, the tobacco, the rum, and more. Other sources, if tangible, would not be overruled, perhaps the new leadership could place a finger on them as well as the future. Also, this resentment of Liberation bears a legitimate cause called 'trust', and in many ways trust is the culprit of truth. People always look at the past. Would they open the doors for the colonists? How would they interpret this affair? Where would it all end up. . . .in autonomy or deeper dependence on foreign aid? Is an effective and functional economy a possibility? *What do we have. . . . ?*

Anton, hand in hand with a man in a black suit and an open white shirt, is watching the parade of the Sea Queen, the annual Queen of the Sea Festival; he is about four now and talking, walking, and aware of his missing parents. The truth is that he belongs to the Liberation and is protected as a heritage. A heritage that nails a landmark in discreet art of active participation; a fact that warns colonel and his men to be straight and open to the opposition. And, still, the Liberation is the force behind controlling the underground while the Coalition only can cover parts of the surface community. Issues like Anton, the son of late Cyrus, prove to be news particles of the revolutionary spirit although hardly known to the average citizen of the Island Nation. Island's daily paper is a show of public opinion. It announces:

"The famous philanthropist vows for more awareness on the island!"

"In recognition of a neo-nationalism the visiting liaison recognizes the crisis to be due to a lack of identity, and speaks for awareness and improvement of the educational system of the Island Nation!!"

"The live print should reach the north and south, the east and west! We are in an age of knowledgeability. . . . !!!"

A committee is believed to be examining the dimensions of bias, poverty, and basic needs on the island headed by the famous philanthropist/philosopher who has had a previous acquaintance with the government of the Island Nation and its short history. He has known Cyrus and has studied his trial. It is like a Messiah to relive the revolution during the pre-election period. What this team signifies is beyond any code of conduct due to its ceremonial nature and inconclusive protection of the colonel's regime. *If it is not a colonel, it is a general!!?* They hope for a fair election-first democratic election-although many political prisoners are detained under harsh and laborious conditions.

Anton stands there celebrating the Queen of the Sea parade like any other citizen of the island. Even in the absence of any arrest however his protector holds his hands from behind in a form of detention, a salute to the man who has started the modern history on those backward dry acres of the sea, his father. Anton has been located by the Liberation and delivered to the provisional army of the party for safety. His mother, no more in existence, has placed him as a member of the revolutionary dynasty that only the heads of Liberation are aware of. The surface of the Sea Queen's body is covered with turtle shells, merely a few; even her voluptuous breasts are covered with small turtle shells as well as her attractive private area so provocative that her spirit rejuvenates the mood of the men whose country is now taking another shot at taking those eternal shells off of a long buried Island Nation.

Along the other parts of the capital, a clandestine motorcade, as usual, takes Casino back and forth to a secondary hideout where he is, not only tenaciously but thoroughly working on a handout, a 'book', to be published without yet knowing why! As exposure has not been a cause until the foreign liaison rampages the limited publicity which always has kept them going. Those people who inform other people and those who ordinarily take it to the streets. Those who can read read it to the illiterate and then they expose it, still, earnestly to others on the island, the neighbors, children and adolescents that would be a force or a source. These philanthropists are making a reputation as being the first group of investigators to delve into the daily life; to express what is to be said and, more importantly, to surprise the socialistic life on the island. The motion to inform-as best as possible-the people is a focus of the Liberation. Casino wants it more than anything else. He knows that the pillars of the media and the available intellect among the islanders would some day rise and thus support the Liberation if he acted accordingly so they sit down and discuss every little detail about the philanthropists' comments, and the know-how that they have cited in their well opinionated presss release. Someone has to do it!!! A possible outcome with positive effects could speak treasures-and many sweet dreams! Finally, Casino offers a handbook to be produced, packaged, and distributed among the citizens who could read by hoping that they would share it with others. This act is to commence a campaign against a critical state of calamity. It is what to be an outline, guideline, and instruction on everything there is. He hopes that reflections of his emotional state would be shared by all of those who can have a hand in the Island Nation's unilateral autonomy.

Ministries, now in a neutral mode, remain dependent on the direct command of the Coalition and the regime. Perhaps, more than ever, the ministers cooperate, perhaps for the last time, to gain control and shift the direction of this unfamiliar yet unheard state of leadership. The smell of burning rubber and that same old routine-terror-covers the pages of a biased daily newspaper. They want to compromise and they want to direct the power into a favorable catalyst and maybe a democratic state on the surface. *Is that what everyone wants!?* Liberation, as always unaccounted for, delivers its last blow before the election through propaganda. I was in charge of working with Casino, and a couple of other members of the party when we are contacted by the notoriously lame cabinet to set up a meeting.

The assassination of Salome has not yet been relayed through the wires, but the Liberation Army has already found out, through their contacts in the government although still unclear as exactly who might have done it. And why!??

So Anton, immature and fresh, stands already as a heritage of this movement and the Liberation, but that is still so unfamiliar while, eternally, this island is sunk in a horror. Something of value now holds the Liberation in an emotional state while the wheels keep on spinning and Casino is aware that they have to move forward and overseeing everything. Elements of foul play are superstitiously evident and the face of crisis is frowning at every heartbeat as backstabbing remains in pursuit through each and every hole and gutter on the island.

Casino has long chosen to be on the democratic platform and remains as civilized as any member of a legitimate political body. The required determination and flawlessness poses a silent dialogue that we have already started to capitalize on. It is history that burns inside the hearts of the Liberation members. They know where they are. Albeit at this stage, a man knows no faith, but the faith that has gotten him where he is and that is patriotism. And peace, remaining to be a pretension, paints the thoughts and intentions of the Liberation forces.

The festival continues to cover the real identity of the Island Nation step after each step. Yet, people seem willing and energetic as an assurance to the hopes of those people one would one day remember as the unsung heroes of their times.

16

At dusk the party headquarters was buried in silence and the corridors held no tolerance for the routine sound of shoe heels and conversations that continued from one end of the hallway to the other. Only promising if at best it could bring the Island Nation to stability. These people had to nail a choice; either lose or thrive and win! It is the last frontier before independence. The elections are months away pending the approval of all three political organs. Casino steps out of his office heading for the conference room. He was holding a number of pages of printed paper that had been stapled together. As he approached the conference room he kept on going through its pages and occasionally stopping to finish reading a sentence or a paragraph. He entered the room as the door was open and there were a dozen or so of the official party heads and activists seated including Harlot who welcomed him by a show of applause while the others followed. Casino remained on his feet as he gently placed the article on the table nearest to Harlot who was sitting to his left.

"They did the best they could and I for one have done all I could to make it clear and easy. . . Out there they are innocent and we are responsible for informing them. . .

I don't find any reason why we should not begin editing it as soon as possible. You can read it. . . you can correct it. . . . or you could destroy it. . . .!! Be it before it's all too late. . . !!!!"

LIBERTY SHELL

(A DRAFT)

AN OFFICIAL PUBLICATION OF THE CULTURAL ORGAN OF THE PEOPLE'S DEMOCRATIC LIBERATION PARTY

-Despite our people's efforts to uphold the principles long ruling this land there are some necessary steps to be taken by each devoted citizen which are nonetheless part of the policy that will be subject to a collective implementation. The objectives of this campaign is to restore and paraise that which aids us in renovating and reconstructing our natural and structural assets in addition to manpower and teamwork. The latter is of utmost importance through all phases of development and upbringing our industry up to par. There will be a campaign towards nationalization and audit underscoring an era that in the eyes of our vast nation will bring excess and corrosion under control. The immediate conversion and establishment of this procedure will help us become more aware of the growth process keeping in mind that there is still a chance our nation shall join the modern world at its best.

-Let the person next to you know what you think of your neighborhood. Share information and be aware! You learn to vote by understanding leadership. 'People' is a word that enables you to feel as one body sharing its parts. Means of unity are around you in every home and shop.

-The ultimate campaign to liberate our nation will rest on the shoulders of its citizens. We will be aware, able, and ready as the process of purification and ideal application of available sources, be it natural or industrial, shape every step and vital phase throughout these paths towards social and economic progress. There are two ways to enhance our efficiency and these consist of proper human acts. Attention and tenacity will penetrate the masses through awareness and unification. Our observational abilities will bloom and become more powerful under ideal conditions that are provided to keep us universally capable of prevailing established standards.

-These steps to an eternal faith will set forth upon the reassertion of our powers; our individual endeavors in a national form that will consist of a collective faith. That which will help us gain indications of repentance and lead us toward a definite destination, one of welfare, trust, and immunity towards crisis and individual shortcomings. Let us hope, therefore, that our land remains rich as today and our roots remain strong while our children yet remain a vital muscle within the process of ascent. Community nonetheless plays a role in shaping our faith in any form be it national, social or else. The extensive process of capitalization of our cultural assets will be commencing through the path to reform; one that will encompass all factors dedicated to common ideals and a unified workforce.

-In our age of innovation and the modernism that endows it we are faced with tangible new and progressive forms. These are not to stand on the way to achievement since a form is an entity easily identified by individuals. These forms will alert us and will shape into new patriotism. You will see the forms according to the tradition and nationalism that have already been part of your endeavor for living together and upholding our social values. How people join hands and decide is a form and how they respect their decisions is another. However, let us classify these forms as a sign of freedom, our deepest hardships, and crises. Forms which pertain to your right of endeavor and hope will be an example of power and civilization in our nation.

-Our rules will be changing. Our society will be on a verge of differentiating margins of economical outcome and, specifically, political evolution that now is an imperative for holding a strong framework to continue with the contemporary nature of a systematic control over our nation's affairs. Now, individual participation plays a vital part of this principle and shall be underscored as the primary responsibility of each and every

citizen of the land. The community will duly take part in this process by providing necessary means by which the latter will be done. The process will be an apparatus built to control our nation's assets such as manpower, loyalty, and most of all individual participation that will increase our awareness. National awareness as well as social and economical will be sustainable elements which shall be rendered accordingly through political participation. This will enhance literacy by teaching each of us about the basic needs of an individual and how efficiency could be improved by timely precautions of interest groups who volunteer to present a new plan as an addition to the status quo. Our patriotism will reflect the significance of this struggle and it will help us better to be ready for the future. Our nation is awaiting us with open hands to pay respect and be the essential part of its entire affair. The structure that will hold the pillars of our economy will be stronger than ever; taking each part of the development that will be a landmark in our history as a total effort. This collective campaign will be a public phenomena and not a private one.

-Living conditions, welfare, and peace in our communities will merely reflect minimal hazards to the wellbeing of our national trust and social form of devotion. That in mind, it is obvious that there is a need for a fresh generation of patriots. Those which put aside self-interests in order to serve others as well as our valued communities. The communities provide a more tangible process of association between officials and the good citizens that play a major role in this mechanism. Our living provisions will be, too, at their lowest rate of waste, chaos, and separation. We should uphold the latter as a sign of rapid modernization and compatibility of our cultural ties.

-Our beliefs always hold an important role in shaping our ways of cooperative existence and compatible living styles. The main

factor in this area of our efforts towards progress is union; this union is brought about based on our existence and individual trust. The decision to believe in certain ways or to choose one from the other can be a lifetime path to proper growth yet let us not forget that an individual can only be responsible for certain elements of belief and not all that he is presented or is told. Thus, the role of a patriot is limited to a group of tasks that are set to fulfill physical and logical outcomes in a manner compatible, accordingly.

-It is a blessing that now we have an actual opportunity to sort and monitor rational options and clear the way for the future masses, be it man, woman, or a child. Let the nation present itself to you as an apparatus for emancipation. The numerous groups that we respect as the clan regiments who lead our stronger national affairs undoubtedly can play a central role in our political system. How we officiate and capitalize them as a force is a choice you are given to practice and respect as your undeniable right. Insofar as our government allows for logical and theoretical evolution, we as patriots and supporters of the former and the latter have an individual responsibility to retain an order providing a balanced environment in the society and the politics of this nation. Remembering our heritage and longstanding history virtually helps us overcome bias and those confusions that come with every step forward. We are equal. We are all parts of a union that upholds individual values regardless of our social, national, or international status. Step forward to express your opinion and freely pass on your message. There is no one allowed to be a barrier against your welfare as long as this nation could depend on individual participation and the autonomy rooted in the hearts of its citizens. Individual values are an exceptional classification that will keep the society in its desirable form. The systematic

China

apparatus including the administrative chapter and various branches that culminate into a conceptual government vitally depend on such classification to survive.

-Occupational fields will be the wheels of our economy turning to supply the market with a higher degree of efficiency. This new economy will uphold professionalism as well as a full scale production line which will include technical and agricultural assembly lines to present pour highly demanded products to the world. The supply will outnumber our previous inventory and will become a competitive token of our new productive system while the concept is sustained in exchange for available manpower. The latter, now a theory, will be a reality as the masses become specialized in various fields of the industry. These applications will further help the nation to renovate and expand the construction of its infrastructure and the public domain.

-Community affairs and inner community activists count for an absolute nationalization of our humane and individualistic assets. Each new color in each of our communities present a step up on the ladder of growth. Progress originates in the hands of men, women, children and elderly, neighbors and friends; even so a classified society within the dimensions of its basic framework requires its communities to maintain uniformity and active participation of all fit, members in various fronts and categories of government and business activities. Communities stand strong because of their participants and they grow when children grow and fathers find work or start a business. Community education is limited but enough so to provide the basic knowhow in order to enable each one of us to provide and strive for life's better opportunities. Those segments of our communities that are significant such as education, culture, and religion are exemplified assets to our nation. Our

efforts to keep them prepared and in use count as a national campaign for the people.

-The horizon is plain to see and lessons to be learnt when the nationalism begins to shine upon all frontiers, bringing alive each and every member of the hardworking and loyal mass of our nation's willing population. The poor and the rich will join hands to cherish the tumultuous movement of economic and industrial growth all equally playing a vital role in this progress; they will raise the standards of our lives. There will be one faith, one direction, and one nation. Our various communities will only believe in progress, liberty, and a national tradition of trust. Belief in one another and joining hands will endorse our nationalistic aspirations and, thereon, the path to a promised economy will be clear. These factors and others as you will encounter them should be amply sufficient and will support the prospective skeleton of an ideal equilibrium in all phases of production. You will find that intellectualism is not unnecessary as that class will remain the iron core of this society. The classes will approach non-stagnant paradise and therefore all branches of the production sector will be equally benefitting from this phenomena. The early shimmers of the light that will identify with a faithful society would only appear if we subsist and remain loyally attached to the principles that have long been followed on this soil.

-Our sources of support and income, today, deliver a difficult pattern that for some could prove tense and out of control, yet opportunity flows on our land with nature, society and a fresh economy stampeding into a new era. Helping a citizen to stand on his feet will be a priority without a cause for greed. The frontiers of education will soon divide us as engines of growth. These wheels will turn as a powerful element that would put the youth on a prime platform to pull forward. Equality is only

steps ahead and will, for years, focus on the labor force; a force which will broaden the possibilities with new opportunities for everyone.

-Your country is the promised heaven that brings innocence and justice to you. Thus, serving the community helps make our nation a better nation. We decide our own fate through our simplest acts that would either improve or degrade the wheels of progress. Each man and woman should consider a day as a chance to render duty and assume responsibility, those which help others and themselves. The leaders carry a two-sided banner that lies or could be truthful as a man will have the freedom to see it either way. Members of our community play the role of justice upon their leaders by creating them truthfully. Pledge your honesty, work with dignity, and play the role of the good citizen as best as you could. This land bears its unique value as a consequence of an earnest struggle throughout history.

-Progress will teach each of us about our ability and those strengths that always help us through the ebb and flow of our lives. Progress is an evidence of true freedom that exists because we create it by just deeds and patriotic individual endeavors. The people are held as the most powerful force in any land, be it ours or any other. They build the social links that educate us toward proper cooperation and strong opinions to improve our lives. We join hands only through complete devotion, and role playing sets the limits that will, in the future, draw the desirable boundaries to an expansive social economy. Liberation always existed and yet exists, in the present, not in the heart but on the plains and farms. It lives on always on its powerful pillars to persuade humankind to believe in the self and implicate the members of that self into better use. Learning about progress redefines economical literacy; it backs our history with evidence of conscious awareness and yet sharing it, as well as defining it.

-It is now plain to see us as part of the world which lays in pride and harmony. Embracing civilization is not a sin. It is a voyage that humans find honorable. The means of progress are only closer and significant. You can turn your back to each other but that is only when you are standing in a line to serve the same purpose in union. Our common goal leaves only a few options for chaos and lack of determination. This land bears many a heritage that will maintain the aforementioned.

-In science and myth, without an exception, the truth is clearly in view. There are no doubts that we are capable; that we are focussed, that we will reach the ultimate haven, that we will take away the victory with dominance and pride. Family will play a significant role in the future as our communities will require moderate and consistent cooperation of their adult members. It will keep us united and pave the way for the youth. Our plan for an ideal home is among the imperative systems of modern times. With collective attempts at completion and application of routine dialogue and essential knowhow that is derived from daily encounters with social needs and public welfare helping others becomes a simple act and will lead us to goal in the long run.

-The main plan will be to capitalize on communicational and commercial channels. For our economy meeting demand is of utmost importance. Outside of the borders is where it all lies, and that should be a simple way of pursuing our goals. Validity of a common denominator among the active forces remains no more a question as we are in an era of national reform. Labor now is a standard word for achievement in the best manner possible. Its age old role that has made progress very conspicuous and will do so in broad terms. Leadership accompanies brackets of skill that, with group support and resistance to bias, will be

assigned based on dedication and voluntary education and training.

-For every man there is a place in this society. Usefulness will be noted in the eyes of the nation and will be respected so the task at the hands of the masses become our direct objectives in the process of achievement. Our goals will deny us many opportunities that are sacrificed upholding our deepest regards for patriotism and comradery. A legitimate path will provide our plan with the required momentum and, then, people could step forward. An important issue to be remembered by all is the eternal link between civilization, progress, and man. It will settle in the flourishing phases of the aforementioned as man gains control of his destiny by observing progress in its purest form. Upon meeting target levels each front will shift into a new category of plans with newer targets. That will help us understand and implement organized campaigns.

-Man's process of thought has long been exemplified as one of the most advance structures to have shaped the evolution of our society. There are other elements that complete this evolution aside from time and nature. The wealth of our land should be accounted for as an elemental force throughout its history. We will not starve to turn the wheels in the right direction. We unite and struggle against each crisis with proper understanding of our principle forces. Those are the ones which do not distinguish man from woman, poor from rich, or weak from strong. The urban efforts always separate us from our compatriots and that, however, will reach a new direction in sharing our different economies. The various classifications of a professional society are divided by skills which are rationed such as literacy. They could enforce an asset-based coordination of masses that eventually enable our government to be accordingly

shaped into an historic form. You, as the people, are all equally responsible for that structure, be it logically or physically.

-Prediction of our future in material terms has many derivatives while the best outcome will always be credited as righteousness, justice, and honesty as many other humanly values that we as a nation should never forget. We will be reminded time and time again throughout this era and later ages that it is the presence of values that helps our country to stand on her feet. Powerful and proud, in good form and prepared, we can do many things without stopping to believe. Those values are collective assets that are found everywhere, among a family in a factory, between men and women and children, or any other directive source of production that exists within our borders. The movements and mass-conversion of our ideas could not be any more progressive as sometimes are the daily events of turbulence and chaos. Our strong belief in each other and a flawless tradition of unity should be enough evidence to pursue the right path and avoid being misled.

-We will unite and call upon our heritage to make the right decisions. We will uphold the rules of our society, respect tradition, and perform the honest rites of this land. Each citizen holds as a right the pleasure and deed of trust and confidence in the other. The morality that surrounds us is a clear sign of the will and the momentum that will expand the horizon and empower us as the root and the evident derivative that always has played a strong hand in our history.

-Those freedom fighters that at the instance of crisis and desperation help us and bring us to our senses will be the sheer force of reason and peace; an invaluable asset to our nation as all of you could join them in a collective effort to correct poverty and deprivation. Our forces will protect the land justly solely

to sustain the mot empirical element of all, that of national security. A peaceful nation is required to pursue all means of stabilization and deciphering outsider forms of betrayal and conspiracy. On land, sea, and the blue skies of this nation the color will be that of calm and prosperity as each of us will be playing its part to present that color in a brighter shade every day. Our future has always been at the hands of the present and owes its existence to the past. A secure nation will rescue us through good and bad, ups and downs, and dark and vivid moments by remaining prepared and alert towards undesired attempts of the hostile forces. The masses of patriots have been blessed with courage and dignity on all fronts; yet this would only fulfill a portion of the required force to immunize a process of utilization which will bring with it a more logical pattern of peace and order. This will include a long phase of assembly and training.

-Our people are of a genuine breed that reflects on our nation as the glares of the sun on a diamond. Many facets of our society can now claim universal standards that are symbolic of modernization. The unity is immense and has resisted social and political turbulence. Our society is no more a battleground. Young and old have joined hands. Rich and poor no more resent each other. A new generation will conquer the frontiers of our civilized society, and reconstruction continues to be in the hands of a powerful mass. We need to be reminded of the strongholds that uphold trust, dignity, and courage at any period of the history as well as the promising future that has already sketched its vivid path.

-A free mind exists. It can think. It can build homes. It can protect us against the acts of nature. It can lead us to unknown frontiers where justice and righteousness will keep our borders immune from our enemies. On our land, leadership is not going

249

to be a sin; we need leaders and politics. Every citizen plays a role in politics and has to feel counted and respected.

In plain view, we should see future first, and then present, and finally take advantage of the past by being earnest and nobly learn to correct mistakes and step forward.

-Those of us who know about the nature and society will be able to teach others same as were taught upon them. Truth will never remain buried; however, the individual acts would reveal it to properly improve welfare and our daily lives. Therefore, avoid loitering and warn others against discrimination. Our society is growing. Our land is precious. We have assets that belong to patriots. They will help us sow the seeds of progress for generations.

-Primitive or advance, thinking minds never reach desired results in any field while practice and hands-on accomplishments have proven to be the ideal method to target industrial and economical positions. Our place in the world should be procured all necessary know-how that solely comes from real results at home. The demand is accessible and sources are available in sufficient shares for production, sale, export, or other means of distribution. Trust your strength in any field or profession that makes a part of our honorable nation. Trust your honest cooperation with those who teach you what they know. Respect is the essence of professionalism, and professionalism is not a game of minds. It is a reality that an actual experience with a medium should introduce its nature to you. This mechanism begins with a handshake as you get to know one another. The economy, however, consists of a collective force to improve the ways of living among many other campaigns that lead to growth and progress. Commonality, therefore, has already begun to

demonstrate these angles through which we can observe and learn from our actions.

-Let us face our political system with regards to its significance toward national security. The political imperatives are nothing more than our daily encounters and what each of us want them to shape themselves accordingly in search of the ideal day. System or no system we always primarily belong to the origins. Those mainstream origins that have shaped the world into what it is now. The majority rule is tribal and a tribe is a social form since early on. The power used to be in the hands of one. Now, power is practiced in all accounts of an administrative system and further divides into good and bad. What is good power now is a phenomenal issue. Is it the practice or taking advantage of it that gives it a name. Or bad power is the one that stands against good power? Power is not chosen but yet implied as a tool of influence and capability. System exists by the degree of its power and it rules our society. Should power be put in the hands of a few or all? Our many efforts to overcome issues have proven to be chronicles of division of power.

-It is our candid thoughts and indisputable loyalty that carries through this age the one element which will establish the desirable order in this society. The union of masses from all parts of this land and a total compromise among them will be a major focus that should be our target. This nation's ability to measure and exceed desired phases of development will soon prove the higher values of our communities priceless. The national pride already rules the home, the family, the schools, and other social institutions. We should remain committed to the ultimate plan which is growth and health in each and every home.

-Do not oversee a revolution and interpret it as a chance toward failure. It is the workforce that is supported by a political

referendum and this force eliminates poverty and destitute. A thoughtful citizen can make a change and among others bring into reality desired results that will play a positive role in our future. Share those moments that help you create ideas towards innovation and progress in the community. Common thought is not a blame. We need to reach a compromise before each and every decision to assure that the citizens of this land live by common methods of participation and righteousness. There is a recognized place for justice at each phase of development however complex the issue. The logic will aid us define the right from wrong. Place your wisdom in an order as simple as the steps that you take toward a friend. Begin with basic logic and learn from your deeds.

-People, rich or poor, young or old, join hands and look forward positively with objectives in mind that will show the right path to you. It is a human justice and being fair that places all men in a higher moral ground. And, do not question your pride or lack of individual ability because we will beat the abyss jointly and live together as a proof to our fidelity. Hold hands in times of crisis and depend on the others as you trust yourself. We are now in an age of inner power. Morale is only one part as are energy, interest, and dignity the collective and componential assembly of our active modern age which we do not need special education to learn how to uphold and profit from them. Group activity will help us put our stronger communicational values forward and follow towards a powerful uniformity of public opinion and social expression of human ideals. Vocal union and joint efforts in various groups and gatherings shall prove to be the imperatives of a political reconstruction for this nation as well as any other. Let us not rest yet place our mind and body into it till eternity.

-We will have a system which will be converted into different methods in order to protect our nation. System is discussed and thus procured in progressive economies. It is what we follow and live by through each and every detail it provides. In order to secure our society and bring it closer to a functional government, it is the system that guides us. System deals with citizens as individuals and not masses. A guideline is the natural part of a system that is legitimately established.

-The theory of unity and movement retains all factual existence of individual opinions and proves them to be the sole elements in shaping change, namely, revolutions. Revolution is not the only solution, however, as it might occur every hour after hour. Production can in any form be a staged revolution as well as new teams and societies of trained labor. Freedom is one form of revolution that will show us its multi-dimensional outcomes in all fields of production such as industrial. There are many ways to achieve optimum levels of mass participation. Those will help the individual to understand and communicate. The results of these observations should be shared and understood; therefore, they will be among the essential principles of our future economy.

-The freedom that will be symbolizing our national trust identifies a few principles that have not yet quite been introduced. Our society, now ready for promotion, will take into body those principles at its various times of procession through crisis or other progressive moods. Our liberal aspirations will once again flourish perhaps in a different from and shape. A profile of all the elements, such as the objectives of a campaign, involved in the aforementioned growth will compile in a democratic nationalism. That which will be comprehended by the lowest of the classes, and even applied by the middle class to direct us to an equality of industrial and economical factions in our nation.

The degree of progress in this marginal development determines the actual strength of those factions and will bring about easier conditions and circumstances towards accountability. We are cautiously entering a new age of industrialization. It will assist us to better see the fate of our proper land and the future frontiers of our constant growth. Progress in this nation as well as any brings about the advantages that point at its speed and legitimacy. We should commit fully to its new and yet unidentified nature, and remind ourselves of the long path left behind. Organizations of our government will be in need of change at any time. We must be ready to dedicate ourselves to those duties that initiate such change indeed with perfect attendance and an appropriate pattern of thought.

-As a whole, the national recognition of the inner structure as well as the outer functions of our collective government will be a desired logical solution against bias. You will be at the center as the parameters will protect our growing society along with its many participant organizations. The system will be an intelligent one and, at such levels, will require full participation and subjective bargaining between itself and the people.

-Our peace has outlasted our history now that we are on the path to freedom. This is a logical resolution that illustrates the consequence to moral struggle that will occupy our daily encounters with many questions. Let us be reminded that a skilled force and the ability to better interpret your social environment is the answer to such logic. This will be an extended hand to aid us and help us find explicit solutions to bring about peace and solidarity in more ways than one.

-Our nation's international role has consistently underscored many prevalent aspects of our noble diplomacy which will assist us in implementing its peaceful nature along with domestic

conditions that can be thoroughly reformed into systematic steps towards promising results. Our world interprets peace in various ways. Our nation will prevail accordingly and will initiate its unique and indigenous means to express peace through every message. The political freedom can be peaceful. Social strength has been tested through ups and downs of a long-term campaign. It will, too, uphold a collective search for a proper pronunciation of an ideal peace. Individual freedom will shape itself based on what future creates as means of production, evolution, and partition with the past. So, peace, too, is a form of progress.

-We will be oriented with the classical society as well as our individual classification through multi-faceted developments that in the long-run will demonstrate a methodical approach toward our ideals. Individual roles are what makes up our present system. Members of the society will associate with such classifications though various modes of progress. Your role in the society will be defined as clearly as such methodical interactions would cooperate to sustain its essential identity. Social communion and practice of imperative rights will categorize our national capabilities in ways as to identify this nation in the world. Let us have the utmost confidence in our society and uphold the principles which make it eternal. The path to unity, ideal cooperation, and ultimately progress will be a result of this formula. It is the fate of our nation, that which is underscored as growth.

-All facets of our society have been growing into progressive modes of existence. We are now in control of our classes. These forms promise future education in fields of scientific, conceptual, and indeed economical nature and, that is, symbolic of our mass effort ahead. We will not deny any class the right to autonomy and social success. They can build this society as it fits into an

ideal path. The society has a nature of dividing us, as people are classified through natural cycles of growth while tending individual campaigns to bring a brighter future for us. This method, as a unique mode of a natural society does not hold as a principle its crucial interactions or diversions towards rich and poor, yet it sustains those elements that support some expertise over the other as it is due and helps our communities maintain desired levels of production, education, and welfare of their members. Classification is an identity that, as a prevalent method of association, could bring illiteracy toward conceptual participation to an end and and proclaim new individual rights that would endorse economical security and, thereby, coordinate the affairs of a nation. We will need active participation on the part of all classes. Each phase of such concept, aside from its logical reality will be a reassurance fro each and every citizen to respect and uphold that which will show us our means of living and better maintain our citizenry toward each other.

-Stability only affords to create a balance in and under conditions of peace that affect the present status of our economical growth. However it could be further developed into its primitive yet new forms to participate in all fields of our national progress towards an ideal modernism. This logic is an action foremost and mainly aimed at the altering nature of our social order nonetheless as a total definition for a planned and thoroughly calculated plan in any nation. We are near a destiny that will be historic and will be illustrating all acts of struggle that we, the loyal citizens of this land, have committed and duly volunteered. Other aspects of a subjective stability explain, through periods of occurrence and constant monitoring, that stability and the logic behind it are themselves unstable. Its nature is volatile and subversive. Yet, we decide what shall suit the status quo of our nation. Its role in the culmination

of the relative elements to bring us to equilibrium has proven that stability is interpreted in different manners. It shapes in many forms and holds vast fields of interaction that have deep effects on our patterns of behavior in agriculture as well as technical areas of our predesignated economic plans. Our eyes will see before long that which legitimizes the chosen fate of our descendants as well as the hopes of the grand predecessors that painted this landscape into our history.

-Past is always in the present; it would return and teach us the good it has done us and it will help us decide on our future. Day begins with strength and determination for everyone as people choose how to put time into the wheels of progress. Rational thought will find its path towards the masses and will aid us in cooperation and division of tasks. Horizon is a form of future that is widely observable to each and everyone. People cover the community; their children, the playground, and this rite is an essential factor in our welfare.

-Our capabilities are based on our social assets and individual role. The era of bias and critical role that economy plays in any land will shift into a new direction by endorsement of the labor force and the muscle that shapes the market. Bless them to be blessed and hail them to be hailed. We will be noted in the eyes of the world that surrounds us the same way as the mainstream nations are recognized. Our target should be justice for all citizens. It will soon be evident that the active participation of people, in all, is the utmost movement that shall occupy tomorrow's frontiers

17

On that humid yet tropically moderate morning Casino and a coupe of other party members were trying to hang Cyrus's enlarged mugshot on the wall of the conference room of the ministry. It had been especially printed and framed for this occasion. The Liberation headquarters, the old ministry, held a central image in the capital of Island Nation. Daily, more and more participants visited this party facility, and some joined while others volunteered to participate in the campaign as well as preparations for the upcoming election. Casino, still awaiting the boards's approval on the distribution of "*Liberty Shell*", was saying a prayer as they were correcting their visual expectations by walking around the hung frame and bending their heads to left and right while interpreting its visual position; they had smiles on their faces as that enlarged mugshot meant a lot. Incidentally, one of the three was a member of the group that had escaped from the Island Nation's prison on that stormy night.

The door was open however a knock took away their attention as it sounded like a hurried sign of alert. Four armed guards with black uniforms forced a man onto the conference room while one kept on slapping him on the back of the head and pulling his ear lobe as the hits had provoked that man to burst into tears; he cried loudly and begged forgiveness. Casino signaled the guard to stop the punishing.

"What is the matter Samuel!? What has happened!? You should be waiting by the car!!" Casino asked.

The guard stepped forward and raised his right hand placing it on his left chest. "It's them!! They were trying to bribe him. . . . we still don't know what they wanted,. . . but Samuel spent over half an hour talking to their people. . . . !!!" He hit him hard on the back of his head and continued. "They either wanted information or were planning something with this idiot!!! Please let us take care of him. . . he is a disgrace to the Liberation! He is a traitor!!! We don't need people like him here Mr. Casino!!!!"

They held him roughly anticipating a task or Casino's command to put him away, but he showed them the door, "You can leave. . . I want to talk to Samuel!!" Casino informed the guards. They stepped out of the conference room where Casino and his comrades were standing under the 20" by 30" mugshot, and there was a six-digit number hanging from Cyrus's neck; his face young and bruised as it had apparently been taken after torture.

"Samuel you've been with Liberation long enough to know that you are one of my trusted men. . . This seems strange!!! What set you to commit to join them!? What do they want? This is the time to tell us everything. . . . You know better than selling yourself to the opposition. . . . . ." Casino was interrupted by a short knock as Harlot walked in with something in his hand. He came closer and raised his right hand placing it on his left chest, "They knew. . . . !!!!" He exclaimed and sighed. "What? What they knew!!?" Casino demanded. Harlot raised the small handbook he was holding and pointed his right hand index to it. "This handbook was being distributed by the Central-Left people at the plaza. . . Don't you get it!!? We have a rat in this organization!!!" He shouted.

"Calm down Harlot. . . Let's not get ahead of ourselves!" Casino responded.

"They knew we were working on a handout. . . They stole our idea. . . here. . . .read it!!" Harlot claimed breathlessly.

"Samuel! Who are these people and what do they want from you!!?" Casino asked.

Samuel cleared his tears as he was still calmly weeping and finally raised his head, "It's more serious than that sir. . . . they will kill my family. . . . my wife, my children,. . . everyone!! They knew everyone and they threatened me saying they would kill everyone in my family if I didn't take a package and put it in the trunk when they tell me so. . . . !!! Sir. . . I believe they are after you, or anyone who rides the party car! I sense explosives. . . . . !! Forgive me but there was nothing else I could do!!! They would murder my family. . . What else could I do!? Forgive me sir! Forgive me please!! You know I would put my life away for you. . . but my children, my wife. . . They are innocent!! Forgive me please. . . . !!" Samuel begged in tears.

"Did they offer you anything else!?" Casino exclaimed discreetly.

"Some money and asylum. . . .they said once this so-called package is placed in the trunk everything would be alright!!! Explosives!!! That's what it is. . . . I am almost sure! The plan is for me to stop somewhere as there will be a roadblock and reach a distance from the car while they would take care of the rest!!! It is a pack of explosives. . . I'm telling you!!! What else could it be. . . . . . !!?" Samuel, Casino's driver, insisted as he kept on drying his tears.

"Let me see that book. . . . I think that the leak is from the board because I had not talked to anyone else during the last few months while I was working on the *"Liberty Shell"*!! For something like this booklet they would need at least a few weeks!! I just brought it up a couple of weeks ago. . . . That someone had known it since I produced the idea and perhaps informed the opposition right away in time to produce something like this. . . . !! Anyhow. . .. since it's been approved we'll go ahead with distributing '*Liberty Shell*' . . . !!" Casino took the booklet and let Samuel go assuring him that everything would be taken care of, and that he was forgiven. The moment was seized while Harlot looked up as he noticed the mugshot. He seemed deeply touched and reminded how far the Liberation had come, "It's too late to lose it all!!!. . . . Really! It's too late!!" Harlot uttering while he left the silent conference room.

Casino, meanwhile, locked the door behind him and sat at his chair. His office smelled of tile and humidity had reached a peak as noon was approaching. He opened the booklet while he was absently adjusting his spectacles. . . .

BEYOND THE CALL OF FIDELITY

(THE MANIFESTO)

COALITION PARTY

Sons and daughters of this land our social progress has long been idealized by the intellectual class. There is nothing to be altered among its multi-facet nature. Idealism once ruled this nation and now we are the initiatives that any idealism or system deeply desires to possess. The commitments of this government are at the discretion of its fate which underscores a structural and progressive phenomena. That being our nation, we shall all remain in pose to prove that unity and trust along with an indigenous method of patriotism as the roots of the political order undertaking the affairs of our country. And that thoroughly noted, the next era will inherit the roots of a logistical regime that has been vehemently surviving the existing opposition. This is due to expert planning and skillful procedures in classification and categorically monitoring this nation. The system always proves righteous ever since the past, and on to the present, and thus to the future. We uphold humanity and equality unbeknownst to the status quo. There are vast areas of contrast that, now as ever, greatly distinguish our nation from others which resemble it in some way or other. This valid land shall be home to the most advance instances of human endeavor; and those will be an addendum to our gold-minted history.

The organs of a ruling regime rely on support and constant watch by the branches of its government. The rules will be set so there is a framework to keep it within boundaries and, thus, a government is left the possibility of outside intrusion. The people need discreet contact by means of participation and supporting the ruling factors that inversely maintain a balance of information and communication between them and the executive forces of this nation. Our land requires a safe haven for the loyal as well as the rebellious while opportunities belong to all. We will surely face obstacles that, however unfamiliar, will keep us alert and remain a factor in pushing forward all areas of our economy. A government, as loyal as any, that sustains years of hardship in order to exceed our expectations will be a friend of people just as peaceful and partisan as a confidante and beloved companion. The elements have always favored us and they solely lead us to the same direction. This nation should be once again reminded that times are a result of dedication when they appear in dignified colors of patriotism, unity, and fidelity. Power will remain in the hands of those who yet remain loyal to our people, this nation, and the future generations. The guidelines are now political and the path to future stays as an issue which has always been debated before falling into the hands of those few. Our society is now a mature entity that has caused a house to house evolution leading to a counter culture still in a primitive phase. It will surely advance and in time persuade and nourish our most immense national ambitions.

Each individual right counts as an important symbol in a fashion now familiar in our present political domain. Both sides respect them so to compromise collectively on decisions that put a direction in one's or all's lives. It is to be upheld and protected with utmost sense of duty and puritan patriotism. We depend on each other to keep the welfare of present and future generations intact and, thereon, look further to answer the wishes of a momentous history that includes many incidents of turbulence and separation. How, indeed, a force could tolerate so much when the world looks upon us as a slim figure on the globe, however strategic and significant. This nation has been on constant scrutiny as, now, it becomes apparent that this important role is being played through our national interests, be it domestic or international. It is only a fact to say that our trust and confidence in our representatives along with national pride which keeps us afoot maintain the security and calm which is required to aid us in our plans for reconstruction, innovation, and probation of the use of force to back our strategic interests. Any essential division among the government officials or social groups that struggle to justify the cause for modernization and a better economy as well as an appropriate cabinet that would overlook such activity is already stipulated in the hands of the few that are not too far ahead of us yet require total support and a dignified show of hands to make a move. The strength of our roots should then reflect its appetite for these crucial encounters.

The natural organisms of our nation are backed by the unnatural one, the government, which is logically a natural part of any political assembly. It is that assembly's organisms which conduct leadership of its entire affair. They are the problem solvers and these members of the government or, per say, the leadership are elected or designated based on a desired degree of loyalty and tenacity to meet the ideals of an established nation. We, as government, or you, as its concerns, will be face to face, or hand in hand undertaking a central plan, that of progress, respect for individual rights, and paving the path for future generations. The domination of the leadership is much viewed as an efficient plan to bring all facets of the government to the people. Backed by a cabinet of dignified ministers and their ministries we present the government as a symbol of unity and command. It is the government that will impose its plan to improve the status quo. An entire nation shall rest in the hands of the government. Your options will be eased into such forms provided by the leadership and put into effect under the political bracket provided by the legislation. Accordingly, the justice will be ruled through the direct allocation of its participants and maintaining its utmost degrees of care in ruling the existing order. Thus, the government will appoint the ministers periodically as the terms dictate; however, the laws remain a secondary essence in leadership because the ministries shall sustain the needed balance to stabilize the legal interactions through the application of these laws.

We shall all respect our ruling ministers. They will uphold the control over various powers of the government overseen by the head of this government. The army will be under direct command of the leadership. We shall all be inspired by the unity and such ideal formation unrivaled in any part of the world. An intense centrality, in addition, will demonstrate the strong demand to avoid corruption, and pull forward in the lines of patriotism and honesty. To serve the people, a government will require its stability as well as an intended flexibility to pass through this tumultuous path which will lead our political system. Its people, a nation knows not to undermine; and by concentrating on our government we demonstrate a legendary nature with open hands to foresee and overcome obstacles whatever they may be. This network will be an effective organ to prevent rebellion as well as regional crises that have been experienced in the near past. Our struggle has yet and always been in familiar patterns that solely point out our basic needs and the intention of the central leadership will be to resolve, prepare, and arm us with those defenses which will establish a mutual peace and balance. The power will be at the hands of those whom we trust; those who dare and step forward to prove their patriotic instincts through sacrifice and engagement.

This age once again takes our fate above the plausible lines that for many years have proven to be a source of reference for all of us. The nation shall be trusted with utmost faith in its long recognized power of identity. Citizens can find the paradise through the words of wisdom that until now have kept us together in a unity unheard of. The leadership always faces doubts in the face of change. Phases of hardship not only bring strength but they have proven to be that flexibility which our nation needs in order to prevail. Confidence fills the hearts of men and women. The moment is a familiar setting that me and you have encountered often to, once again, overcome and tell our children to praise its importance and how the future could benefit from it. The silent frontiers of our nation illustrate the deep peace in the bloodstreams of our yet everlasting social resilience. An instance of critical need will be the example of oneness when it would appear on this precious soil; that is, when we are able to find a familiar reality. Those are what this land has brought us through good times and moments of hardship. Our needs are relentlessly tested and we are reminded to keep the trust that has painted our efforts.

The people and the justice ruling their lives will remain the two elements of our national trust, and it will be up to our government to control and bring peace to the society. The interaction is one of immense results having been naturally tested through history with people as the protagonist bringing a form of individual security to the nation-a nation of basic thought that has gone a long way. The government will put forth the prominent factors to operate upon, or perhaps literally the sole logic of the type of nationalism which is found to be the single efficient mean of keeping the peace and the balance to secure our nation, and put it in the correct path. Justice shall set examples. At homes, offices, public, farms, factories, and other centers of social activity justice will be ruling the people. It will free them from pain and a crisis which always insinuates the roots of our efforts. It shall be the sole organ in the structure of this nation that will separate the good from bad. It will be discreet, resilient and consistently effecting the daily routines of our people in the most intensive manner of performance. It will serve the good as well as preventing the bad from decaying our communities. Such force should not be left overlooked and shall be put into action through available facilities that make up a major part of the government. In retrospect, the justice and the government shall become one to better serve the plans that will set the proper rules for progress on this soil. The sense of just deed and patriotism will overlap and thus our nation will become familiar with the systematic flow of judicial consequence which will distinguish one men from the other based on a set judgements of law.

Serving one's country is a lesson that the people of this land will long be teaching each other and future generations. Along with daily necessities of life and following the principles of being a good samaritan and an existential paradise, our peace is the essential need of this society. It has ruled this nation for ages and has to remain stable and isolated from any critical factor. This peace is thus perceived in its various forms through protection and upholding the laws of the land; the laws executed by a strong front that supports our implementations of a ruling justice. It will form a system that would separate itself from a corrupted structure, not unheard of, by creating a versatile platform by which judgements will turn the wheels of our political, economical, as well as social developments. The system will be on the path to appropriate the needed administrative and field manpower with the knowhow to spread this phenomenal campaign in all and the entire regions of our nation. From the heavens in the sky, and at the edge of the deepest oceans there will be a single force as unique as the elements of our nature to bring us to our ideal destiny, one inspired by dignity and the choice to rule. The justice we are set to speculate and further bring into a real form will, perhaps, for ages overshadow corruption, elements of fraud, and instances of humanly crime; it too is a progressive theory that will be otherwise. By that, we mean a new method, or yet a pure form of a process of resolution which will be dictated within our national dialogues. The judgements will be collective and in shapes and forms attached to and familiar with the outlines of our respectful cabinet of ministers and the central leadership.

Like the organs of a living being a nation too has institutions which help it grow forward and become a harmonious member of the universal community. Upbringing of a growing judicial force along with a central leadership will result in some immensely sensitive affairs that would expedite developments in all fields of service and occupation, not to mention the manpower that ignites our system. The notable portion of the results will be associated with efficiency and acknowledgement of new theories and a logical behavior that will penetrate all frontiers of our new industrial structures. With this pattern, it will be much easier to stipulate future shortcomings and leave our nation in more trustable hands, that of the government. As the ministries will remain a vital part of the legislation, it will be our deeply rooted leadership which will monitor and command the nation according to the guidelines proposed by the cabinet. Let us live up to this framework that is endowed to us, and bring forth the everlasting principle which, forever, will hold the land within the fortress set by this carefully selected paradox. This government, better than any, could outlive all previously or presently established organs in a manner far beyond imagination.

This land has proven, categorically, prosperous yet benefits from a vast haven of resources that have kept it economically fit. Your money is in good hands. It is the government that oversees its activity, availability, and indeed its inflow and outflow towards international markets. The authority which designates this plan and the structure to enact the monetary engine will be one appointed and reappointed based on terms of service; it is overlooked by the central cadre that closely relays its plans and operations to the leader. This will prolong all aspects of a profitable and focused economy, especially our monetary apparatus. Among the active components of this structure, the budget remains to be virtually an imperative element in setting a control switch on what should and should not be done. The class act of budget appropriation is set to be a legislative effort, again as we know, which will be coordinated and monitored by the leadership. Our resources, geographic positioning, manpower, and the diplomatic blueprint will, in time, advance the frontiers of our domestic market to higher levels, i.e. total international recognition and self-sufficiency. According to a precedented practice, the full trust of the people and the history that has recorded its golden moments the necessary monetary capabilities will, at a time, become the root and the essence of the entire planning bracket that would shortly prevail thereafter.

The elements that make up our financial entities are limited yet could be limitless. They will play a major role in the economy and bring us in touch with the international monetary cycle as well as the world financial system. Banks relate to budget and, thereon, improve our life style by taking advantage of the services that are made available by them as our government will allow a number of these institutions to establish offices in our nation. However, we should once more be reminded that it is us, the people, who can decide the fate of our financial ability and take advantage of its dominant stamina. Therefore, your government would be as cordial and intimate as is necessary to manage and provide opportunities based on your needs and the popular demand. Our focus on the budget, as is the majority opinion of a cabinet, is of utmost importance. We believe the final vote will be a systematic quota that would be used to underscore this process at crucial points of its inception. It will be a tool to control the fluctuations of the market and keeping the people in a logically fit framework to become economy's major players. Now, as any other time, would be ideal to plan, look ahead, and step forward in order to view the possible paths one will be able to choose to overcome what future might have at hand. The options will be dictated according to what we can speculate and how an unexpected wave of barriers might sustain an inactive market. That is bad for our economy as well as the hardworking members of the community. Skepticalism in a rich environment as ours could bring sheer power and free us from individual lacks of morale. Our spiritual thoughts rest with you, the people, however our financial organizations and the monetary apparatus need to be carefully considered and constantly improved.

Each and everyone of us labor hardship and preserve our dignified life to earn and make ends meet, provide for the next generation, and most of all, shape the pillars of our economy into its perfection. This demeanor tells and draws a familiar picture but, alas, it took a history to reach its ideal form. There is always time, there is still an oasis in the near distance. The need for security and economic solidarity; the so-called utopia is at its best a very provocative motivation meaning that our muscles are flexing and expanding in different directions. The social class and unity are effective but they are not all that is required to initiate and, thus, seal that package called stability. The expanse of nations demanding bracket which in reality commence this so-called cycle into our monetary systems network activities, solely benefit from a certain group of factors that appear only under ultimate circumstances that requires them or provide an opportunity for them to trigger the appropriate force to activate that particular emission of its phases. For instance, a balanced economy only generates what is required to meet demand and maintain the prices at a desired equilibrium in order to outlast the critical factors which might hurt its evolution into the next cycle. We are required to be more careful yet, perhaps, cautious of the risks that only a skilled team can interpret and analyze in order to emit the proper force overcoming the obstacles, or profit from the right decisions. Our individual roles too are relative and it is in this manner that we could put our patriotic although intellectual strength into use. The cabinet not only anticipates a phase of change and reform, it is certain that a strong leadership would be the sole engine to defeat and prevail any hardship.

The era of stability and power has already started. Lets rise to the ultimate position logically feasible and overcome the crisis that has been in the view at this point of history. The theory and plan both are clear; it is a direct path to an independent nation that could be a claim to fame in this human history. Let all of the potential show us what we are capable of and hope that our children would someday be proud and grateful. Every society is a collective form of different and associated processes that culminate into one conceptual form; that is, the kingdom, not so logically but geographically and rhetorically. That system provides and is self-substantial. It is our future, present and past which will be building into it all components of a fine-tuned society, the ideal life. By gaining trust this regime has pulled through ebb and flow of the world politics especially those regional affairs that set limits on our opportunities for expanding our scope of exports and being able to introduce our production to far away nations. That, by itself, will be a lesson learned. Now we are standing tall and have the right to compete and demonstrate a unity of arms and prove the scarcity of this nation's values. The people of this land have the right to question the integrity of their representatives who are here to answer.

Our forces have never been in a hostile situation, threatened by a legitimate enemy as their position has always been one of peace and patriotic participation in demonstrating discipline and individual skills. Our nation now is in a different position compared with the days of the past. There is more activity on the social, economical, and political level. That all is directly associated with security and stability. The army is blessed with an important role in mediation and maintaining order. The leadership is obliged to plan and outline such operations as is performed and coordinated by the military and its leading command. We have to set target positions to achieve desired levels of foot and mobile forces in a limited timeframe which would bring us to par with the demands of pour geographic and strategic ranks. Our neighbors are becoming more powerful as well; they are a so-called regional community and we have to respond to the needs of such community according to the present international trends. It is to be noted that this regime is not initiating hostile politics or war. We are not and will not be part of the terrorism ongoing on the international arena. Our land will be a symbol of peace and prosperity. Furthermore, the forces will be aiding the domestic projects such as community affairs and internal security. The national economical progress necessitates, along the lines of its vital growth, an order which would sustain and secure all channels of trade, be it domestic or international. This is the primary initiative in the order of importance; it is to be carefully studied and regarded as an imperative in the wellbeing of our commercial market and its constituents. Through an economical cycle such provisions will be answered and cost will be offset by the outcome with which our financial market would perform. It is the intention of this

*leadership to expand and implicate the forces by such elements
as modernity and sophistication in arms and manpower.*

*In the memory of a powerful culture and long-lasting ties among
those of us who fight their enemies with an iron fist and high
spirits to pay their dues to this growing generation there is a
point that should be noted; that is again a substandard that has
for so many years suffocated this nation in many ways that now
is a good time to obliterate and replace it according to the needs
of our promised era which presently flourishes with its wings
open. In order to face this obstacle we have logically stipulated
the outcomes of a present-minded judicial ordinance. Now, we
will be ahead of our outdated ambitions merely by listening to
reason and follow the logical path to restoration and protection
of all that is, as a legitimate capability for forward efforts, needed
to carry this nation to the ultimate frontiers of progress such as
an equilibrium that will outlast our developing economy. There
are a number of phases and there is not much time that could
be spent on the sheer principle phases of this economy. We have
to act and we should stand behind our deepest commitments.
There are still a lot of reasons for an overall scrutiny, and it has
to be overseen immediately and brought under control in order
for us to regain the power to direct the nation toward the proper
path. It will be our efforts along with a fair share of resilience
and resistance that will put this campaign on its promised track.
This is the religion and there will be ample reason to put our
trust into this collective plan. Along with careful planning and
a rotational recuperation of the needed manpower we will soon
overcome ever-breathing fungus that yet lingers in the cells of
our national structure.*

*The logistics of compromise, be it our allies or enemies, will be
a burden that the cabinet will negotiate with our leadership.
It will be a promise on the part of the latter, as always, to keep*

clear against bias, prejudice, and common humanly flaws and use its noble power of judgement to bring such complexities to a desirable outcome. The regime is your regime and it will serve each and every one equally leaving this nation in the celebrated hands of its powerful nationalist intellectuals that will help our nation grow into its perfected political platform. The leadership is unique in a manner by which we will simply be able to measure our marginal steps forward and yet be warned of any critical issues or lacks that might deter the structural evolution by which the community is able to turn its wheels.

Placing justice and safe borders on the list as the imperative principles of the system will in effect bring people and government closer and this association will, at the end phase, demonstrate its beneficial effects. Those would be a higher rate of efficiency in national affairs and an ideal participatory society which would lead to superior individual education and more freedom for those who want to help the system in ways that are to them useful and patriotic. The party has already outlined the future for the constituents that long have been loyal and held the last and final vote for creating the ideal. People have shown many sides of the truth as the storms of [political upheaval and intentions not quite compatible with the nation's almost took us away from our promised direction. The path to paradise is drawn with the tears and sweat of its sacrificial patriots. Those are who we will cherish and trust our fate in their hands. Those are now among you and with you all the way. Just look to the right or the left of you and you will find them. The true life, the ideal society, and the long-envied nation will once and for all reveal its hidden face and bless us and later generations with such optimizations that would devastate all existing standards in any economy or political system. The international arena is a promising model that defines the needs of any nation in order to improve the levels of the universal economy, industry, and diplomacy. Our attention is presently focused on those nations that are compatible and systematically adaptable by our social and political system. We have long kept our eyes on those countries that have achieved ideal and optimum levels of productivity and economical solidarity. This leadership will pursue such manners of investigation and research well through the primary phases of the new era.

The free waters of the world have long proven as the vital part of commerce and strategic planning of all nations. This fact has become a significantly common item of international negotiations and commercial bargaining between the participating nations that for now it would greatly effect our economy as well as an independent member of the marine commerce since so many years ago. These phases of our commercial campaign to improve and let grow our booming capabilities require close scrutiny of all accessible channels to promote its multi-faceted nature. The aforementioned universal network will need extensive studies and circumstantial protection. The safe nature of such continental operation is the sole reason for its survival and growth. This nation, too, as an important member of the marine commercial channels, will need assistance and protection of its floating assets. These ports, under the command of our reinforced leadership, will be protected territories, one kept safe by us and international help as well. In brief, the shores of this nation will be regarded as wealth by us and all others who profit from them. An independent nation in a dependent world that will help it grow into prosperity. Our need for foreign aid has for many years in our history proven to be a vital factor in commercial and political exchanges. The negotiating table will include this iconic demand in numerous forms and items for extensive discussion. A procedural evaluation of the nation's commerce and its participant organizations will give this leadership an elite opinion of the present condition in which our exports and imports are circulating; thus later, we will be ready and aware of how to encounter the wave of economic and financial opportunities that will appear on the charts of our commercial arena; however, securing such categories of national interest will be prevalent under this leadership.

In all, this is the decision of the free mass and the leadership which will keep it free and away from harm and chaos. The nation decides which path would lead her to total victory. In order to achieve satisfactory levels of economical growth we will need to depend on those political organs which could trigger the hidden powers of our society. Putting to work our intellectual forces will be a national effort, and as a responsibility of people they should distinguish the good from bad. During the final moments, it will be essential to maintain order be it an individual effort or a harmony among this nation's devoted citizens. Our politics are elementary yet meticulous and we are struggling to achieve the final paradox by paying the price. From one hand to the other the message is clear. That which will keep us together will prevail in the long-term. Let us be one and remember our age old union against backlash and remain determined to leap forward full-tilt. You have the final moments of this evolution into future in your hands as an individual right with a single purpose, and that is trusting the one next to you and live together. Freedom is praised in its singular character yet it is placed after trust and thereafter it is the future generation that will substantiate over national pride by flourishing in the international arena as a star among others as worthy. Raise your fist to a reliable leadership especially when you can decide on its fate and be a part of this entity.

In our community, one noticeable factor has stood for ages and that is the peace and the devotion that our citizens practice to uphold it. Our tradition, our food, our homes, our family life, and that active part of this society which will again and again prove itself to be a vital element in keeping us united and ready to overcome all obstacles one by one in order to reach a paradox. This ultimate cornerstone of compromise and eternal peace requires care and protection. We worship those pieties that help raise our children, help one another, and keep an innocent conscience yet enemy does not understand any of that and its enemies as well. An enemy is destructive toward our system and our heritage. An enemy is in chaos and the only direction it recognizes is an end to its victim. We will need to keep alert and be aware that we have capabilities to avoid outside intruders from proliferating and penetrating over the line; we should know that all nations identify with such factual patterns as an imperative to the political order. This nation welcomes many different people and should maintain social order despite what happens in our communities. A stable social order helps enhance our commercial channels. We are in need of global attention and are obliged to place the latter in the order of those vital affairs that encompass any of our systems of exchange. Be it individual, industrial, or economical, we have to host all facets of communication in a secure environment. These actions require both domestic and outside aid in any form seen on a national scope. Military, and political protection aside from social groups are among the required parts of this course of action.

THE CONCLUSION

The humidity had begun its friendship with a chill lasting through early morning hours and darkness now was preparing to vanish from the small piece of earth. His bare toes dipped in the mud that was covering the fortress of his immensely modest shack. He meant to tell her everything until about four hours ago when she fell asleep helplessly. He carried his clothes with a pair of shoes to the car and by the time he cleaned his feet and was ready it was almost half past five. The drive to the shore would take him about three quarters of an hour and from that village by the sea he would still have an hour to the headquarters at the ministry. That night he persisted in blaming life for his poor family and hungry children, two girls and a fifteen-year-old boy who always told Samuel to send him to the ocean while he never disagreed although his children knew him for his natural ways of being sarcastic and worn out every time he came back home after work. His children were grown enough to help in the house and understand their father's cause for his volunteering for the party duties. The road was dark and a mist constantly forced him to turn on and off the windshield wipers. He passed through a part of town, the last district of the city before the road led toward the ocean which meant another thirty minutes or so. There were people sleeping on the sidewalks and sporadically a few were sitting by the scarce gutters. They seemed alert in the eyes of a local; Samuel could feel the beat as the election was only a few weeks ahead. He had stored everything in the dashboard. His driver's license, and a handwritten letter that was to be handed to the guards at the village. He was on the outskirts of the beach as the road now ran parallel with the shore where palms and sand stood between his path and water. Most of them knew him well from the ministry, but they had to act official since security had recently become an issue.

After leaving the car he quietly walked to a shack not too far from others like it and knocked on the door. It opened and he was welcome with the barrel of an automatic hanging from the guard's shoulder. He signaled him to enter as he walked behind him toward the center of that small room. There were four men who were not presently armed. Samuel, still refreshed by the morning mist, held out his hand and gave the man standing directly in front of him his documents. He stared at his face as he grabbed the letter and his license, and passed it to the man at his left sitting on a straw stool while another automatic was laying on the floor at his feet. The sitting guard held a short grin and signaled the guard behind Samuel to lower his gun.

"He is asleep!" He informed Samuel.

"Should I wait. . . . . !?" Samuel asked.

"You can carry him in a blanket,. . . . can't you?" The guard suggested.

"Does he know!?" Samuel asked.

"He is a smart kid!. . . . Come with me. . ."

Samuel followed the man on the stool to the room and while he stood aside Samuel picked up Anton as he wrapped him in the blanket covering him.

The man and the boy reached the vehicle as one guard followed them carefully. He opened the rear door allowing Samuel to tuck the boy on the back seat. Then, the guard sat in next to the boy while Samuel relaxed behind the ignition waiting for an order from the man on the stool who was scrutinizing everything. He assured them by raising both hands and showing his palms to move on. The sun was still partly hiding at the horizon; one could merely detect the proliferation of its early rays over the quiet and distant ocean as the palm trees stood still not waving as it was always a ritual with those monsters of the beach. He was quiet and so was the guard. Samuel drove slowly to avoid waking Anton up.

Casino was up early, perhaps to get some work done before the election commenced. Harlot was worried about the recent distribution of *"Liberty Shell"*, the publication which both hoped would turn the tide their way. The conference room still smelled like burned tobacco from the night before while they had everyone preparing and troubleshooting towards the voters; any last idea would have helped. There were a couple of ashtrays on the center table that had remained full of cigar butts. It was Casino that wanted them to celebrate providing his staff with hand-rolled cigars, the island's best. It was about eight when there was a quiet knock at the entrance that jolted Harlot who was not expecting anyone as opposed to Casino who called upon Samuel to come in. He and Anton walked into the quiet room as the two men were sitting at the end of that long table seemingly discussing important matters. Anton looked innocent, he looked as if Samuel had just only wanted to show him off. But Casino had been looking forward to seeing the boy.

"Come in. . . . come in. . . . .good morning Anton! Do you remember me. . . Casino!. . . My name is Casino!"

"Hi Casino. . . . . !!!"

"Samuel you can leave.. . .go home if you want! Come Anton. . . come. . . . sit right here!" Casino pointed at the across the table from Harlot.

"This is Harlot. We are good friends! You might have met him during the festival . . . .! Anyhow. . . . . by the way are you OK if we put you in a new place today!? It'll be just as comfortable as the other. . . You know the election is near and I wanted to congratulate you because your father's dream has come true now. . . . !! You will someday get to know him better and when you grow up you will realize how important this election is. . . but for now let's talk and spend a little time before the car is here to take you to your new home! I thought it would be a good idea to change your residence!! At least during this crucial time. . . . ." Casino explained and held Anton's small hand as Harlot interrupted.

"Would you like anything Anton!? . . . . We have anything you might imagine!"

Anton rubbed his eye with the other hand and asked for water.

"Water!!?. . . That's all you want son!?"

Anton nodded. Casino raised his head to call a guard but Harlot pointed at him to hold on and then asked again.

"Are you sure water is all you want. . . . . how about some cookies or chocolate. . . . !?"

Harlot got up and left the conference room to get Anton some water, and perhaps something for him to eat.

"It'll be a few minutes son. . . . I'll find you something good!!!" Harlot yelled stepping out while those two remained quiet and studied one another.

A guard calmly entered the conference room as he was expected by Casino. He came near and nodded to Casino. "We are ready!" The guard informed him.

"Well! Anton would you like to wait for the water. . . . ?" Casino asked.

"No, I'm not thirsty. . . ." Anton reacted.

"Are you sure son?"

"Yes, I am. . . . . !" Anton insisted.

"Drive very carefully and make sure you keep close to your escort!!! And avoid stops as much as possible! Understand!!?" Casino waited for a response.

"Yes sir. . . . nothing to worry about!" The guard obeyed.

Casino got up and held Anton between his arms and kissed him on the head.

"I'll see you soon! He will take you to your new place and you can sleep some more. . . Go now. . . . !!" Casino nodded at the guard and showed them the door.

Harlot came back to the room with a pitcher of water and a small plate full of cookies, bit it was too late. The boy had already left some time ago. The two men sat face to face, and pursued the discussion about the handbook while considering other options to trigger propaganda around the more remote parts of the Island Nation. It was about nine-thirty as the door suddenly opened and a guard rushed in without asking for permission.

"They've been hit sir!!! They've. . . . ."

"What are you talking about!!?" Casino interrupted by yelling back.

"The motorcade is completely destroyed !!! . . . . They are all dead sir!!" The guard informed him sadly.

"Secure the building Harlot. . . . !!! And you. . . . you tell me what happened!!" Casino asked the guard.

"Someone just called saying that three cars are on fire after being hit by something. . . . He says there is nothing left of them. . . . The road is closed and there is no one else coming forward so far. . . . . !!!" The guard continued.

Casino picked up the papers in front of him on the table and headed for his office where, for a few hours, he sank into deep thought. He felt exhausted from fear and desperate before the big event. He picked up his phone and dialed the dispatcher.

"Sir! What can I help you with?"

"I need the log for all the calls. . . . inbound and outbound. . . . for this morning. . . . !!!"

"There was only one outbound call this morning, sir! That one was from the assistant director's office. . . . ." Dispatcher informed Casino.

"Is that all!!?"

"Yes, sir!"

"Are you sure!!?" Casino demanded.

"Yes sir! It was at eight-thirty-five!!" Dispatcher explained.

". . . . . . Was it a business call!!!?" Casino asked.

"I don't know sir. . . . That number is not on our directory!!" Dispatcher responded.

Three weeks had gone by. Samuel would soon regain lost wealth once his father was freed from prison as others once Liberation would assume the leadership of Island Nation. Many would be able to go back to their businesses and join their families again. They had won by a reasonable majority. Samuel had served the party for his reasons aside from his father's who became a fighter once he, no more, could tolerate the pressure from Chief and likes of him; those hungry scavengers who had no mercy and tolerated no remorse toward the innocent. Samuel had become restless, he loved his father's business more than anything else in his life.

What was it that had to pass and hold a relentless history as prisoner on its knees to, once and for all, embrace a new generation and redirect its bloody canons to tolerance for all. Was it a reason to stop peace and torture them, or was it its inner ambition to ink out in red and lead the familiar resolution not unheard of in so many ages. Alas, the path, rather short, and a will to see the barriers and those who innocently carried the abyss in their minds and presume a willingness to obey what modern man would recognize as the downfall of its race.

They had played the game by the rules. Liberation had used its powers collectively putting into play each and every piece on the board. The silence now had turned into beats of a flaming chime. The opposition headed for surrender was left no reasonable space and no blessings to yet cover its flaws. It was for the last time that they could put one foot forward and cross their sinful hands boasting about the leadership that had cost this piece of earth flesh and blood.

A week ago Liberation had promised, through banners printed in large black print, to build a television station and would proceed to change the island's public diet; furthermore, they assured the voters that the Island Nation would, in the very near future, be able to have the privilege of using personal mobile telephones, that would be paid for by the government, for those over eighteen years of age. One banner, printed in many copies and shown around the capital explained about computer literacy, *"The Ultimate Appliance",* that would bring the world to you. It would be free for public as soon as possible. And many, just like Samuel, knew that the moment was theirs; they now could see and be deductive. The old cabinet gave out early on and a few of them had disappeared through the three day voting period although knowing that maybe one or two could have held on to their seats. *They must have known better!!* The election was a light at the end of the tunnel, this end which settled the long-time score with injustice on this rich and envied soil.

Colonel had to reassure the command based on the decision of the new cabinet. Devastated and deeply shaken, he saw a threat to his stipulations that he would hold on to his past. It was hard to deny his party and, based on the lesson learned, he felt the sound of their boots in the corridors of the palace. The time had come. They had to plan a new protocol, but it seemed almost impossible to get it done in such speed. His tenure would only last a few more weeks once the members of the Liberation settled through ministries and lastly moved into the palace. Colonel had been consulting his ranking officers, but the only way would be to achieve Liberation's trust. However, the army heads decided to invite the elected officers of the new cabinet to an orientation dinner. Colonel felt that he was able to find his way into the new government by denying Chief's ideologies. Colonel believed that was still a bruise in the hearts of those who had to obey him and his regime for so many years. The new cabinet was officially and ceremonially invited to join Colonel and the top ranks of the army at the palace for a dinner only two days before The People's Democratic Liberation Party assumed the leadership of Island Nation.

One invitation came to me as the appointed minister of communication by the cordial request of the top command of the army. We had felt being monitored by Colonel and his men. The notions of politicking were obvious. Army continued scouting the city, the plaza, and the old ministry where we headquartered. We found it hard to believe that soon they had to follow a new leader, yet the path showed its end as the evidence had already proven that morale was at its all time critical low. They were to understand that Liberation had already come a victor over them many a time. A small part of the Liberation's soldiers previously belonged to Colonel's army. The staff had decided to join him in peace as there had been no notion of any discussion regarding the national affairs.

That afternoon there was sound and good people; the doors of the ministry had remained open all day. *Congratulations!* The official cabinet stepped out of the conference room heading for the motorpool. They were to be escorted to the palace and the capital had been informed of this pilgrimage. The short trip was to be taken until dinner time at the palace. The central community were mostly on their feet while there were some chairs set at the edge of the standing crowd for the aged and disabled. The motorcade was slow at its historical pace yet cautious. Flags being waved sporadically but most of the near attendants merely touched the vehicles with a quick prayer. It was the first official cooperation between the army and the Liberation. The latter were to be joined by party representatives of Center-Left and Coalition while the event was distinguishably set to separate the parties from the army!!

Casino had mentioned his plans for a total conversion of the army as part of the prime phase of his term as the president. Although, he had expressed his doubts about a proper dialogue with the present ranking officers of Colonel's forces. At the fortress of the palace the crowd became noticeably scarce as there were army guards at their post lined up all the way for miles toward the gates of the palace. The motorcade, now slower, entered the front lawn area as the escorts came to a stop allowing the official vehicles to reach the entrance where Colonel and his men had been awaiting their arrival.

Casino and Harlot stepped out of their transporting SUV rather informally. They both stepped toward Colonel at the center of reception. Casino shook his hand, and then Harlot approached him with both hands getting a tight grip of his hand and said a few words which only the two could hear. Casino was already being introduced Colonel's staff as among them were many generals and higher ranks than him. The handshakes took more than half an hour and the tour of the palace lasted well until eight-thirty when the last visitation was set to be the famous dining hall. The door opened and on the table were set the most elegant chine. That chine, according to Colonel, had seen many generals and leaders including Chief during his inauguration, and many ambassadors and foreign commissions of international rank and fame. He congratulated the Liberation to be worthy and capable having officially taken claim of the palace and its organs.

The seats were shortly occupied and the finest rum was served with ice in highballs. The Colonel proposed a toast to the future as everyone raised their glasses. Some had downed the whole glass and, shortly, the ambiance was turning more friendly. The guests had commenced conversation although mostly comic and social. Casino and Harlot were rather quiet as he held a smile and kept raising his glass to different guests and saluted them. Casino indifferently took his name card and began writing something on the back of it. When Harlot was finally silent Casino coldly stared at him for a few seconds and then slowly pushed the label card in front of Harlot and began to stare at the card making it clear that he wanted Harlot to read his note. Harlot looked back at him as his impression turned cold and wary. He finally looked down eyeballing the note. . . .

"I know everything. . . . !!!

A guard is waiting for you

outside the door. . . . . . ."

The two men's impression and kinetics brought silence to the room as everyone had noticed Casino's name label in front of Harlot. He suddenly jumped up and saluted, "Hail to Chief!!!" He was trembling when he slowly walked toward the dining hall entrance. A host opened the double door for him. Everyone remained quiet while assiduously observing Casino. He half-turned toward the window. In a few moments there came the sound of a round of machine gun fire from the front lawn.

THE END